Thick and Thin

·rah Harte studied law and French at University College Cork. ·e worked as a corporate lawyer before she switched to writing. ·om Cork she moved to Dublin, where she now lives with her ·sband Jay, their son Conn and Lucy the dog. Her first novel was ·*Better Half*.

Thick and Thin

SARAH HARTE

PENGUIN
IRELAND

PENGUIN IRELAND

Published by the Penguin Group
Penguin Ireland, 25 St Stephen's Green, Dublin 2, Ireland
(a division of Penguin Books Ltd)
Penguin Books Ltd, 80 Strand, London WC2R 0RL, England
Penguin Group (USA) Inc., 375 Hudson Street, New York, New York 10014, USA
Penguin Group (Australia), 707 Collins Street, Melbourne, Victoria 3008, Australia
(a division of Pearson Australia Group Pty Ltd)
Penguin Group (Canada), 90 Eglinton Avenue East, Suite 700, Toronto, Ontario, Canada M4P 2Y3
(a division of Pearson Penguin Canada Inc.)
Penguin Books India Pvt Ltd, 11 Community Centre, Panchsheel Park, New Delhi – 110 017, India
Penguin Group (NZ), 67 Apollo Drive, Rosedale, Auckland 0632, New Zealand
(a division of Pearson New Zealand Ltd)
Penguin Books (South Africa) (Pty) Ltd, Block D, Rosebank Office Park,
181 Jan Smuts Avenue, Parktown North, Gauteng 2193, South Africa

Penguin Books Ltd, Registered Offices: 80 Strand, London WC2R 0RL, England

www.penguin.com

First published 2013
001

Set in 13.5/16pt Garamond MT
Typeset by Jouve (UK), Milton Keynes
Printed in Great Britain by Clays Ltd, St Ives plc

A CIP catalogue record for this book is available from the British Library

ISBN: 978–1–844–88267–0

www.greenpenguin.co.uk

To Rebecca Harte,
Andrea Pitt and Michelle Rabbette,
with much affection,
and in memoriam Evelyn Rabbette

PART ONE
September 1989 – December 1994

'Youth is easily deceived because it is quick to hope.'

Aristotle

I

September 1989

She was a disaster at sex, which wasn't a huge surprise. It was just the latest fiasco in the stumbling journey towards womanhood that had started on the day a teacher had pulled her aside to explain periods after the stain had appeared on the back of her uniform skirt. Her mother was dead so her knowledge of sex had come from garbled schoolyard bulletins and the kind but awkward attempt of a brother's girlfriend to explain the facts of life. Both of them had been mortified and she couldn't bring herself to ask any questions. In the end she had figured out the theory. And now she was finally doing it. Instead of moving her body rhythmically with his, as she had seen so many times on screen, she lay under him on the stale sheets, her brain in overdrive and her body about as animated as a jellyfish marooned on sand.

Those were the things that burdened Clare McMahon as her boyfriend made love to her. Worse, her mind was so jammed with technical questions that she couldn't relax. As a medical student she was familiar with the male anatomy, but she had not felt able to look down. Nor had she dared to place her hand anywhere significant. She wondered if she should show appreciation of his performance as she had seen actresses do. The idea crippled her with embarrassment. It was a short distance from an enthusiastic, sexy groan to a pig-like grunt.

In the run-up to this evening she had rehearsed the scene

many times and had been realistic about how it might happen. Small-breasted and violin-shaped, she knew she was no beauty. In the rare moments when she permitted herself to fantasize about romance – and it was always romance, never sex – she had never secretly cast herself as a seductress using her body to ensnare a man. She had never expected to be told that she was gorgeous. And all the time she had been seeing Joe, she was fairly sure he didn't find her physically irresistible. Indeed, when they had first got together, it seemed that her self-respect was what he most liked about her.

'Some girls are such sluts,' he had said, with disgust, 'throwing it about college as if their reputation was nothing.'

However, more recently she had begun to realize that his regard for her purity was draining away. 'You're not a nun, Clare,' he had said testily, just days before when she had instructed him to stop his exploration beneath her knickers.

It seemed that her virginity, which she had been quietly proud of, had become an albatross. They had been seeing each other for a long time – on a more *ad hoc* basis than she would have liked – but now she knew that if she didn't sleep with Joe she would lose him.

'God,' Marianne had said, when Clare had confided her fears, 'I don't know what the big deal is.'

But it wasn't easy for Clare to step outside the boundaries of her upbringing. When she thought about sex, disquieting images of her father, followed by the head nun at her school, frogmarched their way across her mind. Her father took a dim view of premarital sex and of young girls stupid enough to 'get caught'. Even her eldest brother PJ and his girlfriend Majella resorted to fiction: they hadn't gone on holiday together but had bumped into each other abroad. On the other hand, she wasn't sure she could lead her life according to the dictates of a sixty-six-year-old man.

She had made her way to a department store on Henry Street. There she had fingered the cheap underwear uncertainly. She had felt woefully self-conscious, as if it was obvious to all that here was a virgin picking racy underwear for a night of premarital sex. Was red too brazen? She'd been confused by all the colours and styles on offer. It was a complicated mix of dread, longing and, yes, even a little shame that stalked her as she left, clutching the plastic bag that contained the modest black garments.

Was she a sensual person? She thought not. Sunk in the cinema seat, she had watched the celluloid hero urgently clearing his desk to make space for the heroine he was about to ravish but had focused on the items that smashed on the floor – the waste! And when he fed the woman fruit in foreplay, she decided she wouldn't like that – too messy. Even worse, as the erotic scene unfolded she wondered how many strawberries you could get into your mouth at once – two or three? In a state of arousal, would you manage a punnet?

So, she probably wasn't particularly sensual. She wasn't sexy, either, but maybe with the right partner she'd discover hidden depths. She had thought that Joe would manage things and that she would respond instinctively. She hadn't imagined floating above the bed and eyeing herself as if she wasn't participating in what was going on. Over the bed there was a poster of a topless model with Margaret Thatcher's head pasted to it. Maggie didn't look like a very sensual woman. She was totally drunk of course, having downed drink after drink in the pub in order to steel herself.

'Relax, Clare,' Joe said, in a way that made her clamp even tighter shut.

She had begun to think vaguely hysterical things like 'open sesame, close sesame'. An image of Ali Baba and his forty thieves danced across her cortex in balloon-shaped pants. Clare fought rising misery. She wasn't capable of inspiring lust.

Clare turned out of the Trinity College gates onto College Green and up Grafton Street. After she and Joe had finished she'd wanted to go to the loo but was afraid that Joe might see the stretch marks on her arse.

As a child she had been a normal size, but after her mother had died Clare had started to eat more and, of course, expanded. She wasn't sure why. Perhaps she'd been trying to fill a hole. The previous year when she had been summoned back from Germany, where she'd been working in a cherry factory, she had begun to shrink, and she had lost more weight since. But still she imagined she should wear clothes to disguise her figure rather than emphasize it. She was ashamed that she had been so big – her wrists had been braceleted with fat. She still ran past mirrors and didn't like studying her body.

In the end, with Joe, she had dressed under the covers in a way that was anything but alluring. Later she had cleaned herself up in the bathroom that Joe and his roommate Matt shared. Joe hadn't seemed to want her to stay. 'Matt'll be back soon – he's out with Philip. I wouldn't like him to have it over you.'

It was nice that he had considered her honour. But for once questions of reputation mattered little to her. She had hoped that when she slept with Joe, they would be brought closer. She had wanted to lay her head in the hollow of his bare shoulder and wake up beside him.

Clare walked on, a little dazed, conscious of a strange elation. I am no longer a virgin she thought, making brief eye contact with a man coming out of the Shelbourne Hotel. He muttered at the streets and wove on. She felt that a hangover of epic proportions loomed for her too. They were a rarity with Clare. She didn't like the loss of control that alcohol encouraged – and lacked the money to fund a drinking habit. The irony was not lost on her that, thanks to the booze she'd chugged back earlier, the exact details of her deflowering were sketchy.

Clare sifted through the events of the night again. She was at the age when negatives could be parlayed into the reverse so she gradually found herself feeling more positive. Earlier in the smoky pub, which had been packed with students, tourists and notables from around town, she had won out.

After the college debate, Joe had put his arm around her as they made the short journey from Trinity to the Bailey. The arm stretched out in public represented significant progress. Ordinarily Joe held her hand under the table. While she would have liked to drive a flag into him mountaineer-style to stake her claim – he was slow to admit to what she felt was a relationship – Clare had basked in the glow of possession, unaware of a threat bearing down on them. It had come in a lithe form, with strikingly good teeth, trailing a nimbus cloud of self-confidence and a gaggle of high-heeled, big-haired friends. They belonged to the foreign tribe Clare had regarded with wonder when she had first arrived in college. They spoke in exclamation marks and had known each other 'for yonks', long before they ever stood in line for registration during Freshers' Week.

Over the previous three years Clare had gradually come to understand that theirs was a Dublin world of private schools, rugby and hockey matches, discos and debs balls where first kisses were shared and bodily fluids swapped. There was a look, a lingo and private codes, a sort of argot or shorthand that they seemed to have imbibed with their mothers' milk and which Clare could not have penetrated even had she wanted to.

Clare was not ashamed of where she came from. She had not flattened out her accent as a neighbour from home had, turning West Cork into a sort of strangulated West British. That boy – he was studying dentistry, which had prompted her father to remark that there was 'great money in mouths' – pranced around campus with a Trinity scarf welded to his neck. During her first month or so, when she was casting around for someone to speak to, she had been delighted to spot him outside Front Gate. On approaching him, he had made clear that although they came from the same town, it counted for little in the world they now inhabited.

In the pub the Threat had deftly manoeuvred Joe away, barely registering Clare. Joe had ended up near the toilets, hand against the wall, listening to this girl tell a story that, Clare reflected sourly, almost certainly lacked a point but cast her in a flattering light. The intensity of her dislike had surprised her.

Alone at her table, the Threat's laughter ringing in her ears, she had felt distinctly raddled. Jealousy had stung her into action. There had been another spur of which she was only dimly aware. The Threat's white teeth might dazzle while Clare's were a little jumbled on the lower row, and the Threat's father was a judge while her own was a small farmer-cum-postman. But Clare McMahon came from generations of hardy stock who had seen off invaders, both local and foreign, and doggedly eked out a living from stony soil. She would not be trumped by legal connections or a set of south Dublin delft.

There had been many obstacles to clear on her way to sitting in that pub. Her father did not believe in educating girls to university level because they would marry and waste the investment. He had wanted her to go into nursing, like one of her aunts. But Clare had set her sights on medicine, at

Trinity College no less. She had cycled down the long, winding road from the farm to school each day, face set against the challenges that lay ahead, and fitted school work around chores, eventually securing a scholarship and a grant. Clare had been determined then as she was now. In short, she was not going to go down without a fight. She wondered how to neutralise the Threat.

Instinctively she knew that her adversary was the sort of girl who put out. Clare had drained her drink and made a decision. Tonight was the night she would showcase her new underwear. She would turn her back on what she had been taught and give Joe what he had been angling for.

Now Clare turned into Leeson Street. She and Marianne lived on what was known locally as the Strip. In the early hours of the morning illegal clubs run as shebeens – the gardaí turned a blind eye to the flouting of the licensing laws – disgorged their patrons onto the street, cock-eyed on overpriced wine and with lust. Outside her building, she pushed through the knot of revellers queuing for hot dogs, opened the door and closed it quietly behind her. She stepped forward and fell over a bike that had slipped from where it was propped under a sign that read 'Strictly No Bikes'. She picked it up, rubbed her shin and hit the light switch. Tonight the climb to the third floor seemed of Everest proportions.

As Clare walked into the flat, she was assaulted by the ear-splitting – in her opinion, spirit-sapping – sound of the Stone Roses. Since they had moved in Marianne had played their album on a loop. Clare didn't get the lyrics and the songs went on for what seemed an idiotic length of time. Marianne maintained she was tone deaf: 'They're going to be major, Clare.'

Typically there was a novel in Marianne's lap and a glass of wine within reach. She was smoking a roll-up, flicking the ash onto a chipped saucer. 'Hey there,' she said, looking up and smiling. 'Where the hell have you been?'

Clare turned down the music. 'The neighbours?'

'No complaints so far,' Marianne said, exhaling. 'This strikes me as a kind of party-hearty building.' She added, 'I like the top.'

Clare made a face. 'Sorry – you don't mind, do you? You'd gone out with your mum.'

'Of course I don't mind.'

Clare didn't have the money for clothes. And she found them confusing. She owned two pairs of jeans, one of which did not flatter her bum. If Marianne had not generously opened her wardrobe, Clare would have greeted each day in the same two or three outfits, none of them very satisfactory.

'Has your mum gone home?'

'Finally,' Marianne said. 'She wondered where you'd got to. She wanted you to join us for dinner.'

'She's so good,' Clare said.

'She left the fridge full of food. And told me specially to tell you that there's some of that bread you like in the airtight container over there.'

'Your mum's so good,' Clare repeated.

'I think she finds the flat a bit seedy,' Marianne added.

Clare felt a pang. It was the sort of place she could afford. Their landlord, an accountant, had divided the property into rackety units to maximize profit with little consideration for the lines of the Georgian building. She and Marianne had a dark galley kitchen, with an ancient cooker and a grubby piece of Formica that perched on the small fridge as a work-top. The sink was in the living room. On the draining-board, there was a microwave, with a sandwich toaster and the bread bin.

Because the bedrooms faced onto the street over the

nightclubs, sleep could be difficult, a factor they had overlooked when they'd viewed the place: it explained the depressed rent, which had attracted Clare. Marianne, who lived by an entirely different set of economic rules, could have been somewhere far more salubrious.

'I could find someone else to share with,' Clare had said awkwardly.

'Don't be stupid. I want to live with you,' Marianne had assured her. 'And, besides, it's gritty.' She had conveniently overlooked their position as students in a bastion of privilege and the fact that her supposedly edgy urban existence was underwritten by her mother's largess.

'She met our new neighbours,' Marianne said. 'I could tell she was trying to play it cool but she didn't do a very good job.'

'Which ones?'

Two gay men lived above them. On week mornings they left the building in sharp suits. The previous weekend Clare had met them on the stairs in dungarees and T-shirts, their hair teased into quiffs. She had struggled to place them.

'The pair from 2B.'

'Oh, God.'

The couple who lived below them were heroin addicts. They were whippet-thin, kept odd hours and their eyes were murky and unseeing.

'Where did you get to anyway?' Marianne asked. 'Pour yourself a glass of something.'

'I'd puke if I drank another drop,' Clare said, making for the window. 'It stinks in here.' She was stalling for time.

'I know,' Marianne said. 'I couldn't wait for Mum to go so I could light up. It's weird – the second I'm with her all I want to do is smoke. And drink.'

Clare opened the smeared window a fraction. 'It's because you can't. You always want what you can't have. It's a sort of compulsion with you.' She collapsed into a chair. 'I'm completely wrecked. I have work to do tomorrow so I'd better hit the hay.'

'Clare, I hope you're not going to spend another entire year cloistered in your room.'

'I have no choice. I can't afford to fail.'

Marianne lit a fag and scrutinized her.

Clare was avoiding her eye. She wanted to tell her but at the same time she didn't.

'You haven't answered my question.'

'What question?'

'Where you've been?' Before Clare had a chance to answer, Marianne sat up suddenly. 'You slept with him, didn't you?'

Clare reddened. 'Yes.'

'Oh, my God, Clare,' Marianne said. 'At last. I thought we'd have to take a crowbar to that chastity belt.'

Marianne's approach to sex was radically different from Clare's. A packet of the contraceptive pill was flung casually on her chest of drawers. Even more disturbingly, her mother had put her on it. 'It's called being pragmatic,' Marianne had said airily. 'It's the difference philosophically speaking between "is" and "ought". Gretta gets the distinction.'

Clare doubted that her own mother would have put her on the pill, if she'd been alive, though in fact she had no idea what her mother might have done in any situation.

Initially Clare had found Marianne's sort of liberation troubling. But she had quickly come to understand that her friend viewed sex as a recreational pastime. She had slept with a number of boys and, from Clare's observations, had suffered from no emotional bruising. It contradicted what Clare had been taught at the convent where the nuns had maintained that a bleak fate awaited any girl who shared her favours too freely. However, contrary to their dire predictions, Marianne did not appear to feel empty or used. Quite the reverse, in fact, and if anyone felt cheapened, it certainly wasn't her. There was one boy in particular, an attractive if slow-witted actor, whom Marianne and a number of her other girlfriends had slept with. Marianne had remarked, laughing, that they had 'passed him around like a packet of Smarties'.

'But with Joe Corcoran,' Marianne said now.

'Don't be like that,' Clare said, dashed.

'You can do so much better, Clare.'

That wasn't true. While admiring stares had been the currency of Marianne's college life, the reverse was true of Clare. During her first year she had walked around college as part of the anonymous herd. She had set her bar low. She had aimed not to draw attention for the wrong reasons. In her second year there had been a guy with bad skin who had taken her to the cinema a couple of times. Clearly he had felt he was doing her a favour because she was fat. He had allowed Clare to pay for her ticket, the popcorn and drinks, even though he had invited her. The only other guy she had dated, if that was the correct term for their brief contact, had been a science student Marianne had christened 'Shergar'. 'He looks like he's wearing a bridle. I keep expecting him to whinny.'

'Marianne, please,' Clare said now.

'Okay, okay.'

They faced each other. Then Marianne said, her tone sly, 'So . . . what was he like?'

Sometimes, with drink in her, Marianne would rate her partners' skills, untroubled by the casual intimacy. Clare found this both shocking and gripping. Just recently Marianne had confided in her about a handsome boy, a 'big cheese' on campus. 'I swear, Clare,' she said, 'his willy was half the size of your fingernail. I'm not kidding! This wasn't even a case of size mattering – and it does, let me tell you. That guy has a disability.'

Embarrassingly, whenever Clare encountered him now, in the Buttery Bar or having coffee, she found herself imagining his member.

'That's private,' she said.

Shards of light were seeping into the night sky.

'I badly need to go to bed.'

'Don't be so pious, Clare.'

It wasn't just that Clare felt she'd fallen short with Joe: she'd lacked confidence in her body and hadn't known what to do. The nuns had implied that a wave of emotion would engulf her after she had given herself to a man for the first time, but it hadn't. She'd hoped that sleeping with Joe would cement their relationship. But now, when she should have felt changed, she felt hung-over and sad. 'I'm wrecked,' she said, getting up.

'Marks out of ten,' Marianne persisted.

Clare wanted to ask how you knew you'd had an orgasm, but she was worried she might cast some slur on Joe. 'Ten out of ten,' she said.

The street was silent. It was that time of the morning when the nightclubbers had swayed home and the hum of early-morning traffic had yet to begin. An exhausted Clare was dreaming in the smaller of the two bedrooms. Yet again she was outside the shed, and even in sleep her throat tightened. She rounded the rhododendrons, stepping beyond the lawn and past the thistles to where the moths banged against the glow of the lights that had attracted her. She could almost feel the dew on her bare shins. She stepped onto the dirt track, passing the car propped up on bricks.

Clare turned restlessly onto her side. Now she was looking

beyond the racks of giant tractor tyres, across the oil-stained concrete under the harsh yellow lights. And there it was, clear and stark. He swung from the rafters, his neck horribly stretched. There was a roaring in her ears as she gulped for air –

'Sssh, Clare . . .'

It took her a moment to focus.

'You're having a nightmare.'

The bedside clock on the splintery sun-bleached table told her it was nearly six. Clare felt a gust of air as the quilt was lifted. Cold feet were clamped to the backs of her legs, and Marianne's arms went around her. After the funeral she had said little, just been there. Now she whispered, 'You're okay, Clare.'

2

October 1990

Marianne Dillon was enthroned on a chair in a classic French restaurant, just a stone's throw from where she had graduated that morning. A celebratory lunch in her honour was being held in Les Frères Jacques, with its white linen tablecloths and bow-tied waiters, their accents and attitudes so comically Gallic that they might have come from Central Casting. It was another example of how spoilt she was. At least, that was the silent opinion of one or two of her peers, among the motley crew who had trooped up Dame Street towards Dublin Castle at the behest of Marianne's mother. They were now a little pink, after the fine wine, scallops, duck confit and turbot.

'If Marianne's father, Tim, could have been here today he would be very proud,' her mother said, with a catch in her voice. That her sadness over her father's death was less intense now made Marianne regretful. He had been gone six years and his face had begun to fade. He was reduced to a series of images. She could picture him tall and wiry, standing next to her in the freezing Atlantic teaching her to swim. And, later, she could still hear him telling her she must always swim parallel to the shore. But the memory bank was emptying every day.

Marianne eyed her mother's friend. Boyfriend, lover, partner . . . *You'll never replace him.*

She focused again on her mother's speech, squirming a little because her friends were listening.

'Marianne always loved English . . .'

For Marianne, the elephant in the room was her result. She had entered university with exceptional Leaving Certificate results and had been predicted a first. She hadn't managed it. It was hardly a major surprise to her, and certainly not to Clare, who had never tired of haranguing her about the need to study more. The truth was – and they both knew this – that social success had come at a price.

Did she mind? Not too much. She had been a little humbled, searching for her name on the board, the results tacked on the wall for all to see, and had briefly chided herself, but it hadn't lasted long. It was more that others had secured a first. It was galling that Joe Corcoran had managed it. Earlier he had been like a bantam cock, strutting about Front Square with his billowing gown and degree parchment. She didn't resent Matt's. It annoyed her more that he was currently touching her foot under the table in a way that presumably he supposed to be sexy. All day she had had to angle her neck to hide the hickey he had given her the previous evening. They had been going out for a few months, and Matt was still flatteringly keen, but she was beginning to find him tiresome.

'Tim always had such high hopes for Marianne,' her mother was saying now.

Marianne's eyes were on her plate. Sometimes she wondered if her father had really harboured such dreams for her or if her mother was annexing him for her own purposes. Marianne's mother had been an air stewardess, forced to retire on marriage. That had been the rule back then. As a result she saw college as some sort of silver bullet. And she fostered an almost evangelical belief that Marianne would leave university an educated, culturally enriched, socially aware woman, ready to ascend the dizzy heights.

In fact earlier, standing among the sea of graduates, Marianne had been pierced by doubt. She'd wondered if she'd ever had any ambition, and if she had, perhaps it had atrophied during her college years. She had always been a gifted if erratic student. When her father had been killed in a car crash, she had latched onto her studies as a way to keep a grip on things and had excelled. Perhaps her mother and older relatives had mistaken focus for ambition.

'Here's to Marianne and a bright future,' her mother said, holding her champagne glass aloft.

'To Marianne,' the others chimed.

Marianne looked bashful as her friends whooped, drawing glances from other diners and a frown from the maître d'. People went back to their conversations.

'Coleman is a good man,' her aunt Tess said.

'Yes,' Marianne said, in a tone that was at best non-committal.

In theory she had been okay with her mother dating someone. But that had been when she had assumed it wouldn't last. Two years later he was looking at her across the table.

She followed her aunt's gaze to where her friend Alexandra was expelling a cloud of smoke that wreathed her golden head.

'I'm surprised such a lovely girl smokes,' Tess said.

With her delicately etched features, shining blonde hair and big eyes, Alexandra looked like a heroine in a story book. She had studied the fragrant combination of History of Art and Classical Civilization, which underpinned that impression. What wasn't apparent – and had flown beneath the parental radar – was that Alexandra had libertine tendencies. Her passion for the writings of the French philosopher Michel

Foucault added a pseudo-intellectual gloss to her antics – she could quote his theories about 'limit-experience' and pushing the boundaries *ad nauseam* – but Alexandra had a robust interest in sexual and narcotic experimentation. Only recently she had made her first foray into multi-partner sex. 'Yah, I'm happy to see where it takes me for now. I mean, obviously, I'll end up getting married and all that . . .'

Marianne felt hot. Her face was probably mottled by now, but Alexandra looked perfect. She could sink a vat of wine without any outward effects. Marianne considered her, with her underplayed London style, to be the acme of sophistication. Now that she had finished her degree, she was working as a fashion PR.

Marianne didn't like to be thought of as a follower, but where Alexandra went Marianne tended to accompany her. This meant poring over copies of the *Face* and planning to lose weight while wondering how to imitate the very definite 'look' that graced its pages. Indeed, although Marianne styled herself politically aware and fancied herself as a budding intellectual, the seismic events taking place that autumn were mere footnotes to concerns such as these. A war might have started in Iraq and Margaret Thatcher might be on the way out, but what was really troubling Marianne was the question of how to flatten her boobs. Breasts were out and it was hard to look cool in a disaffected urban way when you had robust country genes. Even when she wore black, Marianne still looked like somebody who was about to smash a ball over a net.

'I very much enjoyed the ceremony earlier,' Tess said, in a way that put Marianne on her guard. Her aunt was the headmistress of a girls' school and conversations with her often turned into cross-examinations. Casual enquiries could mutate into a line of inquiry. Talk might centre on the future or veer onto the 'importance of a well-laid-out curriculum vitae'. She was the least relaxing of Marianne's aunts.

'Nice that it was in Latin . . .'

'Yes,' Marianne said.

'And everyone in black and white.'

At Trinity graduations the men wore dinner jackets and bow ties and the women black or black and white dresses. It was élitist in a way that Marianne publicly derided but secretly relished.

'The campus is so beautiful.'

'Yes,' agreed Marianne, wondering where this was leading.

'You're so lucky to have had the chance to go to Trinity.'

'Yes, I am,' she said, tensing. Tess had a particular fondness for talking about 'the obligations that come with privilege' and Marianne was all for stamping out inequality – she could wax lyrical on the subject after a few pints and speculate grandly as to how it might be achieved – but she wasn't as keen on being told how her own privileged background might imply certain responsibilities on her part.

'I remember the sense of wonder I felt at all the opportunities that lay ahead when I graduated,' Tess said, smiling into the middle distance.

Marianne sipped her wine glumly, wondering what might come next. Tess had a tendency to parables. The fuzzy, festive feeling bestowed by the wine and the occasion was waning.

'Your mother tells me you're going to do a master's.'

'Yes, after I get back from Paris.'

A sidelong glance confirmed what Marianne had suspected. The idea of a sojourn in Paris would seem frivolous and indulgent to her aunt. She didn't care. It had always been her dream to live in Paris.

Typically Tess motored past the Paris reference. 'Yes. And what are you planning for your thesis?'

The question sparked a fluttery near-panic in Marianne. Sometimes she thought that she had settled on the idea of doing a master's, propelled in that direction by her mother and happy to go along with it to postpone the day of reckoning. It seemed impossible to contemplate leaving the womb-like environment of the university.

'Will it be nineteenth or twentieth century?' Her aunt was brimming with pedagogical authority.

'Oh, nineteenth,' Marianne said, in way she hoped was decisive. 'I'm considering something on gender representation in the Gothic novel.'

'Oh. Quite political, then.'

Tess was regarding her in an assessing way that Marianne found unnerving. 'Yes. Something about changed social ideals,' she hedged, fiddling with her dessert fork.

'Hmm.'

Marianne knew that she should change the subject. But she ran on: 'Or I might do something on Virginia Woolf. I need to refine my proposal.' Marianne was certain her aunt would pick up on the doubt leaking from her voice.

'Sounds interesting. The important thing, though, is to be sure of your title and the extent of your enquiry or you may get lost.'

'Yes,' Marianne said, wishing she'd had the foresight to sit elsewhere.

'I presume you're going to teach ultimately.'

'I'm going to be a writer.' She could hardly believe she'd said that.

The waiter glided forward as if on castors and was about to refill their glasses.

'Well,' her aunt said, putting her hand over her glass in such a deliberate way that Marianne wondered if it was a signal to her to slow down, 'better to focus on something more definite first. You can always be a writer later. Get your qualifications and you've all the time in the world to write.'

Matt was between her mother and Clare, brown-nosing her mother. He nodded at anything her mother said. Before he spoke Marianne could see him reaching for a sentence and polishing it before he unloaded it. Clare and her mother listened to him with what seemed like polite detachment.

She wondered if she was still attracted to him. Now that he was reading for the bar, his language had become more flowery. She was no stranger to verbal sophistry herself, but he was taking it too far. Earlier he had used the word 'autumnal' when referring to the golden-brown leaves carpeting the grass in Trinity. And he was far too friendly with Joe Corcoran. This was a definite black mark. Most of all, when compared and contrasted with *him* – which Marianne found herself doing increasingly – he seemed immature and callow.

'I think it's a good idea that they're going away,' Tess said, interrupting her daydream, 'doing it quietly.'

'What do you mean?' Marianne said, tuning in.

'Your mother and –' Tess broke off.

'Tess?'

'I'm sorry if I've spoken out of turn.' Tess returned to the graduation ceremony in an attempt to redirect the conversation.

'They're not getting married?' Marianne interrupted.

She was incredulous.

Tess touched her forearm. 'It's nice for your mother. She's still so young.'

Marianne looked at her mother. She was not yet fifty. A little run to flesh, but still beautiful and vibrant. Marianne pushed back her chair. 'Excuse me.'

*

Later, sitting on the floor at Emily and Fusty's place, Marianne felt despondent. The news that her mother was going to remarry had been a like a physical lash.

'I wish Tess had let me tell you in my own way,' Gretta had said. 'Today was meant to be about you and your future.'

Marianne had said nothing.

'I need to know that you're fine with it, Marianne.'

'Because you wouldn't marry him if I said I wasn't?'

'Marianne . . . don't you like Coleman?'

'He's all right,' Marianne had said, her tone suggesting the opposite.

Pretty soon after that the conversation had wound down. Marianne had refused to discuss the subject any further. He wasn't her father. It was as simple as that.

Emily was yammering on about the 'situation' in South Africa. Fusty sat at a table rolling a joint with the sort of rapt concentration he reserved for weed. On the table lay umpteen Rizla packets, two pouches of tobacco and a giant lump of hash. As the supplier of top-quality weed, Fusty was popular and guaranteed company. People came to him bearing pizza and movies. Sometimes days elapsed before he saw daylight.

Emily – a final-year student in philosophy and sociology – continued to talk, but slower now that she was stoned. Marianne watched her tuck her dreadlocks behind her ears and wished that she would pass her the joint. The red dreads had not been a success.

'In colour terms, I'm aiming for a sort of Edie Brickell look,' Emily had said, lifting her head from the sink where the enamel was spattered a violent red from the henna. 'A sort of Edie Brickell does dreads.' She resembled a glove puppet on children's television.

'She looks as if she's knitted from a giant ball of multi-coloured wool,' Joe Corcoran had said once, to splutters of laughter from Matt, which had irritated Marianne.

Marianne lay back on the floor, a risky move – her head was almost touching a discarded pizza box. Fusty lived in squalor. The flat resembled a cave. A lava lamp glowed in the corner. A leaning tower of plates stood by the sink in the kitchen, decorated with life forms that had been proliferating for some time.

When Marianne had started at college she had dreamed of belonging to a sort of modern-day Bloomsbury set. In her teens she had read about Virginia Woolf and her coterie and pictured herself in a milieu where art and poetry were discussed. During college she had zinged from group to group, flirting with Goth and Punk, but mostly her counter-culture experiments had been expressed in terms of her footwear and eye makeup.

She had hung out in the Junior Common Room, where left-wing types with tattoos and piercings sat on battered old sofas eating subsidized sandwiches. This was where she had met Emily, an almost permanent fixture in the JCR, selling cut-price food and debating politics.

Now Emily was still talking. Marianne thought of something Joe Corcoran had said. She frowned: he planted ideas in a person's head that spread like a fungus. You might never have thought anything much about someone but after a few words from Joe you were zoning in on their previously unnoticed tics and affectations.

'The worst thing that ever happened to Emily,' he had said, one night, 'is Mandela being freed. She's going to have to find another song to play at her parties. You know that her father owns a department store? It'll be off to work for Daddy once she gets bored of posturing.'

Emily could be a little earnest. She often talked about 'anomie', 'construction of gender', 'situations' and American foreign policy. She was, however, high-minded, Marianne thought, watching Emily's mouth move. The world needed people to wrestle with conceptual questions. How much longer was she going to toke on the joint?

According to Emily, Fusty was a deep thinker. Marianne had seen little evidence to support this, but he liked to talk about certain movies in minute detail. Cheech and Chong's *Up in Smoke* was his favourite. He could quote it line for line, assuming the voices of the various actors. He seemed to watch epic amounts of television, rarely making it into college. Clare maintained his monosyllabic conversation had more to do with the amount of cannabis he inhaled rather than any great intellect.

'He's in some sort of drug-induced vegetative state, for God's sake,' she said. 'He can hardly string two sentences together.'

Marianne, thinking of Joe Corcoran's insidious words, sometimes wondered if taking up with Fusty was Emily's reaction to her bourgeois background and in particular to her father, who had probably emerged from the womb in a navy blazer and old school tie.

Fusty was sprawled on the shabby sofa, currently scratching his balls. His pupils had shrunk to pinpricks. He seemed to run off Emily's considerable energy. She was like a sort of mobile generator he plugged into. Marianne knew almost nothing about him other than that he was famous for repeating exams and was from Balbriggan. He was certainly extremely easy-going. He could have done with a good wash.

'Stop bogarting,' Fusty said, in a light but stoned voice.

Emily at last relinquished the joint, and Marianne took a deep puff. Gradually she felt a drug-induced calm suffuse her body and the guilt that was eating her began to dissipate: her mother had been upset getting into the car and Marianne had wanted to make it up with her, but then she had caught sight of Coleman behind the wheel in her father's seat and felt mutinous.

'That's strong,' Marianne said, as her body slackened.

'Shame Matt got ill,' Emily said.

'Yes,' Marianne said, glad that he wasn't there. She had almost definitely decided to break up with him.

When Marianne passed him the joint, Fusty took a drag and expelled a perfect smoke-ring. 'This is good stuff.'

Marianne pictured her mother's anxious face. 'I want to get seriously loaded.'

Marianne was on the verge of leaving Kehoe's. Her cheeriness was counterfeit. The place was thronged. Many of the day's graduates were celebrating. It was an electric night but nothing seemed right.

Emily had stayed with Fusty, who had been impossible to dislodge. Clare had gone off to meet Joe, which had made Marianne even crankier. For somebody who was not particularly biddable, Clare did a lot of what Joe wanted. She and Marianne had had a brief unsatisfactory conversation about Gretta's engagement, which had left Marianne feeling disgruntled. 'But I thought you said that you worried sometimes that your mother was lonely and that she smothered you. Surely it's a good thing,' Clare had reminded her.

'I don't really want to talk about it, Clare,' she had said shortly.

Then Alexandra had arrived with an entourage from a fashion show but tonight Marianne found the animated but aimless conversation dull. Alexandra certainly wasn't equipped to understand her pain. In all the times they had sat on Alexandra's bed discussing sex, life and men – through the fascinating prism of themselves, painting the glamorous futures that lay ahead of them – Marianne had gleaned scant details about Alexandra's set-up. Her parents were divorced. They couldn't stand to be in the same room. Both had remarried. She didn't care much for either step-parent. She felt neutral about her gaggle of half-brothers and -sisters. She was quite close to her brother, she supposed. She was sanguine about what had happened. Most of her friends' parents were divorced. In her teens she had disliked being shuttled between houses, particularly Christmas Day when much time was spent on motorways. But it was life. Alexandra, she suspected, thought of Marianne's close connection to her family as a Hibernian eccentricity.

Marianne set down yet another empty glass. She had been aiming to drink herself into a stupor. But no matter how much she drank or smoked she felt flat. She thought again of the day when the guards had come to the door.

'There's been an accident.'

It had been surreal. In those early days her mother and she had clung together like the survivors of a natural disaster. Earlier today her aunt Tess and Clare had urged her to think of her mother's happiness. But what about Marianne's happiness? Never once had she imagined she might lose both parents.

Marianne had been encouraged to consider her own happiness since childhood. She was an only child, born to parents who had given up hope of having a baby when she arrived. Her earliest pre-toddler memory was of two adoring faces peering into her pram. After her father had gone, it was inevitable that her mother would overcompensate for Marianne's loss. In those first awful years, marked by intense sadness, her doting aunts and Gretta had closed ranks around the sixteen-year-old bereaved Marianne, encircling her and protecting her against further harsh realities. Who could blame her for putting herself at the centre of every narrative?

Marianne looked around the room. The crowd obstructing her view of the bar parted briefly and she saw Joe Corcoran talking to Dervla Feeney, a well-known college personality and embryonic power-broker. She was an agile debater and had run for presidency of the Students' Union on a right-wing, anti-abortion platform.

'She's ultramontanist,' Matt had said. 'Over the hills to Rome in her views,' he had explained, when Marianne looked at him blankly. 'Actually, she's to the right of the Pope. She thinks the morning-after pill ought to be banned as an abortifacient.'

'Then she'll end up with a very big family,' Marianne had said tartly.

'Not before she's married,' Matt had smirked. 'She's against premarital sex too.'

Dervla and her sisters were famous on campus for their strong Catholic faith, their much-vaunted virginity and skimpy clothes. For handmaidens of the Lord, they had a suggestive, come-hither way of dressing. 'There's a lot you can do without losing your virginity,' Marianne had overheard one of them declare in the Buttery Bar one night. She had turned in time to see the maiden Feeney flashing a lascivious smile at two male classmates.

Marianne watched Dervla say something in Joe's ear. Then he saw Marianne. He left Dervla and sauntered over. 'Had a good day, Miss Dillon?' he said.

'Where's Clare?' she said.

'Gone home,' he told her, unfazed. 'She has an exam in the morning. You remember Dervla?' he said. The girl had followed him.

Marianne thought of Clare studying in her room. Most

likely it was cold as she stinted on heating to keep the costs down. Sometimes she fell asleep at her desk from exhaustion.

'Yes, of course,' said Marianne, with a hard look. The virginity thing wouldn't suit Joe. Matt had let slip that in certain circles he was called 'STD Joe' because of his rampant behaviour.

'Before Clare,' Matt had added. He called Joe 'the fanny magnet'.

'You say that as if it's a good thing,' Marianne had said.

'Lighten up, Marianne. It's a joke. Moral indignation doesn't suit you.'

There was something about Joe that sapped her sense of humour. Mainly Marianne wanted to protect Clare. She saw what attracted Joe to her. Clare had a stillness and poise that drew the eye. She was intelligent, moral and loyal. And although she lacked confidence in her appearance, she was attractive in a soft, feminine way. Marianne was stumped as to why Clare liked Joe. He seemed the opposite of the men in her family. But she had grown up in a house characterized by silence and stoicism so perhaps she found his brash, go-get-it ways enticing. Did she feel she needed his pep?

Marianne folded her arms across her chest. 'What are you doing now, Dervla?' she asked, eyeing the fitted suit.

'I'm a trainee solicitor,' Dervla said. She turned to a squat, powerfully built man with prominent ears who had materialized with drinks. His nose seemed to have been broken. His hair was wispy and he, too, wore a suit, pinstriped, with a waistcoat that drew attention to his substantial circumference.

'Cheers, Ed,' Joe said, relieving him of some of his cargo.

'This is my boyfriend, Edward Bell,' Dervla said, in a way that both irritated and mollified Marianne. She talked to them for as long as was necessary to be polite. The talk was mostly of their careers. They were three conquerors, she thought, single-minded, pushy, eyes on the summit, and was reminded of her own lack of ambition.

After she had left them Marianne walked the length of the pub, not sure who or what she was looking for. Then she heard his voice. He was sitting in the snug with some others.

'Well, hello there,' he said.

'Hi.' She raised her hand in a half-wave, then pressed on. She felt dazed. How many times had she dreamed of meeting him like this? She'd behaved like a half-wit. He looked so attractive, in his pale-faced donnish way, which suggested hours spent poring over texts. Among a sea of professors clad in cords and Hush Puppies, he stood out in his beautifully cut jackets. His hair was just the right side of dishevelled. His turn of phrase was exquisite. Here was a man who cared about the classics as much as she did. Many female students loved him but not as much as she did, she thought.

He had consented to supervise her thesis. Surely that meant something. Marianne believed in Fate, in cosmic connections. Life didn't just happen, as Matt had so depressingly suggested. Things took place for a reason. She had spent hundreds of hours contemplating his every look, and each utterance she felt had been directed at her. Sometimes she felt certain there were encoded messages in his eyes specifically for her. At others she doubted herself and was cast back into agony. She thought about him in the shower, shopping for food, putting on her makeup and mooning around college. She often thought about him in bed. She was sketchier on what his naked older body might be like. The imprint of his lips on hers was as far as she'd got. He was at least thirty. And now she had lost her chance to talk to him on a more equal footing. She went to the loo to regroup. She could hardly double-back, she thought, feeling crushed.

Then, on the way back from the ladies, she met him on the

narrow stairs. They stood on a step so close she could smell his beery breath, overlaid with the delicious scent of tobacco. A man pushed past them and Marianne nearly lost her balance. He stretched out a hand to steady her. 'Whoa. This place is crazy tonight,' he said.

'Yes.'

'So, you're off to Paris,' he said. 'Lucky you.'

'Yes,' she said, wondering how she could string out the encounter. 'I'm staying in the Irish college.'

He made a noise. 'The Sorbonne . . . the Panthéon . . . those majestic dimensions . . . breakfast in the Jardin du Luxembourg. I envy you. I love Paris. I love France.'

He seemed a little pissed, she thought. 'Me too,' she said. 'When my father was alive we went to France every year.'

'He's dead?'

'Yes,' she said, her voice suddenly thick. 'He died when I was sixteen. In a car crash. A drunk driver,' she added. 'He'd been playing tennis.' Why had she said that?

'It must have been hard.'

'I'm sorry,' she said. 'I'm quite drunk, I think.' She thought she might cry.

'Don't be silly,' he said, with a smile. 'The majority of the people in this bar are quite drunk. Including me.'

There was a short silence. He was looking directly at her with an expression she couldn't read. Her back was pressed against the wall. She was suddenly dry-mouthed.

'You're beautiful, you know,' he said, touching her cheek. His fingers felt cold. And then he moved the short space to kiss her.

3

September 1991

On a West Cork hill near Baltimore, not far from the town of Skibbereen, Clare knelt on a folded newspaper. She could feel the damp through it. In September life seemed particularly dismal. The dull, unseasonably cold day strengthened this impression. A low-lying sea fog shrouded everything. Beyond the stone walls of the graveyard PJ waited for her in his mud-spattered car. She would stay with him and Majella in their new pub that night.

The rose bushes her father had planted were flourishing. From the condition of the graves it was clear that he visited a lot. Clare felt the familiar sadness seeping in. In this beautiful graveyard, the ghosts of the past weighed on her. The last time she had seen her mother she had been ten. Her mother had raised the Sheila on its pulley until the clothes were near the ceiling, where they would dry quickly. Then she had turned to Clare, who had been eating mashed-up egg from a cup. Donal had already gone to bed but Clare had lingered in the warmth of the kitchen. Seeing that she had finished, her mother had shooed her away.

'Bedtime. Go on, you fairy, you . . .'

When Clare was in her pyjamas, her mother had come up with a hot-water bottle and kissed her goodnight. Later, barking dogs in the farmyard had heralded the arrival of a car and woken her up. She didn't know what time it was, but her bottle had gone cold. Pressing her forehead to the window, she had peered out at the wind-stunted shrubs, decorated with frost as a cold snap had taken hold, able to hear someone being ushered into the house. There had been the rise and dip of voices, doors opening and shutting.

Her mother had dropped dead by the range. Clare's memories of her were faded now and she had few photos. There was one black-and-white snap of her parents' wedding in Rome. On the back it said, 'St Peter's Square, 1958'. Her mother was smiling, wearing a matching coat and dress, a mantilla on her head. After she had passed away the house had died with her.

Clare paused, her eyes resting on the simple headstone. If she tried to focus on the banal, she thought she would be all right.

Sherkin lay behind them. Further out was the Cape. Clare loved the brackish smell of the sea, which she associated with growing up. When she was in Dublin she missed the wide open skies and the view of the islands. Although she liked her life in the city, she was essentially a country person. But she did not romanticize the country as city people did. It could be hard to make a living. Clare's father worked as a postman to supplement his income. Two of her five older brothers 'kept their hand in' at farming, but worked elsewhere from Monday to Friday, coming home in the evening to haul on wellington boots.

She had never had much time for the farm. She didn't miss the smells or stepping over muddy puddles. Nevertheless, she had imbibed her family's attitudes. Dogs lived outside. Horses were bred to be sold. Pigs' throats were slit. As a child she had disliked sentimental films that anthropomorphized horses, whales and dogs. There had seemed to her something cloying and even mentally deficient about them.

She dug a hole big enough for the geraniums she had

bought in the garden centre, enjoying the sensation of the moist brown soil between her fingers. Donal had loved flowers. The ditches around their house were bright with fuchsia, meadowsweet and foxgloves. 'I'd love to design gardens mixing cultivated flowers with wild ones.' He had wanted to plant at the back of the house. 'We could put a table out there,' he had said, in his sweetly serious way.

The brothers had been amused. Their father had said no. 'Are you gone soft in the head?'

In her family it was heresy not to revere the land, but flowers were a different matter. They could not be eaten and did not produce income. Aesthetics came a distant second to functionality and value. Many houses did not have back gardens. People liked to drive to the back door of their homes. Few people ate outside. Meals were speedy, for sustenance rather than pleasure.

Clare picked up her trowel and walked back towards the car. Suddenly she wanted to cry. The funeral was a visceral memory. She looked at the ground to steady herself. She could see, with almost photographic clarity, her brothers and father edging forward with the coffin above their heads. She remembered the congregation getting to its feet. She had followed, light-headed with grief, passing the crowd outside the church with their heads bowed and their hands crossed. The muttering had fallen away to silence. It was that she remembered most.

Country people dealt with life and death on their farms. They were comfortable with it. But on that occasion people hadn't known what to say. The blinds had been drawn as the hearse had inched through their village. They had passed the guesthouse run by two men who were said to be 'light on their feet'. She thought now of the casual way in which they'd called it the Fairy House.

She reached the car and opened the passenger door. 'Thanks,' she said, sliding into the seat.

'No problem,' PJ said.

The light was beginning to fade. He turned on the engine and they drove towards his place. He turned his pale blue eyes on her, a family feature. With his scrawny build and concave chest, Donal had looked nothing like PJ or the other brothers except for his eyes. Twins, she and Donal had favoured their mother's side of the family, though no one would have guessed that they were even related through all the years that she had been fat.

His friend had worked in the Botanic Gardens in Glasnevin. 'Eddie's a horticulturist,' he had said proudly, that day on the Green.

Eddie had had a Dublin accent. He had been tall but slight, with medium brown hair. Did he even know what had happened? She had never tried to contact him. It struck her as barbaric now that he hadn't been told. 'PJ,' she said, 'was there anybody at Donal's funeral we didn't know?'

Her brother glanced at her but didn't reply.

'Any strangers?'

'No,' he said, 'not that I noticed. Why?'

'No reason,' she said, leaning forward to turn on the radio.

When Clare was at home she had a habit of viewing the place through the lens she imagined her Dublin friends might use. When they spoke of 'West Cork' they didn't mean life on a small farm. They meant Baltimore where, in the summer months, visitors stomped about in life jackets shouting holiday hellos at each other and messing about with boats, or Glandore, where a mixture of tourists and blow-ins meandered about.

She wouldn't have liked to bring people home. She wouldn't

have felt relaxed trailing around Skibbereen after a crowd of Dubs, with their slightly too loud voices and ceaseless enthusiasm. The locals were glad of the tourist revenue but they didn't want to be gaped at as if they were exhibits in a museum.

Her earliest memories of the town had been on fair days when the old men came with their horses and carts and she waited with Donal for their father. She had thought of the town as a metropolis. Always they stood next to the Maid of Erin statue, with the plaque that read.

> Start Not Irish born man,
> if you're to Ireland TRUE,
> we heed not race, nor creed, nor clan,
> we've hearts and lands for you.

This version of Skibbereen was hers.

Now in the pub, Clare saw a neighbour pat the empty stool behind her. 'Now so, girleen. Sit here and talk to me. You're down from Dublin?'

'I am.'

'Your father will be pleased.'

'He will,' Clare said, wondering if he would come to the official opening of the pub. He rarely went out now. 'You keeping well, Madge?' she asked.

Madge's great size meant that her flesh overflowed the edges of the stool, and that she wheezed rather than spoke, her weak chest strained in carting around such a load.

'Yes,' she said, in her sinus-y way.

'How did the Stations go for you, Madge?'

'Erra sure grand, girleen. Father Levis did a great job.'

Shortly before her mother had died they'd had Stations. Having Mass said at home gave her mother a great excuse to spruce the house up – walls were limed and distemper used liberally. The world of the Stations was radically different from anything her Trinity friends had grown up with, Clare mused. It was a significant event in a community like hers. The Stations brought together people who might not otherwise meet. Neighbouring women contributed different types of cake, some of which had gone out of vogue, like Madeira and caraway seed – after the religious part, there was a party with people talking late into the night in the kitchen.

'And what do you make of your brother's new venture?'

'It's great,' Clare said.

'They have the place looking well.'

'They have.'

In reality, although the place was scrubbed clean and had been painted, it looked much as it had done under the previous ownership. The rooms over the pub where PJ and Majella lived were basic.

'We had to get out from above and make a start on life ourselves,' Majella had told her.

'I can understand that,' she had said. And she did. The gravitational pull of the farm and their father was strong. Majella, she sensed, would not be cowed.

'With what we've sunk into it,' Majella had said, 'we have to make do.'

'We'll tip away at it bit by bit,' PJ added.

'If anybody can make a go of it, it's Majella,' Clare said now to Madge.

'Right enough.'

Majella and PJ had met through Macra na Feirme at the Miss Blue Jeans Festival. Majella had once held the title 'Queen of the Land'.

Clare watched her now behind the bar, which was besieged.

Earlier Majella had drawn her aside. 'You don't think it's too soon, do you?' She had rushed on, 'We don't mean any disrespect, Clare. I know PJ's worried about it.'

Of course, he had said nothing about this to Clare. They had driven back from the graveyard in virtual silence. They didn't talk in their family.

'What with the opening being so close on the heels of the anniversary?'

Clare had given her a clumsy pat on the arm. 'I don't, Majella.'

It was three years. Yet he was with them all tonight, she knew, even with their brother Aidan, who had arrived at the pub with the exhaust of his beloved Opel spewing fumes and was now horsing around with his petrol-head friends.

'It's some undertaking all the same,' Madge said, making a whistling noise through her teeth, reluctant to let success and good cheer dominate entirely.

Madge was happiest when dealing with sickness and tragedy or discussing her ovaries, which had caused her much trouble. After Clare's mother's aneurysm had killed her, the McMahons could do no wrong. In the aftermath of Donal's funeral she had tried to wriggle in but had been kept at bay. She had sulked, like a dog denied a juicy bone.

'And how are you, Clare?'

'Couldn't be better.'

Madge looked vaguely dissatisfied.

'I think I'll go and give them a dig out.' Clare glanced towards the bar.

A voice stopped her as she made her way through the tangle of people. 'You're looking well, Clare.'

'Mossy.'

'Since you lost the weight.'

'Thanks,' she said, not really believing it. Recently her

confidence had ebbed, like water from a sink after the plug's been yanked out.

Mossy Jennings had been the first boy she kissed. He had escorted her to her debs, arriving half drunk with a box of Milk Tray and an orchid he had fastened around her wrist. In honour of the occasion she had had a corkscrew perm and jammed herself into a royal blue crushed-velvet dress that had pinched under the arms. In the photos she resembled a well-upholstered armchair. At the end of the night she had found that her blue eye-shadow had melted down her face. Nobody had told her. Mossy, with his streak of a body and long, narrow feet, had been as thin as she had been fat. By the end of the night they were being referred to as Stan and Ollie.

Donal hadn't been there although it had been his debs too. Mossy and she had tried to persuade him. It was hardly a surprise that he had refused. Day after day he had been taunted. It had only been a small group of culprits but they had been relentless. Feet had been extended so that he had gone flying. And there had been the names.

'How are things up in the Big Smoke?'

'Grand,' she lied. 'You're well, Mossy?'

'There is no fear of me,' he said.

There was a pause.

Images began to unspool in Clare's head. It had been a late summer's day with cottony clouds. Later the three of them had gone out to Sherkin in the boat. It had been a fortnight before the debs. They had been drinking all night, first at the Jolly Roger and afterwards at a house party, returning home at dawn. The small outboard motor had broken down so Donal and Mossy had rowed back. Clare remembered the banter, then the conversation dying as the boys had exerted themselves. She could almost hear the musical beat of the oars splashing against the water as the small boat cut through the sea. Donal had seemed content. It wasn't true that he had never been happy.

Their father had been waiting on the pier.

'What were you thinking?' he had roared, and Donal had gone the colour of porridge.

'You took the boat without asking. And only one life jacket. Jesus wept! Have you a scrap of sense in that head of yours?'

Afterwards Mossy and she had waited at a short distance. Clare had seen Donal kick a stone in a rare display of temper.

Now Mossy cleared his throat. He was thinking of that night too, she decided. 'Can I get you a drink, Mossy?'

Early next morning she was up before anyone else. She longed to be back on the train. After she had helped with the last of the clear-up, Majella and she had a cup of tea.

'Do you want a lift up to the house?' Majella asked.

'I'd like the walk.'

Clare didn't meet a car on the sleepy road. She passed the shed without turning. A swirl of images assaulted her but she made it into the house, bile rising in her throat. The smells were the same. The place seemed smaller and shabbier than she remembered from her last visit. Every time she came, the house seemed to have shrunk.

Her father was in his chair, in keeping with the unbending rituals of his day. He talked about the pot-holes that bedevilled the local roads, the weather, the GAA. Two lads from the parish played on the Cork team, a matter of local pride. 'Will they do it this year?' he wondered, not expecting an answer.

He barely mentioned her life in Dublin: he had a farmer's mistrust of the city. When it was obvious that he was going to say nothing about the opening of PJ's pub, she said, 'The opening went well.' There was no response: perhaps he hadn't heard her.

She made excuses about why she had to get back to Dublin. The guilt was like lead in her veins. She resented it. She couldn't help it if she didn't want to be at the farm, if she couldn't bear to be reminded of what had happened.

She looked at her snowy-haired father: did he ever think of the fight they'd had in the yard that day? Did he ever wonder how a son might feel when his father found him a disappointment? Then she looked at the lines etched on his face, the dead eyes, and had her answer.

When she was leaving he put on his cloth cap and slipped his feet into the wellington boots outside the back door. He clamped his hand on her shoulder, pressing it just before she walked away. He was still there as she rounded the corner.

They were talking about France. Boring stuff about monuments and restaurants. Clare had never been to Paris. Then, somehow, they had moved on to theatre.

'The Trocadero is steeped in the grand old tradition of the theatre,' Professor Patrick Kingston said, placing his knife and fork together and draping his arm over the back of the seat.

Clare had rung Marianne from a telephone box. 'Change of plan. I'm coming back early.'

She had heard Marianne smile into the phone. 'Oh, great. You've got to come and meet him. You'll love him.'

Marianne mentioned him in every second sentence. 'I presume you saw the comedy and tragedy masks above the restaurant door when you came in?'

'Yes,' Clare said, adjusting her position and sinking even further into the plush red velvet chair.

She tried to gauge his age from his face, and watched

Marianne give an open-mouthed laugh. In Clare's opinion, she was sitting too close to him.

'You'll see photos of famous Irish actors and small-screen stars dotting the walls,' he was saying.

Clare found it easy to picture him in the pit of a lecture theatre, striding up and down the stage, talking. He liked to talk.

'You haven't been here before, Clare?' he was saying.

'No.'

Clare had rarely eaten in a restaurant. Seven kids had meant that restaurants were beyond her family. She had once been to the West Cork Hotel in Skibbereen, courtesy of an aunt, to celebrate her place in Trinity. They had had high tea, with as many chips as she could eat, which had been a lot. Clare cringed now at her delight at the waitress and her stainless steel scoop which she delved repeatedly into the vat of golden chips for Clare's open gullet.

'The Gate will be putting on a full retrospective of Beckett's nineteen stage plays during the theatre festival,' he said, 'in conjunction with Trinity, which, of course, was Beckett's *alma mater*.'

'That sounds wonderful,' Marianne said. 'I'll definitely have to catch a few.'

Theatre wasn't really Marianne's thing although she had implied that it was. She read voraciously, though. Her room was filled with newsprint and novels.

Clare said nothing. She had once seen part of a Beckett play on television. With its minimal action and long silences, she had found it monotonous and incomprehensible. As a university student she had felt duty-bound to grapple with it, but had soon given up in favour of a soap. As he was a professor of English and paying the bill, she decided it would be rude to say so.

Clare didn't read much. At school she hadn't enjoyed English. She had found it excruciating to read out her cack-handed attempts at poetry or her plodding essays. She didn't get Emily Dickinson and her weird 'ellipsis' or the genius of Thackeray. A lot of literature left her cold. She had preferred the relative certainty of facts, figures and science.

Marianne's thesis was on 'The role of women in Victorian England, as reflected in *Jane Eyre*'. 'It's perfect for me,' she had told Clare. 'It has feminist undertones and Patrick Kingston's a feminist.'

'He's a man,' Clare had said.

'I just mean he's enlightened about women. Men can be feminists though.'

The lunch was nominally to celebrate progress on the thesis. Since she had come back from Paris, Marianne hadn't settled down. She went into college and dressed with more care but Clare wondered how much work she was producing. Since her mother's wedding, of which she had said uncharacteristically little, she had seemed restless. She refused to acknowledge that she might be jealous or fear being displaced in her mother's life.

'That's such balderdash, Clare,' she had said. 'I never had you down for an amateur psychologist. I just don't like the Ad Man.'

Coleman worked in advertising and Marianne loathed him.

Marianne and her professor were still banging on about Beckett. Clare was of no interest to him, she could tell. She wondered, with a sharp, almost physical pain, where Joe might be. Was he with somebody whose sexual horizons were broader than hers?

The previous month they had been to see *The Commitments*. When the lights came up Clare had said she'd loved it and wondered whether it would work in America with all the bad language. She hadn't seen it coming. While she had been looking at the screen, digging into their shared popcorn, he had been making his plan. As they stood outside the Savoy she was still talking about the movie when he had spoken the words she wished she could make him retract.

'I want a break.'

'What do you mean?' Clare had looked at him dumbly.

'I need some space, Clare,' he had said.

'I thought we were grand,' she had said, feeling a quiver in her spine.

'I'm moving home to live with my folks. It's more cost-effective for the moment. And I can work in the local pub. Nobody in the Inns will clock it.'

Joe was training to be a barrister. Pupils at King's Inns were forbidden to work in a shop or pub to support themselves. 'Apparently it would lower the standing of the profession,' he had told her. 'Of course it's to keep it nice and élite and the likes of me out.'

Clare had not heard the rest of what he had said. She had walked home numb.

After their split, her days had seemed formless, although they were anything but. She had a strict routine of work and study. That he was living with his family meant she couldn't track his movements. She couldn't loiter outside his rooms or flat as she had done in the past. It was not their first rupture, and if she was patient she would get him back, she told herself.

When Joe Corcoran had first asked her out she had looked behind her to see if he was speaking to somebody else. He had been a significant person on campus and he had chosen her. When he was elected president of the Phil, a debating society of which John B. Yeats, Bram Stoker and Oscar Wilde were alumni, Clare's pride on his behalf had been even greater than his own.

Joe was not particularly good-looking. He did not come from a well-known family or from money, so he wasn't pointed out in reverential tones as the scion of such-and-such. It turned out that his background was even more modest than she would have guessed: solid northside Dublin working class. His father worked in a factory and his mother part time in the local shop. But to Clare, Joe Corcoran was distinctly top drawer, even a bit of a rock star in the circles in which he moved. And she had sufficient ego to want Joe for his glamour and because he made her more interesting.

Long before they had ever spoken she had studied him on the ramp outside the Arts Block. Clare, like many of those who studied in the Science Building towards the back of the campus – Siberia – considered that ramp the epicentre of Trinity 'cool'. It doubled as a sort of catwalk, where people swished along to kiss each other on both cheeks in the continental style that Clare couldn't bring herself to ape. 'Sweep on, ye fat and greasy citizens,' Marianne liked to joke, assuming a theatrical voice whenever Clare joined the stream of students plodding down towards the Science Building in sturdy shoes and sensible rain gear. When Joe was holding court, Clare would watch him, not daring to wonder whether she might have a chance with him.

'I honestly believe you're better off without him,' Marianne had said.

How could she explain to her friend the ceaseless longing she felt to be near him? Marianne had broken it off with Matt and seemingly not given him a second thought, although he still waylaid Clare, desperate for information. Clare did not dismiss the unpalatable truth that she might have a capacity for humiliation: she would have taken Joe back without thinking.

In the early hours of the next morning, when the usual post-nightclub circus was taking place, the Bob Dylan tribute singer stationed himself under Marianne's bedroom window and began to busk.

'I warned him,' Marianne said, tugging the quilt off Clare's bed. 'You're helping me. I can't carry the water on my own.'

Protesting, Clare struggled out of bed and went with her to the kitchen, where they filled the washing-up bowl and staggered with it across the tacky lino. 'It's a terrible thing to do.'

'Shut up and heave.'

It had taken a few seconds for the water to fall the three storeys. 'You mad bitches!'

Marianne craned out of the window. 'How many times have I asked you nicely? How many times have I told you to sit on someone else's steps?'

He turned the air blue, swearing, and Marianne shouted: 'By the way, the seventies called and they want their music back. Bob Dylan is yesterday's man.'

'Like you'd know, you big culchie,' he bawled, pawing at the collar of his drenched shirt.

'The poor fella.' Clare felt sorry for him.

'That's not what you were saying last Saturday night.'

After they had shut the window, they fell onto Marianne's bed, laughing.

'Marianne,' Clare said, a little later, 'you often give me advice.'

Marianne zoned in on her. 'And now you're going to give me some?'

'You're not sleeping with the professor, are you?'

'Don't be silly.' Then she said, 'I like him because he's a great teacher.' As Clare tried to read her face, she continued, 'I admire him because he's so cultured.' She added, 'He's brilliant.'

'Is he married?'

'No.'

'Nonetheless he's your professor. There are rules against things like that.'

'Things like what?'

'Professors getting entangled with students.'

Marianne sighed. 'Rules, rules.'

'So you *are* sleeping with him?'

'Nope,' Marianne said. She grabbed a pillow and hit Clare with it. 'Quit worrying.'

4

April 1992

Eight people were squeezed around the table in a room filled with smoke. In fact, it was two tables of varying height over which a bedspread, masquerading as a tablecloth, had been flung. Seven of them were engaged in dinner-party chat – barely disguised one-upmanship about restaurants and films. Marianne was mainly silent. She forced herself to sip her wine so she didn't draw attention to herself.

'The hamburger at Wolfman Jacks is the best in town,' Matt said.

'I disagree. You can't beat the Miss Piggy Burger at Garibaldi's,' Philip threw over his shoulder, as he carried plates to the sink.

Scrawny, open-faced Philip was the nicest of Joe's sidekicks. Marianne watched Clare and him co-operating at the sink and wondered, not for the first time, if there was more to Philip's gallantry with Clare than just good manners. Four weeks previously she and Joe had reunited.

'Don't say anything,' Clare had said.

That Joe had split up with Clare during the week of Donal's anniversary had incensed Marianne. Now he sat, like an alpha dog, on a suitably high stool. He gave the impression that he was superior to everyone else. She watched him respond to the splashy laughter of Dervla Feeney, with whom he had arrived, so Clare had had to set another place. Dervla tossed her head back so that her big chest rippled beneath her red dress.

'Who does better chips? The Manhattan or Gig's Place?'
'The Manhattan.'
'How can you say that?'
'Come off it! Gig's every time.'
Marianne was glad when the conversation moved on to books.
'I really like *The English Patient*,' Alexandra said, her teeth stained purple-blue with wine. Even though it was summer, she was swaddled in a fur coat with a large artificial flower in her hair, dangling a cigarette from her lips. 'It was my grandmother's,' she'd said, kissing Marianne on both cheeks, 'so the animals died before I was born.'
Clare had visibly tensed at Alexandra's arrival, drawing Marianne aside and saying in a low, urgent voice, 'Tell her, absolutely no smoking dope.'
Alexandra brightened up a room with her whimsical humour, and she was always generous. Tonight she had brought two bottles of wine and a vast bouquet of lilies.
Clare's smiles had become mechanical – earlier she had been chipper. It seemed to Marianne that there was anxiety in Clare's every glance. She was like a punctured balloon. Marianne had offered to cook, although she hadn't felt like it, because Clare was not gifted in the kitchen. It was clear to Marianne, although nothing was said, that she had invested a lot in the night.
'Let's just do pasta with arrabbiata sauce and a green salad,' Marianne had suggested.
'Sounds brilliant,' Clare had agreed.
To save money, they had trudged down to Moore Street to buy the tomatoes and lettuce, where the traders yelled, 'Ten for a pound, love.' Clare still lived on very little and Marianne did not like to embarrass her.
Once or twice Marianne had made half-hearted forays

into the conversation but mainly she was trapped in her own worries. A part of her – the part that had been raised on fairy-tale endings – hoped that the handsome prince would rescue her from the tower but another part knew the outcome would be bleak.

'Me too,' Anne-Marie said. 'That story's a little slow-moving but beautifully written.'

Marianne was sitting beside Matt's new girlfriend. She liked her. She was funny, unfazed by Matt's use of obscure words, and able to tease him out of his pomposity. Marianne was relieved that she was no longer the object of his affections but was also glad for him.

'Ondaatje's Sri Lankan,' Matt said, his arm flung round Anne-Marie. After a pause, he added, 'I'm re-reading *War and Peace*.'

'I'm pretty sure I saw *Fever Pitch* on your bedside table,' Anne-Marie said.

Matt blushed.

There were hoots of derision. 'Matt, you pompous arse,' Philip said.

'You're very quiet, Marianne,' Joe said, from his end of the table.

She had felt his gaze landing on her from time to time but had decided that he was too self-involved to be monitoring anyone else. She shrugged.

'Anybody seen *Basic Instinct*?' Joe asked.

'It's pretty sexy,' Matt put in.

'I have – and I can't believe it was shown at Cannes,' Marianne said.

'Marianne's tastes are very arty and highbrow,' Joe said, to Dervla, 'courtesy of her time in Paris.'

Joe never missed an opportunity to send her up.

Dervla gave a conspiratorial laugh. Earlier there had been

legal talk, banter about judges and senior lawyers, in-the-know jokes. Joe had talked about the senior counsel that he was devilling for. He was well known for his socially conservative views. 'He's quite brilliant,' Dervla had said. 'And extraordinarily successful.'

It was convenient that Joe's faith would lead him down lucrative paths. He was a networker *extraordinaire*. Marianne pictured an older version of Joe chasing golf balls with other movers and shakers. She could see him with a cigar clenched between his teeth.

Her compassion for Clare was tinged with irritation. She listened to Dervla's hyena laugh and Joe agreeing with everything she said. It was like a mating dance. For all Dervla's supposed sexual unavailability, it was not hard to imagine her propped up in bed next to Joe. She felt like prodding Clare. There was something masochistic about her inaction.

Dervla tapped her wine glass with fire-engine red fingernails. '*Basic Instinct*'s awful,' she said, in her clipped northern accent. 'I'm sorry but I think it's a disgrace the way it portrays homosexual –'

'Homosexual!' Alexandra broke in, her eyebrows jumping.

'– homosexual relationships as if they're normal. The main star is bisexual.'

'Off with her head,' Alexandra said.

'Seems a bit extreme, Dervla,' Philip said.

Marianne eyed Clare. She never mentioned her dead brother's sexuality. Clare sprang up from the table and went to the kitchen area. 'I find that offensive, Dervla,' Marianne said.

Dervla's smile was challenging. 'I'm sorry if I'm out of step with the *zeitgeist* but I don't believe that homosexuality is a legitimate lifestyle option.'

Alexandra held out her glass. 'More wine, Philip, please.

And make it a big glass.' Then she said, 'Has anyone been to Shaft? The gay club on Ely Place?'

Clare slid back into her seat. She monitored Joe's expressions as if she was watching a film.

Marianne smiled at Alexandra. 'Not yet, but I'm planning to.'

Alexandra had a slug of her wine. 'I'd highly recommend it.'

'It's ironic that Shaft's in the basement of a building that is also headquarters to the Knights of Colombanus,' Marianne added.

'You're kidding,' Philip said.

'No,' Marianne said. 'I'm not.'

'The Knights of who?' Alexandra asked.

'Pointy-headed foot soldiers of the Vatican,' Marianne said. 'When they shut up shop for the day, having done God's work, the building is infiltrated by homosexuals with their poppers and ecstasy and unholy music.'

'I love it!' Philip laughed.

Joe was looking rattled now.

'I happen to believe we're at a crossroads in Ireland,' Dervla said, reaching for a lighter. 'Do we choose Shaft and hedonism or family values?'

'Hedonism every time,' Alexandra told her. 'Dervla, have you ever tried ecstasy?'

'Of course not,' Dervla said, tight-lipped.

Marianne saw Clare wince.

'Then you don't know what you're missing. You haven't lived until you've been neuro-chemically high.'

'That's a pretty fatuous thing to say,' Joe said.

'How can an experience be valid if you're not in your right mind?' Clare wondered.

It was a debate she and Marianne had had many times. Clare was anti-drugs but she let Marianne smoke dope in the flat.

Her father's death had impressed upon Marianne the transience of life. He had returned videos to the shop on time, consumed alcohol in moderation and never broken the speed limit – in fact, he had driven maddeningly slowly. How ironic, then, that such a cautious driver should have been cut down by random bad luck in the shape of a drunken young oaf who had refused to relinquish his keys to his friends. The thought lodged in her mind that it was futile to advance through life carefully measuring and weighing every risk.

'Well, you can apply that logic to drink, too, I suppose,' Anne-Marie said, 'although I've never tried drugs myself.'

'Part of the thrill is in its illicit nature,' Alexandra said.

'Where do you find these drugs?' Joe asked.

'Well, if you don't have a dealer you can get them down the alleyway by the Stag's Head. Next to Sides. It's like an open-air drug market.'

'I'm assuming you buy them from the likes of the young boys I teach,' Anne-Marie said, 'which I think is exploitative. You take drugs, adopt their lingo, have a bit of fun and then move on. They end up in prison or worse.'

Alexandra made a *moue*. 'Like everything else, where there's demand, there's supply.'

'And all this from a movie,' Philip said, bringing cups to the table.

Marianne had lapsed back into her own concerns by the time the subject she'd been dreading came up.

'Let's not go there,' said Matt, with a dramatic groan. 'We all know where we stand on it.'

'I agree. People's opinion on abortion is usually whatever they've been brought up with,' Anne-Marie said.

'This case will shape our society,' Dervla said.

Marianne felt transparent.

'I'm telling you, the Supreme Court was told to get into

that room and come back with the correct verdict,' Dervla said knowingly. 'It was a political hot potato.'

Marianne could see that Joe was primed to speak. She shrank back in her chair.

'I'm sorry,' Dervla continued. 'Irish people will never introduce a law that allows the destruction of a child's life.'

Marianne interpreted that as a dig at Alexandra.

But Alexandra looked amused. 'When you reduce what you're saying right down – because I read about this X case with fascination – you're pretty much saying you'd stop a fourteen-year-old girl who's been raped by her neighbour from travelling to a foreign country to have an abortion? I'm sorry, I know I'm English, but I think you Irish are absolutely mad when it comes to stuff like this.'

'Ireland is a Catholic country,' Dervla said flatly.

Joe nodded. 'When you get down to it, this debate is about values. Do you respect the right to life or not?'

Anne-Marie said, 'I'm not in favour of abortion on demand but do you not support abortion where a pregnancy is incompatible with life?'

'Where there's life there's hope!' Joe shot back.

Marianne looked at him with hostility. Colour was mounting in her cheeks. To have to listen to one of his harangues now. How could he judge women unless he had walked in their shoes? Marianne thought of Joe's disrespect to Clare, the plight she was in, and wanted to needle him. 'You sound like that professor you love so much,' she said, referring to a man who was known for his trenchant stance against abortion. Joe liked to parrot him.

Joe looked at her. 'You can talk – loving professors?'

Marianne felt the blood drain from her face. She glanced at Matt but he looked away. She and the professor had run into him one evening leaving the Lincoln Inn. Afterwards she had regretted agreeing to go to a pub so near Trinity. 'The best place to hide is in open view,' the professor had said. Marianne had felt Matt's eyes hot on their backs as they'd left but had said nothing.

Joe and she stared at each other. Marianne considered slapping him across the face. Instead she picked up her glass. A moment later Joe was shaking water from his hair like an angry dog. There was total silence, which Alexandra broke with a throaty laugh.

'You're such an arsehole, Joe,' Marianne said, standing up.

'And you're mad,' he said.

'I think you had that coming,' Alexandra told him.

But Marianne had barrelled out of the room.

She sat on the loo lid.

A minute later Clare opened the door, came in and turned on the taps. The partition between the living room and the bathroom was so thin that it was possible to hear the most intimate and embarrassing noises. Ordinarily when unsuspecting guests went to relieve themselves Marianne or Clare turned up the music.

'I didn't tell Joe about you and Kingston,' Clare said.

'I know.'

'What's going on?'

Marianne started, 'Clare . . .' She began to cry.

'Marianne, what's wrong?'

They heard laughter through the wall.

'Oh, God, Clare, I can't tell you. If you told Joe . . .'

'Marianne, please, you're frightening me.'

'Promise you won't tell Joe or anyone?' She wept.

'I promise.'

Then Marianne said the age-old words that spell either great joy or terrible regret.

'I'm pregnant, Clare. I'm bloody well pregnant.'

The next day Marianne and her professor sat under a beautiful Harry Clarke stained-glass window in Bewley's Oriental Café on Grafton Street.

'You've got to tell him straight away,' Clare had said.

When she had spoken to him on the phone, Marianne had panned the conversation for hope.

'We'll discuss it when we meet this afternoon, Marianne.'

The hours had crawled by. She had worn the blue spotted dress that now felt tight across her chest but which he liked. She had taken care with her makeup and twisted her long blonde hair into a bun he had once admired for showcasing her 'swan-like' neck. He had offered her tea. 'A sticky bun?' he had asked, with a politeness that scared her.

Now she listened to him recite once more the compelling reasons as to why she should have 'a termination' and why this must be the end of their relationship. His fingers were interlocked. It was as if he was giving a presentation. It wasn't hard to picture him plugging in an overhead projector to show slides.

'A termination is the only option, Marianne. I must stress the need for absolute discretion, for both our sakes.'

She scoured his face for any feeling. 'I love you,' she tried again.

He was looking at the nearby tables. 'Marianne,' he said, pushing away her hand. 'Please.'

Although there was a fire she felt cold. She thought of previous times when he had touched the side of her face and kissed her, when their bodies had touched. 'But I love you, Patrick. We love each other.'

'Marianne, this talk is doing us no good. I thought you understood I was never going to leave my wife. Of course you're special, and I hate to be cruel, but I was never interested in anything else. Any man would have done what I did . . .'

Marianne looked at him. She tried to make sense of what he was saying. Was she going mad? How could she have misunderstood him so badly? She'd thought they were soul-mates.

She remembered her shock when she had discovered he was married. She had been beetling across Front Square at the Trinity Ball and they had been coming towards her, arm in arm. She had stared at them stupidly.

'This is Jane, my wife,' he had said, the use of the personal pronoun scalding her.

She had not known what to say or where to look. She had blurted something, then escaped to get so drunk she had almost blacked out.

He had come looking for her the following Monday in the library. She had told him to leave her alone. For a number of days he had lurked outside the Berkeley Library, stepping forward from the shadows. 'Let me make it up to you,' he had said. 'She and I married young. Too young. I'm an ass but I'm crazy about you, Marianne. I'm obsessed with you. I think of you all the time. Whether I'll catch sight of you . . .whether we'll have an opportunity to speak . . .'

Marianne had taken this to mean that he didn't love his wife. She had grown to dislike the English rose pushing her into the role of adulteress, hating the pretty colour in her cheeks and the silky brown hair.

It was Marianne whom he had brought to London on a conference where they had made love in a bath, their knees banging against the enamel. It was there, she now thought, that the condom hadn't worked and they had conceived a child. She had believed that all that had happened between them was a prelude to their life together. But he would go back to his wife.

'You're a lovely girl and any man would be delighted to be with you, but I can't offer you what you want,' he was saying, his voice devoid of feeling.

She left while he was still talking.

The bus made its way through the dismal streets, the rain hammering down. Marianne was glad of it: it meant fewer people were about. Still, she kept her face averted from the window. They had told everyone they were going to Cork.

Clare had made no recriminations. They had hashed it out a number of times. Then Clare had gone to his office and extracted the money from him.

'I'm coming with you.'

'You can't – your finals.'

'I'm coming. That's an end to it.'

They had lapsed into silence. If she was truthful, his lost feelings for her were as painful to her as the prospect of the termination. Across the aisle, a man sat with giant headphones and a box of records on the seat beside him. Marianne avoided his eye. She had rung a doctor on the north side of the city, away from college and the flat.

'You do understand that if I think you're going for an abortion I'll be forced to notify the guards?' he had said, stony-faced, as she sat opposite him, her chest tight.

Alexandra's mother had arranged the appointment at the clinic.

Marianne thought of all the things he had said to her. She pressed her mouth together with a thumb and a finger. But the tears came anyway.

'I thought he loved me,' she whispered.

'I know,' Clare said.

5

Easter 1993

Clare had a hazy sense that Dublin was changing. Bars, restaurants and coffee shops were springing up all over the city. The economy was steadily improving and the streets teemed with confident, aspirant young people. She, though, was an overworked junior doctor at the Meath hospital and had little time to enjoy the new Dublin or do anything but work, eat and sleep. This was not the case with Marianne, who appeared to be aspiring to an unofficial PhD in nightclubbing.

Sometimes Clare felt she didn't really know the city apart from her narrow patch. She went to the hospital. She came home and slept. On the rare occasions she and her colleagues went for drinks, it was to Cassidy's down the road from work. Otherwise she walked down to Joe's flat on the quays. It was then, as she crossed O'Connell Bridge, that she was most aware that the city throbbed with new rhythms she knew nothing about.

She told herself that if she had blinkers on, as Marianne regularly implied, she needed them to get to where she wanted to go. Sometimes she worried that her strategy of deferred gratification might mean she was missing out but she didn't have the luxury of a second chance. Unlike Marianne, Clare had no back-up. She was on her own. In some ways this was a good thing. It certainly gave her the impetus to work and drove her on. And there were comfort and security to be had in routine and her limited horizons. In her small amount of free time, she allowed herself to dream of a life that was fragmented not by death, sorrow and regret, but instead by new beginnings. And at the centre of this vision of contentment was Joe.

The previous weekend, on a five-minute coffee break, she had read of a forthcoming marriage in the paper.

Dervla Feeney – Edward Bell

Mr and Mrs William Feeney of Kilcannon, Ballyhacket, Co. Donegal are delighted to announce the engagement of their daughter Dervla to Edward, son of Mr and Mrs Alec Bell, Ennis Road, Co. Limerick.

Now it was Good Friday, a rare day off for Clare, and her chance to consider the significance of the announcement. Though she had tried not to obsess about Dervla and Joe, that notice was the most uplifting piece of news she'd had since she'd won her place at Trinity. The day had begun on such a positive note that she decided she would dedicate it for once to doing very little. She would put off wondering whether or not to make the trip home on Sunday to see her father.

She would also park her mounting worries about Marianne. Ditto her less pressing but more or less constant concern about Joe and where their relationship might be going. Since her internship in Limerick, when she was permanently anxious about how he might be occupying himself in her absence, she had tried to train herself not to think about it. As Joe had said, 'A relationship cannot survive without mutual trust as its base.' When he talked about his glittering future at the bar, she didn't ask where she figured in it. While she was ordinary, Joe was extraordinary. He admired her independence. He didn't carp when she had to study and work. Although this was helpful on a practical level, she would have liked him to fight for more of her time.

The problem was, the more elusive Joe became, the more she wondered where he was and with whom. Clare had a strong impulse to love and be loved but she wasn't very good at it. But this was a neurotic, unhelpful way to think. She wouldn't waste her free time brooding in this way.

She might ring a colleague from the hospital. She couldn't really call Orla a friend – they enjoyed the odd coffee together and once or twice they had gone to the pictures. There had been talk of other excursions. They got on well but Clare had never been particularly good at friendship. Since playground days she had struggled to understand the underlying currents. People fell out of favour, bright new alliances sprang up around her and she never got to grips with what had happened.

She might look into getting her hair cut – her split ends were multiplying – but grooming came way down her list of priorities. Maybe she'd stroll through St Stephen's Green, sit for a while on a bench and enjoy the daffodils and ducks in the spring sunshine. She was not particularly dewy-eyed about nature, but spring had been her favourite time of the year at home, with the new lambs and the hedges growing green. Maybe she'd duck into St Teresa's, the church down the little lane off Grafton Street. She might treat herself to a bite somewhere if anywhere was open. Later she would throw herself down in a chair, watch television and eat a hot cross bun, maybe even two.

When she was planning this day of relaxation she hadn't bargained on bickering with a spiky, only partially *compos mentis* Marianne. There was invariably static in the air when they met now. Sometimes Clare kept to her room if she heard

Marianne banging around in the living room. Once recently she had eaten her meal sitting on her bed.

At a quarter past eleven Clare heard Marianne stirring. She immediately felt cross: there had been an empty milk carton in the fridge, which meant she couldn't have her cornflakes without trekking to the corner shop. Nor had there been any butter, and in the bathroom the shampoo bottle had been full of soapy water. The agreement was that if an item ran out the last user replaced it, with kitty money. Also, when she had surfaced the living room had smelt like an ashtray and the sink was full of dirty dishes, including a saucepan that had been impossible to scrub even using a scouring pad. She had found a glass of red wine on the kitchen table with a fag end floating in it. She was tired of being Marianne's factotum.

When Marianne emerged from her room, she lit a cigarette. The smoke wafted in Clare's direction. 'Morning.'

'Hi,' Clare said, studying her.

Marianne was dressed in a tiny T-shirt, which read 'Pretty Vacant'. It served to reinforce how blade-thin she had become and how her once generous chest had all but disappeared. She was wearing it with a pair of sequined micro-shorts, which were chafing her skin: an angry red rash mottled one concave thigh. She looked clammy and there was a distinct sheen on her forehead. 'Any news?' she asked, with a slight slur.

A number of things were apparent to Clare. Marianne hadn't undressed before falling into bed. And she probably hadn't been there long. She was either drunk or experiencing withdrawal from some illegal substance.

'Not much. Good party last night?'

Marianne had sunk to the floor and was hugging her knees. 'Yes. Any news you?'

'Not really,' Clare said, returning to her paper. She would

not, she decided, mention the milk, the shampoo or the mess. She didn't have the energy. And actually, she thought resentfully, she baulked at the idea of being forced once more into the role of Clare the Enforcer of the Rules.

Then Marianne said, 'I was thinking of having a get-together here later.'

Now Clare looked up. 'I'd prefer it if you didn't.'

'Why?' Marianne said, frowning. 'It's Good Friday so all the pubs and clubs are closed.'

'Like you said, it's Good Friday. I won't be drinking and I really don't want anybody else doing it in my home. Plus I'd like the place to be quiet.'

'You're kidding me. A ban on booze? Are you for real, Clare? Seriously?'

'Marianne,' Clare said, with a small sigh, 'I don't mind if you drink somewhere else. It's none of my business. I'm just asking you to respect my beliefs.'

Marianne pulled on her cigarette petulantly. She looked bug-eyed and out of it. 'You're a scientist, Clare. I don't get it. I mean, c'mon, do you actually believe in Adam and Eve and the idea of some sort of mystical overlord?'

'Faith and science are different things. I believe in both,' Clare said, noticing that Marianne's pupils were extremely dilated.

Marianne said, 'Is this Joe talking?'

'No.' Clare missed the robust, cheerful version of Marianne, who had bounced in the door and gabbled about her day, about life, imagining what the future might hold for them: she would be a famous writer and Clare would be a doctor, who would find the cure for some form of cancer.

Clare had first come across Marianne during their first week at college in the hostel where they were both living that year. Marianne had been cursing into the payphone about her bad luck at being shoved into an establishment run by nuns. 'It has a curfew and a no-gentlemen-callers rule . . . I know . . . I'm serious. I have Aunt Tess to thank for having me dumped in this shithole.'

Clare had been taken aback by her coarse language. She had been brought up strictly, with the belief that bad language was unladylike. A moment later she was also struck by how brazen the other girl was in complaining about the head nun so openly when she could have materialized at any moment: 'I swear she's not human. She sneaks around the place silently with her big, bulgy eyes. It's creepy.'

This observation amused Clare because it had the ring of truth. The nun's shoes never squeaked on the highly polished floors and she seemed to spring from nowhere.

'The one funny thing about this hellhole is that at college it's called the Virgin Megastore. With good reason.'

That remark had made Clare feel self-conscious. She had been moving away when Marianne swung around.

'I wasn't listening,' she had blurted.

Marianne smiled. 'Okay.'

Clare felt exposed.

'I need to get out of this place. Do you fancy going for a pint?' Marianne added.

Clare had been pleased and anxious in equal measure.

They had hung out quite a bit in the first two weeks. While Clare was glad of Marianne's companionship, she had assumed she would be phased out as Marianne established herself in college and made friends higher up the social pecking order. When this had not happened as their first term ended, she marvelled that the freewheeling Marianne had chosen her. By the Darwinian principles that drove college life, and made you 'somebody' on campus, Marianne bested Clare on all fronts – she was fashionable and socially confident while Clare was none of these – yet they had become firm friends. She decided it was a mystery why two people gravitated towards each other. Who could say what particular alchemy caused one person to choose another?

From that first night Clare had always been conscious of the vaguely thrilling whiff of sulphur around Marianne, her aura of glamour and possibility, and how, in an indirect way, it might reflect well on herself. But there had never been this dark undercurrent.

'I suppose you're off to Mass,' Marianne said, expelling a cloud of smoke belligerently. Her fingers were yellow with nicotine. What had started as a social thing now seemed to be a habit.

'There's no Mass on Good Friday,' Clare said, 'but, yes, I will be paying a visit to the church.'

It was easy to mock the intricacies of dogma and doctrine, to find fault with the institution, but Clare found peace in church, with music and words that often floated over her head but satisfied some inner need. Sometimes she felt renewed simply from sitting in a pew alone in the silence.

Clare's memories of religion were positive. She and her mother had gone to Sunday Mass at eight, just the two of them, without her father or any of the boys. Her shoes would be waiting by the back door on a sheet of newspaper, one pair in the long row polished by her father the night before. On the way back they called into the shop to buy cream for Sunday dinner, the papers and a bar of chocolate for Clare to be eaten later. After her mother's death, and again, more strongly, after they'd buried Donal, Clare had thought, Why me? But why not me? That was what her faith had helped her to understand. Why should somebody else have been chosen to bear those crosses? And in this thinking Clare found a sort of solace, as she did in the idea that she might one day be reunited with her mother and brother.

'I think it's primitive,' Marianne said, 'that there's no alcohol sold on Good Friday. What a backward little country this is.'

No drink was sold on only two days of the year in a country where people drank all the time. Was it really so oppressive, Clare wondered. And in some hazy, not very well thought-out way, she saw this custom as a link to her upbringing and heritage.

'Off for a good bout of self-mortification?' Marianne continued crossly.

It was Marianne who was engaged in self-mortification, Clare thought, feeling a complicated mixture of emotions that included anger and sadness.

'I don't know how you stick it,' Joe had said. 'She's putting you at risk by taking drugs in your flat. You should move out.'

Clare had considered it. She didn't relish coming home, cross-eyed with tiredness, to overflowing ashtrays and the Happy Mondays – who sounded anything but happy. But she couldn't leave Marianne.

Post-London, Marianne had slouched around in the flat for a week, not getting dressed, watching television. She had said nothing about what had happened, which for Marianne, who liked to talk everything out, was disturbing.

A number of weeks later Clare and Marianne had been in the Marx Brothers on George's Street, enjoying what was becoming a rare moment together. Clare's exams were finished and she was on the verge of moving to Limerick.

Marianne picked at the doorstep of a sandwich. Clare was glad she was eating. She seemed to survive on a diet of vodka and cigarettes and God knew what else. Then she had doubled over in pain and had been barely able to walk. Clare had had to coax her into a taxi to go to hospital.

'No way, Clare,' she had managed to gasp, 'after that last doctor. They'll be judging me and looking at me.' She had not been for a post-abortion check-up so Clare guessed there was a link between that and the pain.

At the hospital they had cleaned her womb and found a piece of tissue that had been lodged there since the abortion. 'The endometriosis has spread from your Fallopian tubes to your uterus. You may never carry a baby to term,' the doctor had said. 'It's hard to be accurate about the percentage chance but you may be infertile.'

Clare had held her as she howled. After that Marianne had turned away from her and begun drinking in earnest. Night had become day. The details of daily life seemed not to matter. Now and then traces of the old Marianne emerged. Once, Clare had found her sifting through old photos. 'This is my dad,' she had said.

But in the main Marianne radiated misery. Clare thought of the waiting room at the abortion clinic and the eyes that had never met. Marianne seemed hell-bent on self-annihilation. Her body got tinier and her spirit had withered.

Clare had come back from Limerick to discover that Alexandra had virtually moved in and that Marianne had bleached her hair.

'You know, like Courtney Love. The girl with the band called Hole. She goes out with Kurt Cobain.'

Like two tops, Alexandra and she spun from the Chocolate Bar to the Globe to Hogan's, drinking brightly coloured cocktails. With her job in fashion, Alexandra got them in free to functions and openings. It seemed that social pre-eminence was everything. Alexandra was the only part of her old life that Marianne hadn't jettisoned. She was held out as a

Bohemian pioneer, fearlessly exploring life, but to Clare Alexandra seemed jaded and lost, incapable of self-regulation. The luminous beauty was dimming and Clare thought she could see the middle-aged woman she would become.

They went out dressed in knee-high boots and what looked almost like bikinis, over which they threw coats until they reached whichever club they would party in that night. If Clare voiced dissent, she was told she was tragically staid. Maybe she did need to be jolted out of her dull routine but she didn't want to stumble through life half intoxicated. What were Marianne and Alexandra doing but blocking out reality?

Clare often came back after a long shift to find Marianne holding court in the smoky flat. Alexandra and she colonized the living room so that Clare felt like the outsider in her home. Alexandra often ended up passing out on the sofa, wan and twitchy, her breathing ragged. They talked about going to Manchester, the epicentre of a music and clubbing scene they professed to love, yet never made it. Their conversation had become rambling and repetitive.

'How's Emily?' Clare asked now.

Marianne shrugged. 'Off busying herself with East Timor, I'm guessing.' She lit another fag.

She had acquired new friends to whom Clare wasn't properly introduced. Emily, with her philosophizing and ideas, was no longer interesting. Marianne didn't even read any more. Her talk of becoming a writer had died. All other activities had been sidelined in favour of the relentless pursuit of pleasure. And Clare, who was in a different orbit, was completely cut out, which hurt.

'You don't like Alexandra,' Marianne said sulkily, like a teenager. 'That's why you're asking about Emily. You were never that hot on her before.'

'I don't dislike Alexandra,' she said, wondering if that was true, 'but she drinks too much.'

'You think everyone drinks too much,' Marianne said, picking at her rash. 'Do you never want to have fun, Clare? Take drugs . . . experiment?'

'I don't believe in taking drugs. And I have to work to earn money to live.'

'Pointed,' Marianne said.

A beam of sun hit Marianne's face so she squinted. The skin under her eyes looked bruised.

Clare decided to brave it. Although she was tired of being viewed as a dull parental figure, she would say the unsayable. 'When was the last time you made it into college?'

'Dunno.'

College was a remote land that Marianne never visited. In theory after London she had requested a change of supervisor. But in reality she had never gone back. And yet the subject was taboo, as were the abortion and the professor. A line had been drawn under the entire episode. But the fiction was maintained that she was working on her thesis.

Marianne got up a little unsteadily. 'I'm going out. See you later. Or not, as the case may be.'

Clare heard a tap being turned on in the bathroom. She was fairly certain that the backdrop to this was Marianne vomiting into the loo. It seemed to Clare that her friend was walking a high wire and that she was bound to fall off.

When Clare found Marianne, she was crawling around on the gurney, wanting to get over the metal sides. Her face was grotesquely swollen and her lip split. Clare felt a catch in her chest.

Marianne thumped the side of the cot. 'I want to go home to the flat with you,' she moaned.

'You're going to be fine,' Clare said, trying to soothe her. 'When you're better we'll go home.'

The call had come from a nurse in the Meath hospital. 'Your friend has been in a car accident. She asked us to call you.'

'She's been given morphine intravenously,' the nurse warned, when Clare arrived puffing, having run most of the way, 'so she's a little bit out of it. She was drifting in and out of consciousness in the ambulance but she's stable now. She's been calling for you all the time.'

Clare lowered her voice. 'Do you know what happened?'

'No,' the nurse said, 'but I gather she was cut out of the car by the fire brigade. And she was severely intoxicated. She was lucky.'

'Was there anybody in the car with her?'

'Two others. They've been discharged.' She continued: 'We're assembling a team, a surgeon and an anaesthetist, and they're going to operate on her ankle as soon as they have a theatre.'

When Clare spoke to the consultant, he explained that Marianne's ankle was badly fractured and he had to put a pin in it.

Later, when Marianne had calmed a little, Clare pieced together more of what had happened. Marianne had crashed her on–off boyfriend's car. He had been beside her in the passenger seat and seemed more of a drugs buddy than a boyfriend. He had once been an amateur boxer and now he was a body-builder who moonlighted as a bouncer. His pumped-up biceps were encircled with tattoos. When they were drunk, he and Marianne fought. Then there were steamy reconciliations. Clare couldn't see that they had anything in common apart from drug-taking. Alexandra had been in the back.

Marianne slurred, 'The guards want to talk to me, Clare.

I was driving with no insurance and I had a bottle of vodka between my legs. We crashed into the back gates of Trinity.'

'Very rock 'n' roll,' Clare said, aiming for a levity she didn't feel.

Marianne winced. 'I've really messed up.'

'Well, at least the car wasn't stolen.'

'Stop making me laugh, Dr Death,' she said, using a nick-name Clare hadn't heard for a while. 'It hurts too much.' As Marianne was wheeled away she said, 'Clare, I'm sorry about everything. I really am. I don't want to lose you. You're my sister.'

Clare had never been able to stay angry with Marianne. Just when she had alienated you she made some gesture, like a lovely note tacked to the fridge, the gift of a lipstick or a book that Clare would never get round to reading.

Clare went outside to think. Smokers chatted in a little huddle around the door. There were times when she almost wished she smoked so that she could casually strike up con-versations with strangers. Now she tried to focus on the decision she had to make. If she went ahead, Marianne would be very angry. She might see it as a big betrayal. But what had just happened was not some isolated mishap. Marianne's recent escapades had got steadily crazier and she regaled them to Clare with a glee that bordered on maniacal.

'We went skinny-dipping at the Forty Foot,' Marianne had said, falling through the door, her hair a wet tangle, her eyes glittering in a way that wasn't natural. Clare had a vision of Marianne in the rough sea off the rocks. Swimming at the Forty Foot at midnight on a November night, with the tem-perature close to zero, was crazy, but Marianne had just treated it as a lark: she seemed to have no sense of the danger she was courting.

Another night Marianne seemed to lose control of her

limbs. Her balance was off and she crashed into the furniture. 'I've taken ketamine by mistake,' she'd said, shivering on the couch in the foetal position. 'Call Alexandra.'

Clare had been horrified. Ketamine was a horse tranquillizer used by vets, an anaesthetic.

'Call Alexandra, Clare, please. I need her to talk me down. I'm freaking out here.'

Another night they had come back from a club off O'Connell Street called the Asylum. Clare didn't need finely tuned antennae to know that they were completely out of it. Even Marianne had seemed shocked by what had gone on in there. 'Somebody pulled a gun on the guy sitting next to me,' she said, subdued.

On St Patrick's Day a crowd of them had driven to Cork to a rave. They had returned at six in the morning, high as kites.

'Anto lost concentration at the wheel,' Marianne had laughed. 'We ended up on the wrong side of the road. If I hadn't woken up we would have smashed into a lorry.'

A line had been crossed a long time ago. Now Clare was appalled that she hadn't recognized it. Or more accurately, she thought, for recognizing it but doing nothing about it. She was left with no choice.

Clare remained at the hospital while Marianne was in surgery and was by her side when she woke up. And she stayed at her bedside until the door opened and Gretta walked in, her face collapsing at the sight of her daughter.

'You didn't, Clare,' Marianne said.

6

July 1994

Sexy-bum guy had disappeared into the ether. Marianne felt disappointed. There was a weird vibe at the party anyway. First off, there was the question of location. They were stuck in the damp basement of what had probably been a nice house. It had clearly seen better days, but now it was tumble-down, with cracks and damp patches creeping up the walls. This was presumably why Emily's cousin Susie and two or three others got to rent such a big place on the beach in Sandycove.

Next up was the bizarre crowd, some of whom seemed to be auditioning for Stereotype of the Year. Marianne was having difficulty in working out the mix. It was as if the remnants of different cliques at college had been mingled in some weird cocktail. First, Susie and her boyfriend were swanning around with pastel jumpers knotted around their shoulders. They had been the doyens of the business course at Trinity. Susie, Marianne suspected, would dot her i's with hearts. The library was one of her stamping grounds: there, she displayed herself, whispering theatrically, beside a stack of pinkish ring binders containing what were probably very neatly written notes. The boyfriend drove an MG and, in Marianne's view, could have done with a couple of holes drilled in his head to let in some air. Their presence accounted for the preppy contingent in white jeans and bright tops, scrunchies and loafers.

Then there was a more rural-looking bunch, mainly male,

galloping around and intermittently tossing a rugby ball in the garden, with the odd girl shouting, 'Hi, lads.' She'd been told they were vets. Emily had come with a group of shabbily dressed social-worker friends, who were dancing at the edge of the room to the lame music. She was grim-faced, trying to break up with Fusty. He lay like a sack of dreadlocked spuds in a corner, with drooping eyelids, too stoned to be overly perturbed or to give her the sort of juicy breaking-up conversation she craved. Emily loved talking about emotions, which Marianne had gone off.

'Okay, man,' Fusty kept saying. 'Okay.'

Translation: *Please stop wrecking my buzz.*

The beer was vaguely warm. The wine was gone. A guy with bad skin stood sentry over the music system in the corner.

'Do you have anything decent like Blur or Portishead?' she had asked him earlier. 'Or Jeff Buckley . . . or anything basically that isn't what you are playing? C'mon . . . seriously.'

Every now and then a plump girl – presumably another flatmate – in a curiously old-fashioned nightie and slippers came into the room and shouted about keeping the music down, which wasn't helping to get things going. This was what happened when flatmates decided to hold a party as a group effort. There was no continuity.

Marianne scanned the room again for the cocky guy and felt roundly depressed. She missed Alexandra, who had been hauled home to England more or less permanently when Gretta had contacted her mother and related the incident of the vodka, the car and the Trinity gates. Although she and Clare were getting on better now, Clare was a poor substitute on the partying front, especially since that prime bollocks Joe had broken it off with her again.

'Don't ever take him back this time, Clare,' she had said. 'You're worth ten of him.'

Marianne's partying had severely contracted anyway. When Clare had opened up – sometimes in her darker moods Marianne applied the word 'ratted' – to Gretta about Marianne's lifestyle, Marianne had been forced to make a long list of promises, some of which she had honoured.

Tonight she had swerved a little from the path of righteousness. She had taken half an E, courtesy of Fusty, although she hadn't come up at all. As a consequence she felt pissed off at her failure to get high and racked by guilt. It was a lose–lose situation. The second she'd popped the small white pill with the dove imprinted on it, she'd thought of her mother and Coleman. How dare he lay down the law? She would take correction from her mother but *not* from him.

In the main she didn't regret her clubbing experiences. The problem was that if you weren't completely off your tits there was no point in it. When you took ecstasy things that might once have seemed banal were fascinating. She had read an article in the *Face* that suggested house music had emerged in response to the Thatcher years. The theory was, roughly, that while the rave scene was about feeling 'loved up', people retreated into their own mental space, not really communicating. There was something in that, she thought, visualizing the lines of dancers fused by the music yet lost in their own bubbles. I don't need E to be lost in a bubble, she thought, feeling low.

Gretta had cut back her allowance drastically. 'I have to,' she had said, when Marianne had been recovering at home, hobbling around in a cast on crutches with Coleman driving her mad. 'You had too much money and you went mad. I blame myself.'

And I blame Coleman, Marianne had thought, although this was illogical, she knew. It felt good, though, to hate Coleman. When she pictured him lying on her father's side of the bed, his grey head denting the pillow where her father's should have been, she felt angry. She was adept at finding things to power her dislike. The smell of his cologne, the fact that his car was a little too ostentatious and not one her father would have driven.

Marianne had worked in a series of casual jobs to supplement her funds. One waitressing job followed another. Usually she left before she was fired.

'You finish your master's,' her mother had said, 'and you go away for a while to get yourself together. Then I suggest you come back and think about doing a H Dip – you'd make a good teacher.'

Marianne hadn't finished her master's but she was going away. Her master's was now a bad joke. It had been years, but she still refused to acknowledge that she might not complete it. Very often she got up determined to make progress on her thesis, but by the time she had dressed and trailed into college, her motivation seemed to have dwindled on the way.

Marianne still thought of the bastard. No matter how hard she tried to convince herself that she had put the experience behind her, it reared up in her consciousness again and again. She told herself she didn't care, but in some way it had detached her from her life so that now nothing seemed to matter very much.

The sorrow and fear had been so overwhelming. A wave of grief had engulfed her. Just after he had dumped her she had bitten the tops of her arms in a frenzy so that they bruised yellow and brown. When she had heard she might be infertile she had briefly considered throwing herself under a bus. She still wasn't certain if she had contemplated the idea as a melodramatic gesture or as an actual possibility. She wanted kids. The prospect of perhaps being unable to have them had clarified that.

She had loved him completely, or so she told herself. Sometimes she wondered if she would ever get over him, if she was condemned for the rest of her life to have feelings for him. His rejection had stoked the fires of her obsession. It didn't matter that somewhere in her psyche she knew he was a coward, who was not worth it.

She had dumped Anto in accordance with Gretta's instructions. She didn't miss him or any of their so-called mates. Those relationships had been almost entirely based on booze and drugs. They had been good-times friends. It was amazing how much more interesting people were when you were all out of it. You sat around telling each other how amazing you were, stroking each other and holding hands so that you remained earthed. It was always a shock to see how less attractive people looked in reality, how the house you were partying in was a dump, how the music began to grate as your serotonin levels plummeted, thanks to the pills.

'"Johnson's Baddy Powder,"' the sexy-bum guy said, reading the legend on her T-shirt. 'I like it.'

Bingo. And not a bad opener either. She had clocked him almost immediately on her arrival. They had thrown each other a number of surreptitious glances over the previous hour or two. And she had thought, Game on. Then he had disappeared.

It was galling that he had taken so long to drift over. But here he was. He was good-looking in the square-jawed well-built way she tagged as conventional. Marianne had always told herself that she wasn't into looks but deep down she knew that was untrue. On the downside his shoes were only okay. And his jeans weren't great. He had, however, an inescapably epic arse.

She lit another cigarette.

'You're a chain-smoker,' he said.

'Sue me.'

'Cancer sticks.'

'Jesus, Dad, it must be nearly time for your bedtime,' she said. She caught the faint, pleasant smell of soap.

'Would you like me to get you a drink? I'm getting myself one.'

'Go on so,' she said, assessing him further. 'I'll have a beer.'

He took his time and she began to wonder if he was coming back. She applied some lipstick and hoped, annoying herself, that he would come back.

Then he was there, offering her a bottle.

'Cheers,' she said.

'What's your name?'

'Marianne Dillon.'

'Peter Campbell,' he said, stretching out a hand, 'but you can call me Pete.'

'Hel-lo, Pete.'

'Who are you friends with here?' he said. 'Let me guess. It's the homicidal bird who keeps screaming for the music to be turned down.'

Her face cracked into a smile. 'I'm here with my friend Emily. She's breaking up with her boyfriend in the corner.'

'They look happy.'

'Don't they.' Then she added, 'I've taken an E and it hasn't worked. It was probably a bloody aspirin. You know yourself.'

'I don't do drugs,' he said, sitting down beside her.

'Just say no, kids,' Marianne said.

'I kind of think drugs are for losers,' he said, 'not that I'm one to judge.'

'Right, yeah. Which kind of tells me you've never done any. Because if you had, matey, you wouldn't be saying that,' she said, in the knowing, urbane way that suggested she'd been around.

'And that's where you'd be wrong,' he said.

She looked at him.

'Is that a Cork accent I detect?' he asked.

'Might be,' Marianne replied.

'I'm thinking you're from a posh part of Cork.'

'And I'm thinking that's a lame thing to say.'

He did a poor impression of a Cork accent.

'Don't give up the day job,' she said.

The comment seemed to glide over him. He crossed his legs at the ankles and sipped his beer in a relaxed way. She was used to guys making more of an effort around her. She wanted him to feel a little jittery.

Then, indicating the corner, he said, 'If he plays "Things Can Only Get Better" one more time, there's a high chance I may have to beat him to death.'

Marianne laughed again, and was annoyed with herself for rewarding him so easily.

'Where do you live?' he asked.

'I'm not sure that's any of your business. I'm not in the habit of giving strange men my address.'

The guy raised an eyebrow. 'Okay . . . Em . . . I was asking because I wondered if you'd like a lift.'

'Pretty early to be going.' She didn't want him to leave.

'School night for me,' he said.

'God, you're fun. What do you do?'

'I'm a banker.'

'Exciting.'

'You really are very rude,' he said. 'Did your parents never teach you manners?'

'They tried,' she said.

'What do you do, Marianne Dillon, that you can be so quick to cast judgement?'

'I've flunked out of college, more or less.'

He said nothing.

'I slept with my thesis supervisor and it didn't really work out . . . He was married,' she added.

She wondered if this was some sort of self-sabotage, if she was trying to derail something that might make her happy because she didn't deserve it. Or was she just testing him to see if he could deal with the real her?

'That wasn't very smart,' he said. 'Although I've no doubt that the fault lay on his side. He sounds like a dick.' He stood up. 'So, lift or no? This bus is leaving now.'

She didn't move. 'Good luck.'

'See you,' he said, giving her a jaunty little salute before turning on his heel.

She tracked him across the floor. He stopped briefly to say goodnight to some guy with a hawk nose. He was walking out of the door. She had thought it a bluff. She had sensed an erotic charge between them. It didn't matter.

But then she heard herself shout, 'Wait. I'll take a lift.'

He turned, as if he'd been expecting it.

'Anything's more exciting than this place,' she tacked on.

He looked down at her as she drew near. He was openly admiring her, she saw, and waited for the compliment.

'You've lipstick on your teeth,' he said.

For three weeks after that night Peter Campbell had refused to come up 'for coffee'. She had become a little paranoid, wondering how it was that, unlike the majority of men she'd met, he wasn't launching himself at her.

As he had driven her home after the party, she had watched his profile in her peripheral vision, the way women can. His face looked relaxed. But she felt sure he was interested. She had considered sleeping with him that night and decided that almost certainly she would do so.

On arrival at the flat she had commented on his decrepit car. 'Pretty shit jammer for a banker.'

'Baby banker,' he corrected, 'but I'm on my way. Some day in the not too distant future I'll be able to swap it for something better.' Then he had stretched out his arms and yawned. 'I'm going to have to let you go, Marie,' he had said, to her astonishment. 'Home time for me.'

She had got out of his car, thrown and a little angry, unsure whether the mistake had been deliberate.

Two days later she'd met him on the pavement outside the flat.

'I suppose you're just getting up,' he'd said, looking at his watch.

It had been lunchtime. 'No,' she had lied.

'I was just passing,' he said.

'Really?' she had said, sceptical.

'Yup.' Much later he would admit that it had been deliberate. 'I work just down there on the Green.' He had asked if she wanted to go for a beer.

Sitting in the Globe on George's Street next to the Angel, he had said, and she flushed, 'Tell me why you want my body so badly.'

'You must have been smoking crack if you think I want to swap bodily fluids with you.'

'Sure,' he had said. 'I thought that was your department. Smoking crack.'

That he had kept her guessing had driven her wild. She had wondered whether it was him she wanted or that she wanted him to want her. Sometimes he left it a day before he rang her again, and she watched the phone, willing it to ring, resenting anybody else calling. When he did ring she had to force herself to let it ring out before she answered.

He was confident in a way that she found appealing. It was all very well saying you had to have equality in a relationship but she didn't want a man who did her bidding and who was too in touch with his feelings. She seemed far too able to quell her boyfriends so that they soon learned to submit to her will. Not Pete. He had, she thought, just about the right degree of swagger. He came across as robustly masculine but in a low-key way that wasn't macho and didn't seem to hint at underlying insecurities. Plus he was a worker. She felt the stirring of a comparison with her father but shied away from it: thinking about a potential boyfriend like that was disturbing.

And here they were, finally in bed, three weeks after the party. It had been a long lead-in for her in terms of seduction. Her motto had always been 'Road test them straight away.' If you didn't connect in bed, what was the point in prolonging it? They had ripped each other's clothes off and it had been the best sex of her life. Instantly she had downgraded all previous partners.

She watched him swing his legs out of bed. He had an impressive body but not so perfect that it screamed, 'Narcissist!'

'Don't go anywhere,' he said. 'I'll be back.'

In a couple of weeks she was going to India. The ticket had been bought. Her long-stated desire to visit the subcontinent had evaporated. She felt a surge of panic at the idea of leaving him. She didn't just fancy him: he had lain over her and she had listened to his heart beating fast against her chest. At that moment she had known that he was The One. It had been that simple. Game over.

7

Early December 1994

Clare wondered if her secret was, in fact, secret to anyone. It seemed unlikely. She sat in the bedroom that her mother had decorated with the flower-sprigged wallpaper that was now mildewed. Dawn had come before she'd managed to doze. The rain outside continued to drum on the roof, its volume steadily increasing. The wind howled and a gate was banging somewhere. Clare tried not to think that the bleak day was an omen.

'It's a day for ducks,' her cousin Cait said. 'We'll be grand once we're inside. Sure you wouldn't be out at this time of the year anyway.'

Clare thought of her father waiting downstairs to drive her to the church.

'Does Daddy know?' Clare had asked Majella.

'Of course he does,' Majella had replied. 'Nothing's been said, of course.'

'Oh, God.'

'He'll have to get on with it,' Majella had said, in a way that made Clare think they had exchanged words.

Clare's great fear was that Matt, as best man, might make some reference to it in his speech, but Joe had assured her he wouldn't. The pregnancy would not be mentioned until a ring was on her finger and a certain number of months had elapsed. People would do the maths but that was okay.

Such an idea would seem quaint to many of her peers.

They might point out that it was 1994 and that Ireland had emerged from the era when unmarried mothers were sent away to have their children in mother-and-baby homes out of sight of society. This was all very fine but it was not how things were at home, at least not in her family, where doing things in the right order still mattered. And where being low-key and discreet was still valued.

'You look beautiful,' Majella said, putting the finishing touches to Clare's makeup.

'Beautiful,' Cait chimed. Clare was not sure Cait was in a position to judge: her maroon bridesmaid's dress did nothing for her, except to emphasize her solid arms. Clare had let her choose it.

No, Clare decided, she looked pinched and she was putting on weight at an alarming rate. She had never been one to shy away from the truth about her physical limitations. She was unsure about her dress, which had been bought for two reasons. First, on the day in the bridal shop, with Majella and Cait in tow, she had felt herself unequal to the task of choosing, and as she had felt her insides heave, she had taken the first that they seemed to think looked half decent on her. Second, the dress had a full skirt, which would conceal what would soon become evident to everyone.

Clare felt almost too sick to care whether she looked nice. She was overcome with crushing tiredness. Even standing up was an effort. Her makeup looked wrong but she couldn't identify why. She relied on Marianne for that sort of thing.

They had not been able to contact her at such short notice. Clare had agonized about what to do. But she couldn't delay. She wanted to get married before she began to show. Marianne had written to her from India, describing the sounds and smells, and Clare imagined her sashaying down dusty trails, dressed in a bright sari and chanting in ashrams. Marianne, she felt sure, would have fixed a *bindi* to her forehead.

Clare had read the letter happily until she got towards the end: 'As for Joe, I can't pretend, Clare, that I'm sad you've broken up. You've always been more upset than happy with him.'

Even though she dreaded her friend's reaction to her marriage, it was a matter of immense sadness to Clare that Marianne was not there. It cast an even greater pall over what was already a difficult day.

After six months of working in Casualty she had learned to expect the unexpected. Last week she had dealt with a patient who had a light bulb up his rectum. Casualty in a busy hospital was the melting pot of humanity. But she had been shocked to discover she was pregnant. It was embarrassing, too, because she was a doctor.

Conception had been the result of taking a chance on a drunken night. Joe and she had been on one of their many Joe-instigated breaks. There was another girl in the frame – a girl with a foxy smile. Clare had seen them together. She had bumped into him in town. They had both been drunk.

'I miss you, Clare.'

That had been enough. They'd gone back to his flat. And now this life was growing inside her. After that night he had said nothing about getting back together.

She had met Joe at the airport. He was on his way back from a stag party in Prague. 'I'm pregnant,' she had said.

A pause. Then: 'You're joking.'

'No.'

'Jesus Christ, we're screwed.'

At her suggestion they had gone to the Bad Ass Café in Temple Bar. There, over burgers – the smell had made her gag – she had attempted to massage him into the right decision.

'What do you want to do?' he had asked, pale-faced.

I want you to want me and our baby. I want you to introduce me to your family, whom I have never met. I want you to push that other girl out of the picture for ever.

'You're against abortion,' he had said.

'Yes,' she had said. 'Aren't you?'

There had been a fatal delay in his response. As socially conservative as he purported to be, she had known then that he would have overlooked certain things were she prepared to free him.

'Of course,' he had said, not looking at her directly.

She had waited it out until she had elicited the correct response, the one she wanted.

They did another lap of the town. The hairs on Clare's arms were raised. Joe had not arrived.

'He went out to get some air,' Matt had said, sounding too casual.

Beneath her veil Clare didn't dare to look at her father. Her own anxiety had shaded into doubt. If she had doubts, his were almost certainly greater. The idea of being left at the altar was dreadful. She began to think inconsequential hysterical things – would they still eat the wedding meal without the groom?

The night before there had been a small do in the pub. The wedding was family only. Matt, as Joe's best man, was the only non-family member. She had considered having people back to the farmhouse but it hadn't been touched since her mother's death. Sometimes Clare had wondered if her mother's clothes still hung in the wardrobe in her father's bedroom.

'Don't you worry one bit,' Majella had said. 'I'll have sandwiches and soup laid on, and we'll offer them a few drinks. PJ and I would like to do that for you, Clare.'

Clare had almost wept with gratitude.

It might be less awkward in the pub, less intimate. As it was, she dreaded mixing the two families. She had been fearful that conversation would run out. Her father was not a sociable man. She doubted that there was much common ground.

Clare had visited Joe's parents in Stoneybatter just once. For so long she had wanted to be introduced to them, to meet the people who had created him, who looked like him. They lived in a two-up, two-down terraced house. It was spotless and cosy, but without a patch of ground, which would be anathema to her father. He couldn't understand how people didn't need to feel soil between their fingers. Joe's family seemed to think of 'down the country' as a foreign land where people might be a little backward.

PJ had picked up Joe's parents and sister from the railway station. Mr and Mrs Corcoran didn't drive and Joe was in the process of learning. He had come down with Matt.

They had mixed all right, considering. Her father, though quiet, had good manners and he had done his best. Matt had been great, wittering on and filling gaps in the conversation.

'Where's Marianne?' was the first question he'd asked, and she wondered if, Anne-Marie aside, he still carried a torch for her.

Majella had been brilliant, moving about making sure that everyone was looked after. The drink had lubricated things. Joe's father was almost entirely silent. He rarely spoke. When he was asked a question, he sometimes smiled fleetingly but his answers were always monosyllabic. It was not that he was instinctively wary of questions, as her father was. It was more that he had a knack for bludgeoning the conversation to death with his hesitation and then his deafening silence. He seemed more or less oblivious to his surroundings. He sat there, a stooped whippet of a man, quietly nursing a drink and smoking cigarette after cigarette. Clare felt she knew where Joe's hatred of smoking had come from. After a while people realized that it was best just to address his wife. Even Majella couldn't seem to break through the edifice of his silence. This had been the case during Clare's visit too – she felt moved to ask Joe if he disliked her.

'He doesn't. He's like that with everyone. He was an orphan brought up in Artane, an industrial school.'

Clare's relief was undercut by deep sympathy for her future father-in-law. His upbringing seemed to have had a major effect on his personality. Apparently he had experienced terrible hardship, though he never spoke about it.

Joe's sister was quiet too. She wanted to be an accountant, she said shyly. His mother, Mary, was a fluttery sort of a woman with a weathered face. She talked a lot and Clare decided Joe had inherited his loquacity from her. That was where the similarities ended. It was hard to see how Joe had sprung from these people.

There was a strange dynamic between him and his parents. He was scrupulously polite to them, in a way that suggested he was dealing with strangers. At one point, when his mother was telling some anecdote in her strong Dublin accent, Clare thought he looked uncomfortable. His father was as inscrutable with Joe as he was with everyone else, but it was obvious that his mother was fiercely proud of her son. She had worked nights in the postal sorting office, on top of her day job, to earn money for extras like music and elocution for her son and daughter. She seemed a nice woman and Clare was delighted when she drew her aside towards the end of the night and said, 'You're a lovely girl. We're delighted with you.' She had added, 'It'll all work out great.'

She wished Joe had said something like that. He was jumpy

and flat at the same time. He sat there like the sacrificial groom. Clare found herself thinking inappropriate random things – that there was no divorce in Ireland, or that her child would be vertically challenged: the Corcorans were small and slight while her family, if stockier, were close to the ground as well.

She wondered that Joe seemed not to care that her ordinarily low sex drive was now non-existent. He hadn't touched her since the night she'd got pregnant. And she worried when she saw PJ and Majella's little one waving her arms about: she didn't cluck naturally over the baby as she had seen other women do. She couldn't see herself bustling around a kitchen with a baby on her hip. And how would she juggle a baby with her medical career? She drew a complete blank when she tried to tap into maternal feelings.

Clare wondered if she would have felt as unsure if she had seen any spark of delight in Joe. The years of second-guessing him were over. He would soon be hers. But it was hard to take joy in marrying a man who gnawed his lip and stared into the middle distance as if he was somewhere else. It was wedding jitters, she told herself. They'd be fine.

She felt her stress level rising at the thought of the long day ahead. Her father was paying for the entire wedding. He had insisted. 'I have only the one daughter.'

The reception was to be held in the West Cork Hotel. She knew it would do a good job but she hoped that people might relax a little and that she wouldn't transmit her strain. Marianne would have put aside her misgivings about Joe and brought her natural sense of joy to it. She would have said something like 'Let's get this show on the road.'

Clare looked at her father as they drove through the town again. The tension in the car was almost palpable. She didn't get the feeling that Joe would be making the trip from

Dublin to West Cork very often or that her father would be visiting them. On a previous visit, Joe's first, Joe had said very little as PJ drove them down the long, bumpy drive to the farmhouse. She had watched his eyes roam around and she had wondered what he was thinking.

Passing through the town, he had said almost nothing. She had hoped that he might have mentioned Field's, a fine-looking premises fronting onto the street, with a supermarket that stocked everything and a coffee shop where you could get a cake from their bakery. Joe had been meticulous in his manners while not really engaging. He had asked questions about the farm that seemed perfunctory and which her father, a man of the soil, would surely think stupid. Her father had been civil, of course, but stern. And afterwards he had passed no comment on Joe.

She and Joe had come down to meet Father Levis. There had been no time for a pre-marriage course and he had talked to them one afternoon. 'That'll do you both.'

Afterwards, when Joe had said he would like to walk round the town, Clare had stayed with the priest to discuss the arrangements. They had sat in a pew in the church.

'Your mother would have been so proud of you, Clare.'

'Thank you,' she had said, her voice cracking a little.

Father Levis had christened her, he had been at her confirmation, he had buried her mother and brother, and she thought that, no matter what, he would baptize her child.

She felt suddenly homesick, reminded that she was breaking away from her roots. She was marrying a Dub. Not that Joe would thank her for describing him so. Without saying it outright, he had implied that the label was beneath him.

Clare thought of Donal. It had been six years, but the fact that her twin brother was not there on her wedding day was still unfathomable. It pained her that he had never met Joe.

She still lifted the phone occasionally to call him, only to be assaulted by brutal reality once more. She placed her arm on the car door handle to steady herself. In her wedding dress Clare felt entombed.

The car approached the church again. Matt was sheltering under a large umbrella. He gave them the thumbs-up and, whatever her doubts, relief coursed through her.

She was standing at the back of the church in the porch. The small congregation turned so that there was a rustling noise. At the top of the aisle she could see Father Levis smiling encouragingly. She could see Joe straightening up, Matt to his right. She had a fleeting image of coffins being carried down the aisle.

Her father took her arm. His florid face was fixed so that she couldn't read it. He cleared his throat. 'Ready?' he said.

She heard music. She must move forward. Her throat felt swollen shut.

'Yes,' she said.

She took her first step towards her new life.

PART TWO
August – October 2011

'How easy it is to judge rightly after one sees what evil comes from judging wrongly!'

Elizabeth Gaskell, *Wives and Daughters*

8

In the dying days of that summer, on a humid, clammy day that clawed at her, Marianne felt that her best days were behind her. It was strange, she had thought earlier, peering out from behind her living-room curtains at the photographer snapping her house, how you had an unwelcome moment of clarity and saw your life as it really was. It wasn't simply that she was a fugitive in her own home, thanks to Pete's fall from grace. Or that they had been forced to scramble over the back wall of the house to avoid being seen in their party finery by the photographer and having their faces splashed across the paper. There was more to it than that.

It was about how you grasped that you were no longer part of the tribe of bouncy, successful people upon whom Fortune had shone. It had been a long time since she had filed through the gates of the university with other young graduates, degrees in hand, high on ambition and hopes for what the bright future held. Now the degree parchments were lost or gathering dust somewhere, the youthful hubris long since punctured by what life had dished out. All Marianne could hear was doors slamming shut. How, she wondered, had it come to this?

Two months previously, with great fanfare, police cars had driven through the gates of the bank Pete worked for. There had been talk of criminal prosecutions. Pete's name had not been mentioned in this context but in the papers he had been implicated by association, thanks partly to old photos that had been dug up showing him as his boss's right-hand man.

Socially his name was tagged with those of men who had become poster-boys for financial chicanery and voracious greed. While he might not be going to jail, Marianne had learned that you could be punished in other ways.

Now she stood in the cavernous conservatory of Clare and Joe's home on Palmerston Road, holding a glass of wine in one hand, a social smile clamped to her face, with the twin bedfellows of disgrace and failure slung around her neck. That Joe's sister was sympathizing with her made it worse.

'Sure God love you,' Joe's sister said – she was an accountant with Dublin City Council, which meant her job was so safe she would have had to open fire on her colleagues to lose it – 'you wouldn't wish it on your worst enemy.' She spoke in a low confiding way, which was ironic, given that she mined every sentence for information.

'Hmm,' Marianne said.

Before they had left for the party, the photographer had stood outside their electric gates, his intrusive lens trained on the house. She could visualize the pictures accompanying an article about 'disgraced bankers'. The house would be snapped at such an angle as to make it look bigger and the text would refer to it as a 'luxury residence' or maybe a 'magnificent home'. The tone would be of outrage and the clear subtext would be that its owners and their ilk ought to be ripped apart limb by limb.

'How is poor Pete?' Joe's sister said. 'It's got to be hard to have led such a high-flying life and then to have it all come tumbling down.'

God, she was like a tenacious little dog with its teeth embedded in Marianne's leg. She was the sort of woman who would have enjoyed a good seat by the guillotine. It did not take much to picture her toothless in a mob-cap, knitting and shouting, 'Off with his head!'

'He's very thin,' she said, and Marianne followed her gaze

through the gap in the crowd to where Pete was lecturing a young woman in strikingly high shoes – Matt's new wife. He had traded in Anne-Marie for a pair of bony shoulders from which an emerald green dress hung.

How is Pete? It was a good question. He was weird and growing more so. It wasn't just that Marianne was scared he might lose his job, thanks to a reference she'd read in the paper about the clear-out of senior management at the bank. 'Not applicable to me,' he had said. Or that he had found God, a most unfortunate development and yet another example of how derailed their lives were. Or that he was now almost certainly sermonizing to Matt's wife – 'Too many of us have been spiritually limp,' she had heard him declare to some guests over a plate of barely touched food. She couldn't even blame it on alcohol, as he wasn't really drinking. A mixture of feelings roiled inside her. What the hell does that mean? she'd thought. 'Money isn't everything,' she'd heard him pipe up. 'We should all try to lead simpler lives.'

She had wanted to shriek at him. Marianne would not have had to point out to the old Pete that being anti-consumption was easier when you had no choice: when you were awash with money it was harder to ascend to the high moral ground. In this regard his credibility was dented. She wondered, too, how this new spiritual perspective was going over at work. *Let Jesus into your heart and your account. Let Him manage your interest, your bonds, your derivatives* . . . or whatever it was that Pete did. Marianne had never been sure. When the pay cheques were rolling into their account, like Atlantic waves, she hadn't minded. She was now regretting her lack of attention.

The old Pete would have mucked around with the kids in the garden and drunk lots of beer. He would have chatted easily, flirted in a gentlemanly way with female guests but not so that she – or they – felt uncomfortable. At junctures during the party he and she would have exchanged sly glances in the complicit way of those married a long time. How she missed those moments of shared intimacy, she thought sadly. The new Pete had little interest in such earthly matters. He hadn't even wanted to come to the party.

'It's in bad taste, Marianne, going to a party.'

'It's a family party, a sixteenth birthday celebration for our daughter and our friends' son, and it's being paid for by our friends. It's in their house. I'm trying to normalize things for our children,' she said.

Marianne's sadness segued into anger. The new Pete was on a mission to stun people into submission with his boring lectures and to mark out his family even further as curiosities, if that was possible. This would have been enough to cope with. But Marianne's fears could not rest there. He wasn't sleeping or eating and was progressively more wired. Marianne had a lurking sense that they might not make it through the party without some sort of transgression, so she was trying to keep Pete in sight.

She had fielded calls from journalists. On one occasion she had been out when Pete had unwisely given an interview. This had ended up splashed across the paper and she had wanted to stick pins in the picture that had accompanied the reporter's by-line, his white face, his dark eyes staring back at her. 'Banker's Shame at Wrongdoing.'

Pete's lawyer had suggested that 'wrongdoing' was actionable.

'I don't care, Marianne, about the legalities. As far as I'm concerned I did wrong. And I'm ashamed,' Pete had said.

Marianne had started to cry, then to rail at him, the bank, the journalist and the world at large. Once more their conversation had bumped along well-worn grooves as she struggled to understand how her husband had allegedly erred. 'I'm still in the dark about what you're supposed to have done. You didn't control operations at the bank. You're not off sunning your balls in some other country, riding this thing out, like those cowardly bastards you worked for.'

Marianne was mortified by what had emerged about the bank. There had been protests outside its vanity offices. In private she battled a shame that she could not communicate. When she saw to-let signs dotting the streets and heard of people taking the plane in search of work, she flinched. In public she was more defiant. Pete, she told herself, had been guilty of no more than blind loyalty to the boss who had mentored him, the 'father figure' who had betrayed him. As a result he was being portrayed as culpable along with the men from whom he had taken his orders.

'Pete's fine,' she said brightly to Joe's sister, looking over the party-goers for somebody to palm her off on.

To her relief Joe banged a fork against a glass so that his sister was forced to shut up. He seemed to be looking at Marianne in a beneficent way. She wondered if he was as enthusiastic about the joint birthday celebration as Clare had maintained. Earlier he had given her what had looked suspiciously like a charitable smile. No matter how hard she tried with Joe Corcoran, something inside her curdled. Images hovered at the edge of her memory that would not be banished.

Once the voices had died down and he was sure he had their full attention, Joe began to speak. Marianne decided that he had deliberately positioned himself under a Paul Henry painting. He looked around in a lordly way, like the empire builder he was, a man with no fear of drawing attention to himself.

The birthday girl, Marianne's daughter Grace, and the

birthday boy, Clare's son Finn, had been shepherded into the room by Clare. Both hovered reluctantly on the edges of the gathering. Grace was wearing something baggy and ill-fitting that Marianne didn't recognize or much like, her shoulders rounded. She had failed to persuade her daughter to wear a dress. Grace wore far too much inexpertly applied makeup so her young face looked a little clownish.

Marianne signalled to her to smile. Grace ignored her. Marianne hoped the day hadn't been ruined for her by the way they'd had to leave the house. At the same time she felt frustrated. *Be pleasant*, she wanted to say. *We're virtual outcasts. We're disgraced. We are the villains in the pantomime. At the very least we must try to be charming. We must sing for our supper.*

The charm offensive was going badly. Earlier, Marianne had spotted Holly, her younger daughter, strategically positioned near the dessert table, devouring pavlova. One daughter scowled while the younger ate all before her. Now she saw Pete positioned to the left of some guests caught in a trapezoid of light, illumined like a modern-day saint. His expression was vacant.

Finn gazed out of a window as if the celebration had nothing to do with him. Clare insisted that he no longer touched dope. Not that she necessarily knew. Despite her professional expertise, Clare had been blindsided when Finn had been busted for drug-dealing. She had been just as deluded about her child as many of the other mothers Marianne encountered. To be fair, it was probably hard to tell with Finn anyway. He seemed perpetually to be in a semi-coma, his eyelids heavy at the burden of just being Finn, a popular boy having a good time.

Marianne was fond of her godson. He was easy to like, with his lazy good humour. He was also distractingly handsome in a way that his parents and siblings were not. Marianne wondered if Grace's world-weary seen-it-all-before expression might be a by-product of trying to impress Finn. She had overheard her talking to him about a music festival with false authority, given that she had never been to one. They had been very chummy in West Cork on holiday earlier in the summer.

'You don't think there's anything romantic between Grace and Finn?' she had asked Clare one day, as they stood on the pier in Glandore watching their respective eldest children disappear from sight in a little punt.

Clare had said ruefully, 'Finn would never have such good taste.'

Now Marianne noticed that Clare had stopped orbiting the room. Standing next to Joe, she looked tense: she got keyed up about entertaining. Marianne gave her a thumbs-up to convey that it was a great party. Clare had remained slim, which Marianne hadn't, and although there were discernible lines on her face she had aged well. If anything, Marianne thought, observing her, she looked better now than she had as a girl.

What Marianne really wanted was Clare to herself. She wanted them to sit in a corner with a glass of wine so that Clare could listen to her and tell her that everything would be okay in her measured way.

Earlier Marianne had cornered her briefly to vent. 'Pete spends hours surfing the net. His appetite is gone. He barely sleeps. He lies next to me, staring at the ceiling. He says he doesn't feel tired. I'm exhausted. He gets up at six and bangs around the place, although he thinks he's being quiet. I honestly feel like strangling him. I know that's selfish,' she said, 'but if I can't say it to you . . .'

'It's hard for you both,' Clare had said.

'I'm trying to get Pete to see that he can't be held responsible for the bank's near-collapse or the global debt crisis.

He's like Atlas taking all the cares of the world on his back. He was middle management, for God's sake. He didn't exactly have his fingers on the levers of power. He made none of the key decisions. He hadn't a clue what they were up to.'

'Tell him to come and see me,' Clare said. 'I could give him something to help him sleep.'

'I'll try,' Marianne said, 'but he thinks he's just dandy.'

Marianne wanted them to mark this moment together. Memories kept popping into her mind and she felt a rush of emotion. Through the years Clare's life and hers had intersected again and again. Marianne had miscarried in the loo of the supermarket. She had cried and refused to come out until Clare had arrived to tell her that everything would be all right and she would have a baby. There had been the drama of Finn's suspected meningitis, the test with the glass to see if the spots stayed, the hysterical dash to the hospital and then the hours spent keeping vigil.

Marianne remembered sobbing in rage when the young teacher told her that Grace might need remedial teaching with her reading. Beset by indignation and doubt, she had needed Clare to point out the teacher's youth and lack of experience. It had been Clare who had said how advanced verbally Grace was. They had been through so many dramas together, so many twists in the road, the sorts of things that men often regarded as trivial.

Although he spoke fluently Joe was going on for far too long. She looked at his rapt audience, the men, and thought that quite a few looked like overfed, self-satisfied peacocks. Men were said to age like fine wines but on the evidence of this party . . . Many of the men she knew had grown potato-like, and misshapen, overweight, with the jowls of those who ate and drank too much.

Joe grew ever more expansive and sentimental, evoking

nostalgic memories that today, when everything had gone so wrong, felt like lead in Marianne's veins. It was obvious whom the speech was aimed at. Every now and then Joe couldn't resist looking lovingly at the esteemed judicial fish he had netted: Rory MacEoin was a Supreme Court judge, no less. His presence, it seemed to Marianne, caused Joe to brim with delight and his colleagues to form an admiring little constellation around his legal greatness. In fact the judge seemed like a wry, pleasant man, entirely unassuming and in no way seeking any of the fawning that seemed to follow his every word.

Marianne was only half listening now. She imagined Joe's oratorical skills as a barrister were impressive. Even in private conversation he had a natural eloquence. She pictured him with a curly, yellowed barrister's wig plopped on his head, hands clasped behind his back, gravely addressing the court.

Clare's father sat in a corner regarding his son-in-law. Marianne wondered what he made of Joe, his sharply pressed trousers, his shoes so highly polished that they could have doubled as a mirror. Thaddeus McMahon, who was simply dressed, was small and wizened, like an apple that had been left out in the sun too long. On the few occasions Marianne and he had chatted she had been left with the impression of a man not easy to reach. Clare had implied that he had never got over her brother's suicide. Neither she nor any member of her family would have confirmed it directly. Now Marianne fancied she saw a dubious look on the closed leathery face.

There was an enthusiastic chorus of laughter, with a bit of heckling, mainly from Joe's lawyer pals. In contrast, the sixteen-year-old birthday boy and girl, the star guests, looked unmoved.

'Would you traduce my character thus?' Joe said magisterially, in response to one witticism.

No doubt he and some of his colleagues would benefit from the cross-litigation that would follow if the bank Pete worked for collapsed. A cabal of advisers, lawyers, accountants and auditors had presided over the transactions that were now being labelled as lunatic, if not illegal, but they had melted into the shadows when blame was being apportioned while Pete and others were publicly nailed to the cross.

The professionals at this party, some with faulty investments, were chugging along, broadly solvent. Many of them talked a good show in public about having to economize but when you looked at the fine print it seemed to be business as usual. She had to guard against growing bitter. Only a few of her and Pete's friends were here: the others would no longer accept a party invitation from them.

Shadows lengthened and the gathering thinned out a little but those who remained were drinking heavily. The recession, Marianne had read, meant people drank more. The wine had not mellowed her, although she had been drinking steadily. She went to the bathroom and spent a couple of minutes standing on the landing, listening to the party downstairs move up a gear, wishing the ordeal was over. It was hard to feel light-hearted when you were a social pariah. She wondered when she could reasonably go home without giving offence.

Of course, Matt had waylaid her as she had known he would. 'I was sorry to hear about Peter's troubles,' he had said, looking so grave that she had almost smiled. His voice had been alive with concern and she had felt herself shrink from him.

'How are you?' He had zoomed in on her so that she wanted to swat him away. Ideally she would have liked to tell him to piss off.

'I hear you're doing even better at the bar,' she had said, recalling his fondness for talking about himself.

'One does one's best to earn a crust.' She was reminded of Uriah Heep. It was a line she thought he had used before. Fundamentally she knew Matt was fairly decent but she wondered which type of sympathizer he might be. There were three basic groups. First: the genuine (relatively few). Second: the rubberneckers – fishing for information to retail elsewhere. They were the sort of people to slow down their cars at accidents, ghoulishly glad to be unharmed. Third: the *Schadenfreude* crew, thrilled to see you get your long overdue comeuppance. The jury was still out on Matt, she supposed. After all, she had dumped him. Decent or not, he seemed unlikely to have forgotten such a slight.

Marianne regarded his peeling nose as he sounded off about a holiday 'on a yacht' in Turkey. Where was Pete? She was craning to spot him as discreetly as she could.

'The chef was so talented . . .'

She remembered a weekend she and Matt had spent in a caravan on the edge of a field in Kerry at the start of their relationship. He had been anxious to please, with a fondness for Tayto sandwiches. His other culinary speciality involved wedging unfeasible amounts of chips between slices of white bread slathered with butter and brown sauce.

Now the lover of carbs and TK red lemonade shandies had been replaced by a wine connoisseur and gourmet. He was the type to recount long tales of a 'super little *gîte*' in Provence or a tour of the frescos in Rome with 'a wonderful guide'. Matt gave a loud, rollicking laugh. In college he had favoured jeans and jumpers, although he had become more dandified in the later years. Now, in his white linen suit, he had morphed into a *flâneur*. Earlier she had seen him remove a Panama hat, as if he was unwilling to let the summer go. His features looked a little smudged through the gauze of alcohol. The image of a giant runny Camembert, oozing over the edges of its wooden casket, came into Marianne's mind.

She suspected the beginnings of a paunch beneath the jacket. But who was she to judge? And what did he see when he looked at her? That she was still tall and blonde, with a bust that had held up well, given the two bouts of breast-feeding, but considerably better padded than she had been at college. What he couldn't see were the crenulations on her thighs and bottom, which made them resemble the karst landscape of the Burren. Or her lumpy stomach. Her body felt heavy and water-logged. She didn't particularly care. Marianne wasn't militant about her right to be fat and fabulous. She just didn't see herself as a list of physical problems to be solved. There were worse things than being generously proportioned, as she was discovering.

Marianne no longer put herself at the centre of things. In the painting of her life she had moved to the background and her two girls were firmly in front. She didn't want Grace and Holly to waste their lives wishing themselves smaller, a depressing thing for young women to want.

Marianne listened to Matt jawing on and thought it astonishing that she must once have felt a current of attraction to him. Certain memories almost made her smile. The sex had been relatively uninspiring, she remembered, when compared to what had come after. He'd had a weird thing about flinging her about, making their bodies assume different positions. After they had split up, she'd wondered if it was something he'd seen in a movie. They had been young, of course.

His voice had grown plummier over the years, slightly Anglicized; at college, he'd had a country accent. It was a voice designed to conjure images of heavy decanters with crystal knobs and good port. He was completely content to listen to his own voice and she continued to drift. There was another man at the party, yet another barrister, with whom she'd had a brief fling in college: he used to keep up a running commentary during sex, like the voiceover from a seventies porn movie. She remembered him as a cheerful boy, with long hair, and narrow thighs, dropping acid and having a bad trip. That memory was hard to reconcile with the self-assured, tumid burgher of the gleaming pate now holding forth: 'Look, the reality is you need the wig in court and you need to say things like "May it please your lordship" even just as a stalling tactic. They're necessary props . . .'

Marianne remembered holding his hand as his legs had shaken like pneumatic drills and he'd begged for the bad trip to end. Midway through he'd thought they were in India when in fact they had simply eaten a curry. He had crawled along the floor on all fours, afraid to stand up. She had never done acid during her drugs phase. She'd suspected it wouldn't suit her.

The memory of her drug-taking shocked Marianne now. She had become quite vehemently anti. The idea of Grace ever knowing the details of her wilderness years terrified her. Marianne thought of Gretta: it was hard to imagine her as the possessor of a secret past or of delinquent tendencies. Maybe all children were destined to regard their mothers as pure, half-baked characters who had gone nowhere and done nothing except give birth to and raise them.

'It's frightening,' she had said to a group of women earlier. 'Drugs are everywhere, on every corner, in every park. There's dealing going on in Palmerston Park. I rang the guards about it. We all need to pool our information.'

'Do you think Grace has taken drugs?' one mother had asked.

'No,' Marianne had said, 'definitely not. She doesn't even drink.' She had lowered her voice: 'I was much wilder.'

'I think if you give your children proper values they won't do drugs,' said the slow-speaking wife of a consultant.

'I wouldn't even know if somebody was high,' said another woman.

'Human nature never really changes, though, does it?' Ruth had said. 'Since the time of Romeo and Juliet young people have always experimented and worried their parents.'

Marianne filed Ruth under the label 'colleague of Clare' although over time she had become Clare's friend. It was typical of her to pontificate in a detached, theoretical way. What did she know about child-rearing when she didn't have children? Ruth didn't drink either. Marianne harboured a deep suspicion of people who didn't drink.

'Why doesn't Ruth drink?' she had asked Clare.

'I don't know. She never said.'

In Marianne's view there was a lot that Ruth had never said. She had just materialized one day in response to Clare's ad, giving scant background information, and now here she was, a fixture in their lives.

'Grace is reading *Wuthering Heights* for what I think is the third time. She dreams of meeting her soul-mate. She's basically on the look-out for Heathcliff. For Grace it's all about high minds and theoretical love of the distinctly non-biblical kind. She's a starry-eyed romantic. I'm sure at some point she'll experiment but for now I'm really glad she's sexually delayed. Half the young girls I see going to discos look like porn queens in training and it's depressing. There's something so crass about it. You don't catch young French girls dressing like that.'

'That's a little sanctimonious,' one woman had said, 'if you don't mind me saying. They're just having fun, getting used to being women. They want to do what their peers do. I bet you your daughter takes a bag of clothes with her and tarts herself up somewhere else.'

'I don't think so,' Marianne had harrumphed.

Though she would never say it out loud, Marianne thought she was a good mother. Once Grace had emerged into the world, courtesy of forceps, announcing her arrival with a lusty yell, Marianne had been filled with a sense of purpose. It was as if she had found her calling in life. That night she had shuffled up to the hospital nursery, bruised and battered, unable to pee and therefore attached to a catheter, to seek out her little blob in the row of glass cots. There, clasping 'Baby Campbell, born at 5.05 weighing 9 lbs', she had murmured into the sweet-smelling little neck a series of pledges that, as far as she knew, she had not broken. Grace was to be her anchor. Exhausted and exhilarated though she was, the world had taken on a new clarity.

Marianne marvelled at Grace's abstemiousness. She was proud of her solemn, slightly prim daughter.

'Of course Turkey has more Greek ruins than Greece, you know . . .'

Dear God! Matt was still banging on about his bloody holidays.

Matt's wife observed them anxiously from a corner. She tottered about, wearing a permanently stunned expression. Where possible, she pressed Matt's hand and looked up at him under her eyelashes as if to remind him of her existence. It was hard to see why Anne-Marie should have been relegated for her, Marianne thought. Earlier she had watched the woman's attempt to connect with Matt's children. They had resolutely ignored her. The daughter, in particular, scowled and was clearly determined to be as unpleasant as possible. An emissary of her mother, Marianne mused, briefly feeling sorry for the new wife and thinking of Coleman. She had long since learned to live with him. More than that, she had come to appreciate him: he was a good man and loved her mother. They hadn't made it to the party, which irked her because she would have liked to have them there.

The pitch of the voices had risen. Marianne adjusted the strap of the slimming undergarment into which she was vacuumed and which dug into her flesh. She saw a figure in the garden. Surely not Pete. The rain was hammering down. Matt was keen to talk. She wondered about the new wife again. Earlier she had told a long anecdote that hadn't really taken off. Matt had listened politely until she had finished and resumed the conversation about something unconnected.

Now Matt was puffing a stinky little cigar. He began to take an unwelcome walk down Memory Lane. Marianne felt depressed: she had no desire to be confronted by that earlier, shinier, optimistic girl. She thought of her old pal Alexandra, whom she had invited to the party.

'Another time,' Alexandra had said.

'You were going to live on the Left Bank and be a writer . . .' Matt was saying.

Someone tugged at Marianne's sleeve. There was a crust of something by Holly's mouth. 'Say "Excuse me, please",' Marianne said, in the sing-song voice mothers use to corral their children in public.

'Dad's in the garden, Mum,' Holly said, ignoring the request. 'I think he's really drunk, like you were at Christmas.'

Matt laughed.

'He's acting kind of weird.'

Marianne looked down into her daughter's round face and saw concern. 'Excuse me, Matt,' she said.

They threaded their way through the small crowd. Outside there was a sweet smell of freshly mown grass. She passed the patio-heaters that normally she would have criticized as ecologically unfriendly and thus vaguely anti-social. She heard a child sniggering.

'Oh, Jesus,' Marianne said. She took in the scene as if she was watching something on a screen that was not connected to her.

Pete stood in the centre of the garden, his head flung back as the rain poured down on him. She thought of King Lear. 'Pete,' she yelled.

He didn't respond.

Marianne pulled her cardigan round her and squelched across the wet grass, her heels sinking into a soft mulch of leaves. 'Pete, what the hell are you doing?' she asked, her eyes narrowed against the rain. 'Pete,' she said, reaching out and grabbing his shoulder.

Rain ran from Pete's hair. His face was pink with cold. His eyes burned. 'I'm cleansing my sins,' he said, smiling.

9

The railway station was cold and desolate as the wind whistled down the platform. There was a distinct tang of urine. A sleepy ticket collector was hunched over on his seat. Clare and her father had driven there mainly in silence.

It was a difficult time of year, of course. There would always be something incongruous about celebrating anything in late August. Every member of her family had Donal at the forefront of their mind around his anniversary. Sometimes she thought it was the raw emotion they felt that stopped them talking about it. Other times she decided it was because they were hopeless at communicating. She wondered if she was as bad at discussing things with her own children. She strongly suspected she was.

Then, as they pulled into the station, her father said, 'Cian reminds me of him.'

Her instinctive reaction was to assume she had misheard. But she hadn't. 'I agree,' she said, completely fazed.

A minute later the train drew in. He climbed on and waved at her through the thick glass window. His comment buzzed in her head. Clare backed into a cider can, which stood on the ground, abandoned. Sidestepping the stream of liquid, she thought of the twins: she had caught them gulping the dregs of abandoned drinks the night before. It hadn't come as a huge surprise. They had been sent to bed in disgrace, semi-inebriated, riotous and unperturbed. It was the opinion of their peers that counted. They didn't care what the adult world thought of them.

On occasion Clare marvelled that her youngest sons had sprung from her body, that she and Joe – neither of them big – had produced two such large, violently energetic children. That they were good at sport delighted their father. Joe was not physically gifted. He enjoyed being seen roaring encouragement at his offspring from the sidelines. She would walk into a room and invariably find them playing some graphic video game, watching sport or switching to a programme about cars. Only violence, physical exertion or mechanics seemed to attract them. Nature programmes were of interest only when one species was ripping another to shreds. Boggle-eyed they would stare and she would hear a male narrator say something like: '. . . Attracted by the smell of fresh blood rising from the water the hunters can finally feed.'

They regarded the lies they told as necessary stratagems. When she remonstrated with them she imagined a thought bubble ballooning from their heads: 'She's gone postal. Say whatever it takes to keep her off our backs.'

Sometimes she told herself that the twins' ability to throw a ball or run down a field was evidence of spatial ability. Boys were mentally diffuse. In the end they would 'knuckle down'.

Mainly, though, Finn and Cian, her middle boy, were on her radar this morning. At the party every time she had come upon Finn he had immediately moved off. Her maternal instinct, which had proved far from infallible where he was concerned – and here she paused to feel the usual pang of guilt at her ineptitude – had told her something was awry. Confronting him openly would get her nowhere. It was a question of summoning the energy to play detective.

With Cian, she had also to tread softly but for a different basket of reasons. He was sensitive in inverse proportion to his younger brothers' brutishness and certainly displayed none of his older brother's truant tendencies. It had taken all her resources to coax him from his lair.

'I hate parties,' he had said, when she had finally reached him in whatever solar system he inhabited.

She looked at his sad, flat face and felt the familiar twist in her gut. His glasses lent him added vulnerability, but it was more than that. Cian spent swathes of time staring dreamily into the ether, or plugged into a virtual world where he had friends and status, which she couldn't help thinking was significant. That he had woken her this morning to inform her that he had a pain in his stomach was noteworthy, too, as a new school year had just begun. These pains never materialized during the summer holidays.

All this preoccupied Clare as she watched her father find his place on the train. It was six forty-five in the morning and she was lucky that it was not even earlier as he had been gunning for the six o'clock train, anxious as ever to 'get back'. She couldn't point out that he had no real work to go to and nobody waiting for him in the bleak, damp house.

She watched him place his overcoat carefully on the overhead rack. He was seated opposite a student, whose blue-haired head lolled against the seat; her mouth was slack so she was dribbling, and her ear-buds were in, making conversation impossible. Not that her father would have been one to initiate it. In some sort of genetic throwback to a different time in Irish history, Clare's father regarded strangers as information gatherers and was innately suspicious of small-talk until he felt sure of somebody's credentials.

He took his seat, instinctively straightening his back in response to the sloppiness he was confronted with. In his navy suit and jumper, a cap on his head, he looked like a relic from another age. She had heard him read out items from the paper, marvelling at the lack of discipline among young people. 'A good root up the backside would do them a power of good,' he would say.

If he knew that his eldest grandson had been caught dealing dope he would have been speechless. That terrible time when the school had called, Clare had not known how to react.

'It can't be true,' she had said, repeatedly asking herself how, as a mother and a medic, she had not spotted the signs.

Joe had been angry, of course, but there had been a focus to his fury beyond remonstrating with Finn. He had persuaded the school not to expel Finn, successfully arguing for a suspension instead, implying legal action if his request for clemency was not heeded.

'It's clear Finn wasn't the ringleader. He's a good lad, a bit spirited but nothing that can't be corrected, and I'll be seeing to it that he understands exactly how he has transgressed. He has clearly been led astray. Indeed, I'm surprised that in a reputable fee-paying school such as this it wasn't picked up sooner. You say this has been going on inside the school grounds for the best part of a year, yet this is the first we're hearing about it. I find that worrying.'

She had wondered, too, if Joe blamed her for having been so blind.

'Of course I don't,' he'd said.

But Clare roundly blamed herself. As she had sat opposite the rugby-mad priest detailing what had happened, she had felt on trial as a mother. Society would set the blame firmly at her door if Finn turned out to be a drug-addled drop-out or a joy-riding addict. Stay-at-home mothers might hope to offload a little of the blame, but working mothers carried the can for their children's shortcomings. 'She was never there' would be her epitaph if Finn really messed up.

There were dangers associated with smoking cannabis

when the brain was developing. Had Finn's smoking caused him to be lazy and unmotivated? This was one of many worries that plagued her. Finn was terribly disorganized. She spent her life trekking to the school office to hand over various forgotten items to the secretary. All too often a mid-morning SOS text would arrive, asking her to bring him this or that, ending with a plea that, were she not to oblige, some dire punishment would be his lot. And although she often swore to let him at it, she usually capitulated.

In her calmer, less self-flagellating moments, she told herself that Finn had always been phlegmatic. Even as a baby he had never bothered to crawl. He had sat around happily sucking bottles of milk. He had always seemed strikingly devoid of intellectual curiosity. And his entrepreneurial spirit had been strictly limited to the drug business. Finn was naturally deviant. In former times she had no doubt he would have been sent to Van Diemen's Land. Were he from a poor family, he would have ended up in a young offenders' institution, like Joe's father. Not that Joe's dad had committed any crime, the poor man, other than being impoverished and an orphan. Clare felt sad when she thought of Mr Corcoran. In the years since she had first met him, all this awful stuff had come out about how boys like him were physically and sexually brutalized in orphanages and industrial schools. On those rare occasions when they had met after the story had broken in the press, she had known he found it hard that everyone was aware now how boys like him had been treated. It was as if he was exposed all over again. No wonder he had always been so withdrawn. It was a miracle that he had managed to marry and produce two successful children. That was mainly down to Joe's mother. And, when you thought of it, it was extraordinary that a man who had known such abject poverty and degradation was the grandfather of four such happy – and spoilt – boys.

Clare tried to catch her father's eye as the whistle blew, but he wasn't looking out of the window. He was rooting in his pocket for his packet of mints. She thought of his parting salvo, and wondered if he had enjoyed the party. She hadn't, but she hated entertaining. She had relied on Marianne to help her.

There had been depressing aspects about the occasion too, like Matt being without Anne-Marie. Instead he had brought his new young wife. Clare had been disproportionately upset when Joe had told her Matt and Anne-Marie had split up. Matt had met somebody on a charity walk in Nepal. 'I didn't know you and Anne-Marie were so close,' he said, bemused by her reaction. They weren't particularly, although Clare liked Anne-Marie. She couldn't explain to Joe why the split frightened her. It was too close to home. If two people who seemed to have such a good marriage had failed, what did it bode for other couples, like her and Joe? Ireland wasn't yet like America, where it seemed everyone divorced prolifically, but people were moving on to second and third partnerships. Clare didn't know how she felt about that – but in her family, marriage was for life. There was no such thing as a disappointing union. You got on with it.

Lying in bed, she had asked Joe what he thought about the new wife.

He had shrugged. 'She didn't have much to say for herself. She neither added to nor subtracted from the conversation.'

She had felt sorry for the girl, who had seemed gentle and brittle. She pictured her texting on her phone, her two thumbs flying across the pad for what had seemed a very long time. 'Do you not envy him?' Clare had probed.

'No. She's too young. It seemed more like an owner–pet sort of set-up than a marriage.'

'She's very pretty,' Clare said, testing the water further.

Joe made a face. 'But she looks like if you touched her she'd crumble to dust. Insubstantial in every way.' Joe, she thought, were he to replace her, would require more than an attractive face. He would want a hot-shot career too, and somebody to parry with intellectually. It was a point she had often considered.

He continued: 'Her looks are too showy. She might be all right if she wiped half of that war paint from her face. He'll get sick of her, you wait and see.'

That she felt bolstered at the expense of the young woman made Clare feel queasy. But she was mollified, and savoured the fact that Joe had been in a good humour. Although he had been in a frenzy issuing instructions to the kids before the party about behaving themselves around people – and by this he meant the judge – he was pleased with the party.

'It went off very well,' he said, as they got into bed that night.

It seemed highly unlikely that her father had enjoyed it. She had watched him loitering on the edges, almost exclusively talking to his grandchildren when he could collar them. Of the four grandparents, he was the only one left. Joe's mother had died of throat cancer. She had been followed swiftly by her husband, who never had the chance to enjoy the benefits of the money paid to him by the state in compensation for the horrors visited on him in the industrial school.

Clare hoped that the party hadn't been too extravagant. Although she had insisted on pruning expenditure at home, she knew they lived disproportionately well compared to most people. It made her especially uneasy when she was with her father. She wondered how he viewed their ivy-clad home, with its name, 'Stoneville', etched outside the electric gates on a plaque. Given the state of the world and of the domestic economy, had he thought, as she sometimes found herself thinking, 'Nero fiddled while Rome burned . . .'? Clare had an ambivalent attitude to her home. When she was in the mood to feel quietly satisfied, proud of it, she thought that its squat grandeur was a monument to their hard work. But on those rare occasions her father visited she saw it as the physical manifestation of voracious ambition, with something boastful in its proportions and pretensions. As if they had tipped from acceptable goals to greed.

For a short while PJ had been a small part of the story of the Irish gold rush. He had made a killing selling a parcel of land from the farm and had put the proceeds into bank shares. 'Bank shares are safe as houses,' he'd said, parroting the then common wisdom.

Now they weren't worth the paper they were written on. In addition, the pub's trade had been decimated by stricter drink-driving laws and the smoking ban. 'He's too depressed to come to the party,' Majella had said, 'and that's the honest truth, Clare.'

It would be as hard for him to face their father. Nothing would be said directly but there would be silent reproach in their father's gaze at the folly of exchanging the security of land for a handful of dust.

Clare made a mental note to ring PJ, pushing him to the top of her long to-do list. Next to his name she filed Pete's. His hollow-cheeked appearance had shocked her. Every day she, as a GP, saw people who were depressed and flattened by their financial woes. Men in particular were flummoxed by changed economic fortunes. They often felt unmanned when they lost their job and status. Suicides had increased significantly during the recession, a fact she had not relayed to Marianne, to whom she had spoken already that morning.

'I couldn't sleep,' Marianne had said.

'I'm not surprised. But he'll be fine, Marianne.'

'Clare . . . don't take this the wrong way, but I hope that Pete turning to religion isn't some sign of craziness.'

Clare had chosen her words: 'There are worse ways to get through a crisis.'

She had sensed Marianne holding back. It was one of the hoary old debates they'd had since college. Privately Clare thought that Marianne's anti-religion views had all the hallmarks of a religion, such was her zeal. She didn't dare point this out. Marianne over-reacted – predictably – when you challenged her about religion. When they were students Joe had got endless amusement out of provoking her. She was easily baited.

In Clare's experience it was natural to turn to faith when faced with dilemmas and at key moments in life. She herself had done so.

Pete was under significant pressure. There was the financial aspect but there was also the airing of their problems in the press. Clare had picked them up for the party, waiting in the car in the lane behind their house as they'd climbed over the wall.

'Like *outlaws*,' Marianne had said, trying to make a joke of it for the kids as she'd got into the passenger seat.

Clare considered the outburst in the garden. She would have to suggest to Marianne that Pete see a psychiatrist.

Clare had pushed for the joint party. 'It'll take the burden from them at a time when they're under such strain,' she'd said to Joe. 'It would be a nice thing to do.'

'I wonder if it's wise to be seen in public with Pete at the moment. I mean, I have Rory MacEoin coming and I wouldn't like to put him in an awkward position.'

'Pete and Marianne are two of our oldest friends, Joe,' Clare had said, 'and I don't believe in witch-hunts or scape-goating people, whatever Pete may or may not have done.'

'Marianne, Marianne, let's all keep Marianne happy,' Joe said, in a way that hinted at old unspecified antagonisms.

'Were the boot on the other foot, Joe, I can guarantee that Marianne and, indeed, Pete would go down with the ship for us.'

That had swung it but Joe hadn't been happy. 'Just know this, Clare. Conal and Helen want to go to dinner next week and they do not want to be seen in public with Pete.' Conal and Helen were both lawyers and sometimes made up a six with Clare and Joe, Marianne and Pete. They'd had many nights out over the years.

'Oh, Joe, I already asked Marianne.'

'Well, unask her. Pete may as well have a target drawn on his head. Professionally speaking, it's suicide to be seen with him, and whatever about tolerating him in my home, I won't do it in public.'

This left Clare with the unenviable task of breaking the news to Marianne. She strode briskly back to her car, feeling defeated even before the day had begun.

A full-scale argument was in train when Clare walked into her house, wondering if a coffee might perk her up. She sighed inwardly and went to put on the kettle.

Joe and Finn fought a lot. Joe's relationship with Finn was characterized by occasional, largely abortive, attempts on Joe's part to 'connect' with Finn and simmering rage when Finn inevitably defied him in his low-key way. Lately Finn had taken to calling his father 'Joe' in a semi-ironic fashion that incensed him. 'If I had ever spoken to my father like that I would have been beaten within an inch of my life,' Joe had said to her, although it was hard to imagine the late Mr Corcoran having the energy to strike anyone.

Joe often referred to his upbringing as if it were a paradigm that ought to be followed by all parents. When Clare thought of his sister, with her veiled eyes, ferreting out information, she wasn't sure she liked what the model had produced.

His and Finn's bickering usually centred on a number of topics, from study to Finn's aping of an inner-city Dublin accent and his appearance: 'If you spent half the time on your studies that you do on your bloody hair . . .'

When Joe complained about Finn illegally downloading music, his son would openly delight in mocking him: 'Joe, copyright means nothing any more, you're Jurassic, dude,' which enraged his father. Worst of all, though, where Joe was concerned, was that Finn had declared himself to be an atheist. 'Sorry, Joe, what I can do? I just don't believe in a magical world where there are angels and harps,' he'd say, pointing skywards.

Here Clare sympathized with Joe, agreeing with him that a sort of hard-bitten, world-weary irony had infected their kids' thinking. Everything was dismantled and sent up so that it seemed nothing had any meaning. Sometimes she wondered if they ever felt pleasure in the newness of experience that she remembered from her childhood, or if, having been given so much from so young, their sense of wonder had never developed.

Today, although she very much didn't want to – in fact, she wanted to pick up her briefcase and leave – Clare quickly got the gist of the argument. Finn had stayed up half the night on the Internet.

'Finn, you made a commitment to study and to get up early in the mornings,' Joe said.

'It was, like, my party yesterday. You're a slave-driver,' Finn groaned. 'I'm just about back at school. Chill.' His head swivelled towards Clare. 'Mum, tell him.'

Clare was invariably forced into the role of referee. 'You also said you'd take up a sport. Fit body, fit mind. You're naturally good at sports. What sport are you going to play this year?'

'Is he going to study, Clare?' Joe said, in a mildly accusatory tone.

'I play Nintendo. You don't play any sport, Joe.'

'I play golf when I've time. On the rare occasion I have a window. Normally I'm too busy earning money for this family.'

'Ah, Joe, not the old walked-barefoot-to-school speech. When I'm online I'm communicating with people, posting things . . . sharing stuff about music. You don't get it.'

'You're right, I don't,' Joe said. He launched into a quote: '"The Mind is but a barren soil, a soil which is soon exhausted and will produce no crop, or only one, unless it be continually fertilized and enriched with foreign matter." Sir Joshua Reynolds,' he concluded. He was trying, Clare could see, to batten down his rising anger.

Joe saw himself as the supreme authority in the house. When it came to Finn, though, he was like a puppet government, devoid of any real power. Finn was more or less oblivious to correction. She and Joe had stood in front of the boy, castigating him, as he craned his neck to see around them to the television. He was not so much deliberately uncooperative as unconcerned. He certainly didn't share the urge to please that Clare remembered from when she was at that age.

Joe was right about Finn's hair. It was one of the few topics that really excited their son. 'It's a version of a Mohawk,' he had told her one day, with real feeling in his voice. To his immense chagrin, he was forced to flatten it down during school hours. Finn's school had strict rules about deportment and conduct. The second he exited the school gates, though, his hair was lovingly teased upwards.

'Is he gay?' Joe had asked.

Finn's parent–teacher meetings were marathons in which both parties discussed how they might help him to apply himself. Nothing changed in the wake of these conferences. Finn remained untroubled by his poor performance at school.

Unlike Marianne, Clare had rarely watched her progeny ascend the stage at school prize-givings. Year after year the newspapers broadcast dire warnings about grade inflation, slipping standards and the dumbing down of the educational system. Yet even under these circumstances, three of her boys had brought back no plaudits. Cian was the exception but his accomplishments ran to no more than nebulous-sounding awards for 'computers' and a merit badge for good conduct. It infuriated Joe that his sons had singularly failed to distinguish themselves. 'They dress as if they were about to break and enter somebody's house. I wouldn't be surprised if people avoided them on the street,' he said.

Clare found herself writing endless notes as to why so-and-so hadn't given in his homework. 'Could you not just do it and save all this hassle?' she would ask. 'I had nobody to do my homework with me. I just did it.'

She might as well have been speaking into the ether. How had she produced such unfocused offspring? They had plenty of extracurricular activities, none of which either she or Joe had ever laid on for them. She had assumed then that, with their private-school education and opportunities, they would get on with things.

At other times Clare tortured herself with the idea that she had not spent enough time with them, producing artwork to cover the kitchen walls. She recalled herself dashing in to school concerts halfway through or catching the end of sports days, pretending she had been there all along. Raising boys was like taking a turn on the roulette wheel.

Today she felt differently. She listened to her mollycoddled son's carping, her husband's backlog of complaints and the undertone of blame she felt directed at her. Was it the time of the year? Or the comparison her father had made that had destabilized her? Was it the fact that she felt a chasm between her and her family?

She accepted that, like a lot of women, she was sometimes overburdened, her time torn between the competing demands of home and work. Or that she often felt invisible in her own home, like a ghost ship sailing along on a sea of maleness, an intangible provider of food and drink. Today, though, she felt short-changed and angry.

She remembered Donal and the games they had played growing up. For what seemed now to have been long, happy hours, they had swung back and forth on an old tyre that had been tied to the tree in the haggard. Sometimes in the summer when the light was fading they had raced across a field as fast as they could, avoiding the cowpats that were dimly lit against the grass. Those had been different times, of course. It was not strictly fair to compare them with today. But she was doing just that, standing in her high-end kitchen pressing her fingers to her temples to block out the sniping.

Then Clare did something she had almost never done in her life, as either a mother or a wife. 'Just shut up, the two of you, will you?' she had said, and stalked out, leaving her menfolk to stare after her.

10

In a Georgian townhouse on Sandford Road, about five minutes from where Clare lived, Marianne was in a funk. She had opened that day's paper to be confronted with a story about failed attempts to extradite Pete's boss – Deep Pockets, as they called him privately – from Argentina. It was accompanied by a deeply embarrassing shot of her and Pete quaffing champagne with him and his assortment of flunkeys and flatterers at a U2 concert in Slane.

She rang Pete. 'You saw the paper, I take it?' she said, looking at the by-line.

'Yes.'

'They're persecuting us. How many more times are they going to run that bloody photo? They're making out that we had some hugely lavish lifestyle when we didn't. It's unbalanced reporting. It's not fair.'

There was a pause. 'Pete, are you there?'

'Yes,' he said, sounding vaguely stoned.

Clare had prescribed Xanax to help with his anxiety. She had also made an appointment with a shrink, about which Marianne had mixed feelings.

'You don't think he'd off himself, do you, Clare?'

'No, I don't,' Clare said, in her doctor voice, which Marianne found reassuring.

Then she did something that was uncharacteristic for Clare and made Marianne feel less reassured: she leaned over and gave her friend a hug.

Part of Pete's core attraction had always been his self-assurance. It was the first thing that had drawn her to him – that and his bum. Later, when they had become a couple, he had said, 'If you ever play away you're out.' It was the simplicity of his approach that had hooked her.

There was no deconstructing what he meant or agonizing over hidden meanings or wondering how far she could push boundaries. With Pete, roses were red and violets were blue. She'd had a surfeit of boys singing about roses (in her I'm-with-the-band phase) or opining about them (in her junior-barristers phase) or, worst of all, contextualizing them (in her college-professor phase). She had correctly intuited that the certainty Pete offered would allow her to be a chameleon. He would ground her without choking the life out of her. And she'd been largely right, until now.

Marianne looked at the paper and cursed.

There was another silence. Then Pete said, 'Don't speak like that, Marianne, please. It's ugly.'

Who was this stranger who disapproved of bad language, this man who spoke so slowly that she wanted to finish his sentences for him? She gave the phone the finger. It was childish but satisfying. 'Where are you anyway?' she said. 'Is that the Luas I hear?'

'I've just nipped out,' Pete said.

'Why did they have to put that picture in?' Marianne wondered again. 'They keep rerunning it as if we did that sort of thing all the time. That was a once-off. It's like the way they present the house. We have a nice home but it's not the pad they make out.'

'Well, we did go in a helicopter to that concert with those people so it is the truth, like it or not. And I seem to remember that at the time we were more than ready to do so.'

There was no denying it. There they had been for all to see in their finery, Marie Antoinette-style, with grins stretched across their foolish faces.

'So, big deal,' Marianne said, unwilling to surrender the point. 'You didn't funnel off money here, there and God knows where. You didn't leave a giant bloody hole in the bank's reserves.'

In her view Deep Pockets was the central cause of Pete's undoing. Her face hardened as she thought of him and his greedy little stub of a wife, hiding out in Argentina where extradition laws protected him. She felt a deep hatred for them that she knew was unhealthy.

They had holidayed as his guests in Spain. They had been flattered to be asked. Marianne could almost smell the mimosa. She pictured Deep Pockets practising his swing on the constantly watered lawn. There was no going back and making different choices.

'I'm almost certain that Pete won't be mentioned in any file sent to the DPP,' Pete's lawyer had said. 'He wasn't senior enough. Any such file will centre on breaches of company law by the directors. Pete wasn't a director. Once the file is sent, there will be some huffing and puffing, but most likely it won't come to anything. And if it does it won't concern Pete.'

'He means,' Pete said afterwards, looking pained, 'that white-collar crime is rarely prosecuted in this country, which is plain wrong.'

'You just took orders from that crook.'

'Like the guards at Auschwitz were "just taking orders". I could have blown a whistle,' he said. 'I colluded.'

Marianne lay back on her bed. It was almost as distasteful to her that Pete might have been a hapless pawn as a wrong-doer. She didn't want to think of herself as married to a man who had either barely circumvented the criminal law to further his career or passively followed orders.

'I was on the wrong path, Marianne,' he said, yet again.

'Pete, you've got to lay off the martyr routine. I must go,' she lied. 'Somebody's at the door.'

She dialled Clare. 'Did you see the paper?'

'Yes. Ignore it. Put it out of your head. Tomorrow's chip wrapping.'

'At least I hadn't seen it when I was dropping the girls off.'

Marianne wasn't sure if she wanted to be ignored or spoken to at the school gates. The other day Holly had forgotten a book and gone back into school to fetch it. A mother had rapped on the car window. 'How are you bearing up? You're so strong,' she had said, when Marianne had opened it. 'I wouldn't be able for that at all.' She was a big woman with an outsize head, and Marianne momentarily pictured a giant vulture beating its wings. 'It must be hard, though.' She was so close that Marianne could smell something stale on her breath.

Marianne had offered nothing, intent on camouflaging her feelings. So the woman had pushed it further: 'And to think we used to envy you and think your life was so glamorous. It just shows. Chin up.'

Such people caused her to feel unpatriotic. In her darker moments she thought her fellow Irishmen and -women were a vindictive bunch. She wondered if there was anywhere on the planet they could go to escape what had happened. She said to Clare now, 'I should get a bell for Pete's neck and mine too, then shout, "Unclean, unclean." Let's face it, we're social lepers. I don't know what to think, Clare. The bank encouraged employees to invest in shares. Pete did that and lost his pension. Did he make decisions as an individual or did he just go along with the culture? He always felt part of a family.'

'I know,' Clare said.

'I just feel like I'm going mad sometimes, wondering what to think,' Marianne said. 'People don't forgive stuff like this.'

'I'm not sure that's true.'

'Forgiveness is a Catholic idea. It's a nice concept but it's a fairytale. It's sort of fake. People never forgive and never forget what you've done.' She gave a deep sigh. 'Speaking of Catholicism, Pete went to Mass again this morning. He goes most days.'

'You know, it's possible, as terrifying as you might find the notion, he finds some comfort in it,' Clare said mildly.

'Hmm,' Marianne said, restraining herself from further comment. She knew that Clare's Catholicism mattered to her, which Marianne had never understood. Like any good liberal, she was careful to pay lip service to the notion that she respected all creeds and beliefs, but she found religion suspect, the preserve of people who couldn't deal with the idea of death.

Marianne had sent both girls to multi-denominational schools where children of all cultural, social and religious backgrounds were equally respected. Clare's sons attended a fee-paying Catholic boys' school. Marianne had once attended a Christmas concert there, standing in for Clare when she was late at work. The small narrator had read out, 'And after Mary and Joseph were married, Mary had a baby,' which was misleading and retrograde, if not downright creepy, Marianne had thought. When Clare was told, she had appeared to find it amusing. In Grace and Holly's school they had pieces about the origins of Christmas, the Jewish Hanukkah and the Hindu festival of Diwali. Those concerts had gone on for a bottom-numbing length of time, but they were pluralist and accepting. To Marianne, the idea that her husband might stand around chanting repetitious phrases in a near trance was disturbing.

In what was obviously a change of subject, Clare said, 'Now I presume you saw the item about Joe and Dervla Bell, Feeney that was, the no-to-same-sex-marriage campaign?'

'God, no,' Marianne said, scrambling for the paper.

'Page three.'

'Jesus,' Marianne said, 'she's aged well, I'll say that for her.'

'Well, she has no children, so that might be the secret. Couldn't have them, apparently.'

'Kind of ironic in a way,' Marianne said. 'I'd say the secret is more like the Botox needle.'

'Bitchy.'

'Yes,' said Marianne. She had never liked Dervla.

'Well, her marriage is gone and she's living back in Dublin.'

'Gosh, I am surprised.' Then: 'How do you feel about that?'

There was a short silence. 'What do you mean?' Clare said, in a voice that made Marianne quail.

She couldn't say she felt uneasy at the idea of Dervla being back on the scene as to do so would remind Clare of Joe's chequered past. As she wondered how to move the conversation on, a memory edged its way forward. In the spring of 1996 she and Pete had held Grace's naming ceremony in a marquee in the back garden. Apart from their *ad hoc* secular ritual it had been no different from a boozy south Dublin christening party. Clare, exhausted from working in Casualty, had left with a fractious Finn, but Joe had elected to stay on and the party had become more raucous as day gave way to night. Marianne had gone upstairs to feed the baby and had heard murmuring in a room nearby. Pushing open the door, she had seen two interlocked hands break apart. There had been the flash of a nipple. Pete's younger slutty sister Melanie had tried to make an excuse but Marianne had silenced her with a look. Joe had busied himself with the pile of coats on the bed as if he was searching for his. He had seemed casual and almost unconcerned. His cheek had been marked with lipstick.

'I take it you're going home, Joe,' she had said coldly, before turning on her heel.

The incident had never been mentioned. And certainly she had never said anything to Clare, who would not have welcomed any such confidence.

'I was just wondering what you felt about the no-to-same-sex-marriage campaign,' Marianne fibbed, although in fact she was interested in Clare's answer.

Clare was less clipped: 'I don't know. Obviously I want to be supportive of Joe.'

Here Marianne allowed herself a little eye-roll, thinking again of Joe with Pete's sister.

'But I'm not sure I agree with it. I'll have to give it some thought. And on that bombshell I must go. I have a full surgery.'

When she had showered, Marianne went downstairs, her feet bare, her hair wrapped tightly in an angry screw of a towel. She tried to separate out the things that were upsetting her. The idea of a newly separated returned Dervla Feeney was not good. Ditto being in the paper again. That Pete did not seem to be engaging with what was happening to them but instead took refuge in pieties was not good.

In the hall she bent to retrieve the post, gritting her teeth at the menacing brown envelopes, harbingers of bad news that Pete no longer opened, simply tossing them onto the growing pile and forbidding her to tackle them.

There was a bland card from Ruth, with a bowl of flowers

on the front, thanking her for the party, which was nice in an annoying way. Marianne frowned. Naturally Ruth would follow protocol. She was polite to a fault.

Ruth had wormed her way into Clare's life. No matter how much she tried to suppress it, Marianne was irritated that Clare's conversation was sprinkled with what she identified as Ruthisms. She was also piqued that Ruth's smile faded too quickly when Marianne was being witty. With her shorn hair and staid blouses, there was something distinctly ascetic about her. Marianne's career at her convent boarding-school had been full of incident – to put it diplomatically – and Ruth made her feel as though she was back in her beady-eyed headmistress's office, in trouble yet again. Ruth, like Sister Fidelius, seemed impervious to her charm.

'Ireland is full of English people with "no past",' Marianne had remarked to Clare.

'That seems a prejudiced thing to say,' Clare had commented, 'when you think of all the Irish people who have gone to Britain.'

Marianne did not like to imagine that the fact Ruth was English added to her mistrust. She saw herself as open-minded in her impulses. She disliked the sort of politics that involved hostility to their nearest neighbours on the basis of 'eight hundred years of oppression'. The Queen of England had visited Ireland and had been a resounding hit, overshadowing, in Marianne's view, the visit of the American President. The people of Ireland had loved her. Marianne had watched every second of the visit on television, liking to imagine her roller-skating along in her tiara and jewels. She had seemed so dynamic. And as a result of the visit, history had moved on, which, in Marianne's view, was a very good thing indeed. Age-old grudges were rightly buried.

The fact remained, however, that, nationality aside, they

had scant details about Ruth's history, except that she was English and had some vague unspecified medical past.

Matt had also sent a card: 'Thanks to you both for a wonderful party and to Clare and Joe. Marvellous to catch up as the summer fades and gives way to autumnal delights . . . We might manage a coffee some time perhaps. My email is . . .' It was good of him. She felt oddly touched in spite of the overblown language.

Then she frowned. Matt had reminded her that she had wanted to be a writer. It had been gnawing at her since he'd said it. Marianne went into the kitchen, telling herself that everyone's life narrowed as they grew older.

Emily, Marianne's friend from college, was now a bigwig in the art world. Once Marianne had overhead her say, 'If I had a daughter, I'd almost prefer her to be plain. Pretty women are tripped up by their faces in a professional sense. Good looks are limiting: it makes it more likely that a male will provide for a beautiful woman. Plainer ones, like me, are driven to succeed as they can't bank on male patronage.'

The observation had stung a little. Marianne wasn't sure what to think. At some point her ambition to be a writer had stilled. Her desire to be a full-time mother had taken over. What was wrong with that? Why was she regarded as somebody who had wasted her potential? She tripped over the cord of the iron to see that the dishwasher was still unemptied. Grace had had a free period that morning and Marianne had asked her to put away the crockery. Whenever she asked her daughter to do something, she often dragged her feet. 'If you ask me in that tone, I won't do it,' she would say, so that Marianne wanted to screech, 'I'm asking in that tone precisely because you aren't doing it.'

But generally Grace had been reasonably biddable. Now she seemed in some sort of retreat from her family.

'It's the age,' Clare had said, when Marianne had moaned. 'Teenagers are typically self-involved. They always think their experiences are unique, that nobody understands them. It's a phase. The boys never open up to me. I think they're embarrassed by me. Ideally Finn would like me to tag along ten paces behind him in a burka. On the rare occasions he consents to go anywhere with me.'

Marianne felt she had a different relationship with her children, although she didn't voice the thought. When it came to parenting, you got out what you put in. That was the harsh fact. Clare had not been around as much as Marianne had so, in Marianne's private reckoning, her children would be different animals, the bond between them and their mother less intense. Marianne prided herself on her rapport with her girls. She had rarely spent any significant time away from them.

Of course there had been the usual mother–daughter dramas: when she told them that their curfew was such-and-such, teenage theatrics of a particularly female variety followed. Passionate accusations would be levelled at her:

'You don't understand how important my friends are to me.'

'You don't get me.'

'You're so mean.'

'Nobody else has to be in by eleven.'

According to Clare, boys didn't favour histrionics in such situations: 'They just ignore you.'

If a daughter – invariably Grace – asked her for an opinion on something she was wearing ('Does my bum look big in this?') and she intimated that something else might 'flatter your shape more', there were sure to be ructions.

'What you do you mean? You're saying I'm fat.'

Now Marianne felt ill-used.

Someone had butchered a loaf of bread. She glared at the crumbs decorating the counter and the floor. The pungent smell of burned bacon hung in the air. A dirty frying pan lay on the hob, with a pool of pockmarked oil. Smears of butter glistened on the worktop – the culprit hadn't bothered to use a plate.

Over the years when she had been asked at countless social occasions what she did, Marianne had parroted that she was a homemaker. 'And I love it.' Since the change in their fortunes she had realized that this statement came with a qualification: provided I don't have to do all the cleaning and ironing myself.

In the later years of her marriage she had had help in the house. Now Daina had gone back to Latvia and Pete had said not to replace her. He had lost money by investing in the bank. He had also invested in property without apparently understanding what he was ploughing his money into. The grim news was that the members of his property consortium were being asked to supply more money as property prices tumbled and the communal pot needed filling. Marianne was sketchy on the details. She understood three things, though.

These terrifying demands were called 'cash calls'.

They didn't have the cash to satisfy them.

And that Pete, as a newly God-fearing man, was no longer exercised by such matters, inhabiting a higher, more spiritual plane.

Of course Marianne characterized herself as a feminist. She had kept her own name. Anything else would have been a travesty! But in an unthinking way she had been glad to leave the more routine, logistically tedious side of life to Pete. She knew far less than he did about their finances. Domestic economics and matters like insurance had always been his preserve. She had been more about childcare, food, entertainment and the things that gave colour to life. Marianne found that temperamentally she wasn't suited to cutting back.

She had been more like America, as far as consumption went, while Pete had resembled China in being industrious.

Marianne thought of the aphorisms she used to trill. *It's only money. Money isn't everything.* Both statements were true when you had surplus. And it was easier to love your husband when the family finances were in good order. It was hard to feel sexy and loving when the ironing basket was overflowing, the floors were filthy, the dog needed worming, your child stumped in saying there were head lice at school, and there was nobody else to deal with it. Marianne had always viewed herself as a kind person, a care-giver, but it was definitely easier to be kind and caring when life was going well.

Scooping up the detritus, Marianne had the unsettling thought that she had spoken a lot of bullshit in her time.

'Seize the day,' she could remember herself saying about life. Which was baloney of the first order if your day consisted of matching socks, ironing shirts and cleaning the oven – literally the worst job in the world – for no thanks. She had genuinely loved her role as homemaker when it was lubricated by enough money for treats and breaks.

'Why does Dad never nag us?' Holly had whined, a few days earlier.

'Because he doesn't do anything for you in the house,' Marianne had said. 'Do you think freshly laundered clothes appear by magic?'

Exchanges like that depressed Marianne. She was tired of playing bad cop to Pete's good cop. That had always been the case. He had floated through the door at the end of the day and the girls had carolled, 'Hi, Dad!' But now she felt that she was called on more and more frequently to use the hectoring tone she hated. *I'm a fun person*, she wanted to say. *I'm not just some harpy who nags. I'm cool.* Grace in particular would mimic puking at her annexing that word. Mothers, Marianne thought, a little self-importantly, advanced the human race and not just in bearing children but in their raising of future generations. And they didn't get much appreciation for it.

Marching to the bin, she lifted the lid to find a rasher, an egg and a piece of toast perched atop the heap of rubbish, virtually untouched. This was unacceptable. She felt a spasm of fury. An image of Grace seated at the table, pretending to eat, came to mind. Other children starved, she thought, composing a lecture.

Running up the stairs two at a time, she called, 'Grace!' The other day she had found her weeping over a Merrill Glass poem. 'Grace, what's wrong, honey?' she had asked.

'This is so sad,' Grace had said. 'The poet's lover doesn't come home from Vietnam.'

'It's beautiful, all right,' Marianne had said, 'but you mustn't get so overwrought. It's just a poem.' Inwardly she had been pleased at this evidence of Grace's sensitivity and what Marianne termed her sensibility. Once Marianne had recited a W. B. Yeats poem –'He Wishes for the Cloths of Heaven' – to her own and Clare's kids while driving them to the beach in West Cork. They had been crammed into the back like a bunch of sandy skittles. She had rounded off the last line.

'That's so gay,' Finn had piped up to laughter from his brothers.

Now Marianne thought less of poetry and more of the dirty kitchen. She could hear strains of melancholy indie music. The sort that made you want to sit in a hot bath and slit your wrists but which she had once loved.

The night before, as Marianne was folding a pile of laundry, she had looked up to see Grace slouched against the door jamb. She was sloppily dressed with a stain down her front and Marianne, who wasn't particularly smartly attired, felt unjustly annoyed. 'Yes?' she had said, trying not to sound impatient.

'Nothing.'

'Come on, out with it,' Marianne had said, in a too-brisk voice.

'Nothing,' Grace had repeated morosely.

'Grace . . .' Marianne's temper had been rising.

'It's okay,' Grace had said, before melting away.

Marianne was tired of Grace skulking around and refusing to say what was wrong with her. Clearly she'd had some sort of falling-out with her friends. She had noticed that they were not clogging up the kitchen as usual, with their curious blend of high-minded, blue-stocking talk about books and scurrilous gossip about others, which sometimes made Marianne wonder if girls were genetically programmed to bitch and tear each other asunder.

'Grace!' she repeated, knocking on the door. She turned the knob. 'Grace, why did you leave that mess on the counter? And I found perfectly good food in the bin. Are you deliberately not eating?'

Grace lay on her bed facing the wall.

'Grace, I'm talking to you. Turn around, please.'

Marianne was not above cursing at her children when her finite reserves of patience had run out. Now she could feel herself working her way into a volcanic fury, for reasons that were not just to do with Grace. 'For Christ's sake, Grace,' she yelled. 'Answer me.'

Nothing.

Marianne prepared to vent again. But Grace rolled over. Her face was distorted from crying. Then she said, 'I'm pregnant.'

11

Clare sat in her surgery at four o'clock, speculating on how a day that had started averagely well had gone askew. There was a certain irony in these thoughts as she had no idea that things would get so much worse.

Earlier she had been trying to calculate how long it was since she and Joe had had sex. It had been ages since she'd seen him naked. She considered this fact, turning it over in her mind. She was reasonably trim. She put concerted effort into maintaining her weight, ordering salads without dressing and other dishes with the sauces on the side or not at all.

Marianne had grown fuller-bodied over the years. She made intermittent but short-lived resolutions to eat less and exercise more. Clare was surprised at her blasé attitude. She had expected her to mourn her figure in the way that pretty women tended to lament the departure of their bloom.

Although she guarded her weight, Clare accepted the face she had been given. She had deep grooves on either side of her nose with lines fanning out from the sides of her eyes. She was conscious, however, that in spite of his corrugated forehead, Joe had aged better than she had, retaining a boyish look.

She was indulging herself in such frivolous thoughts when Cian's dean had called. The word 'homo' had been emblazoned on Cian's bag. Cian had been distraught and had gone home early. Clare had said, her throat dry, 'Who did this?'

'I can assure you, Mrs Corcoran, the matter is currently

being investigated and we will punish the perpetrators once we root them out.'

Clare and the dean had met before. There had been a series of incidents. In the course of their conversations he had said, not unkindly, 'Cian isn't a good mixer. He doesn't participate in group activities. He's a good lad, bright, and never causes trouble, but it's possible he comes across to his peers as aloof.'

Clare wanted to contradict the idea that Cian might think himself superior. He longed for friends. She would see him gazing wistfully at clusters of kids walking along the pavement, jostling and having fun. Cian wanted badly to be a member of a herd, any herd.

At one point he'd had a friend, a quirky guy like him. They'd been building a computer together, although Cian had been the driver. Then the other boy had drifted away. She'd heard his name mentioned less and less. One day she had seen him walking down the road chatting to another boy. She had wanted to open the window and plead, 'Don't desert Cian. He needs you.'

Clare had suggested to Joe that maybe they ought to move him. 'Not every school fits every child. Maybe we should send him somewhere smaller with less sport. I don't think Cian's a team player. The world needs individuals too. Maybe he doesn't want to have to thunder down a pitch and have his head shoved in the mud.'

Joe had been firm. 'Nonsense. If you mollycoddle him you'll make the problem worse in the long run.'

Sometimes it seemed to Clare that the thrusting masculinity Joe expected in a son was missing in Cian. She sensed that Joe and the dean felt Cian was being difficult in not fitting in.

Joe had said, 'They're picking on him because he lets them. He stands around looking weedy so they see him as a victim, as a weakling. He needs to stand up for himself. If he allows himself to be bullied, they'll bully him. He needs to thump them back.'

Clare had driven home to see Cian, careful to skirt around the offending word. 'We need to talk about what happened at school,' she said.

'There's nothing to talk about,' he had insisted, his chin disappearing into his chest.

She had tried again but he had cupped his hands over his ears. In the end she had given up. She would have to talk to Joe. There were things that needed to be said about Joe's campaign and about Cian. Those things were now connected.

Clare was Catholic in an easy-going way and, like a lot of Irish people, suited herself when it came to the Church's teachings on matters like contraception. But she was embarrassed by its attitude to homosexuality. Actually she resented it. And she felt that she must say so to Joe.

Her phone rang.

'Marianne.'

'Clare . . .'

There were tears in Marianne's voice.

'Is Pete okay?' Clare said, alarmed.

'Grace is pregnant.'

And then the life-changing words.

'It was Finn who got her pregnant.'

'*What?*'

'Clare, Grace is pregnant by Finn,' Marianne said. She began to sob.

'How in God's name?' Clare tried to think. 'Has this been an ongoing thing?' she managed. She waited for Marianne's crying jag to tail off.

'No,' Marianne said shakily. 'Apparently it happened once. Of all the lousy luck.'

'That night in West Cork,' Clare said. 'When we went to O'Callaghan Walshe's.'

For fifteen years the two families had holidayed together, renting a house by the sea in July for the same week. Each year on the penultimate night of the trip, the adults went out for dinner. This year Finn and Grace had been allowed to go to a disco while the younger kids stayed at home. Snatches of the night came to her. She could picture the restaurant in the square of the quaint village. The black-and-white frontage, with its hanging baskets, was more reminiscent of an old-fashioned country bar. The menu hung whimsically from a clothes line in the window. Behind the lace half-curtains there was a room with exposed stone walls and old fishing nets draping from the ceiling, the mismatched furniture interspersed with shelves of wine bottles and nautical paraphernalia in an eccentrically pleasing way. The food, mainly fish bought straight from the boats, was fresh.

After the meal Clare had suggested going home: 'We'd better get back.'

Marianne had wanted to go on to the pub, although they had already had too much to drink. Clare had thought of the teenagers. 'I think we should call it a night.'

'Ah, c'mon, Clare,' Marianne had protested.

On the way home they had hurtled up the twisting road, over the humpbacked Roury Bridge. The taxi had whooshed through the darkened summer night, under the low-hanging lush green branches, rabbits diving for the verges. They had passed the sign that had 'British Queens' chalked on a board, which always prompted Marianne to wonder aloud if English tourists were baffled by this sign for potatoes. The driver, whose taxi they always hired, played his usual choice of music, including Kenny Rogers's 'Coward Of The County', which caused them to nod knowingly at each other. But Clare had been anxious. She remembered that. She had never imagined the children having sex but she had wanted to get back, some instinct driving her home.

'We didn't go home.'

Marianne sniffed. 'You're not blaming me, are you?'

'No,' Clare said, a fraction too late. 'I'll ring you straight back,' she added, then made her way to the sink in the corner.

Her legs juddered as she tried to sip water in an effort to calm herself. Now she had a contrary set of images of the two perpetrators. First she saw them before their loss of innocence, Finn and Grace naked in a paddling pool, their soft limbs plastered with sun cream, hats on their little heads. She thought of them holding hands at their birthday parties before they realized that they were girl and boy and migrated to the camps of their own sex. And then she saw a graphic image of Grace pinioned under Finn in some revolting incestuous parody of sex. She dropped the glass. 'Dammit,' she said, as it smashed.

Picking up the fragments, she cut her hand. Red drops fell on the white tiles.

Ruth came, attracted by the noise. 'Leave that, for goodness' sake. I'll get the dustpan and brush.' She turned to leave. Then she stopped. 'Clare? Are you okay?'

Clare fought for self-control. 'I've had a shock,' she said. She went back to her desk and sat down.

'Can I help?' Ruth asked.

'If I could have something sweet maybe.'

Ruth left the room, and Clare sat there shivering.

12

Marianne and Clare met in Slattery's pub midweek. It had become a tradition. They mulled over the events of their respective weeks, acting as sounding boards for each other. They derived comfort – some might argue of a feminine sort – from discussing things without necessarily finding solutions or reaching firm conclusions. Their purpose was to talk things out.

This week Marianne sat in the snug, as usual. She waited for her friend, agitated and unable to settle. Her temples felt tight and she was beset by anxieties she didn't want to name. How would she and Clare grapple with this? She stared down the length of the bar through the hatch but was only peripherally aware of the other drinkers. As she slugged back her vodka, she resolved to get very drunk.

Earlier she and Grace had gone to the Well Woman Centre on Pembroke Road, and some time later they had filed out, clutching a raft of leaflets. Grace was eight weeks gone. Marianne had tried not to stare at her daughter's belly. How could something so flat contain a budding human being?

When Grace had told her of the pregnancy Marianne had had some sort of panic attack and rushed to the loo. 'Grace, wait here, please. I'll be back in a minute.'

She had locked the bathroom door. The ceiling seemed to lower itself and she thought she might suffocate. It was hard to understand what Grace had said. The idea that her daughter would have to go through what she had endured – for Marianne had no doubt as to what the outcome of this disaster would be – was devastating.

Fleetingly she was that girl in London with her legs in stirrups and a needle in her arm, counting until she was knocked out. She remembered the shame and confusion, and afterwards the perverse longing for a baby. History had repeated itself in the most terrible way.

The bathroom seemed airless, like some hermetically sealed chamber.

It was the death of innocence and of her illusions about herself as a mother. Both she and Grace were tarnished and would never again occupy that uncomplicated mother–child space in which needs were mainly physical and love passed back and forth unfettered and unblemished by the concerns of the real world. Grace's adulthood had begun too soon and there was nothing Marianne could do to protect her. In fact, Marianne had failed to protect her.

Grace had come to the door.

'Mu-um,' she had said, knocking. 'Mu-um.' She was crying softly.

Marianne had swung into action. She had tried not to unleash a volley of questions. 'We'll sort this out,' she said, feeling as if part of her had been gouged away.

After the appointment Marianne had shepherded a tearful Grace to the car.

'Grace,' she said softly, when the doors were closed, 'we need to talk about your options.'

But as Grace began to speak, Marianne was seized with fear. The idea that Grace might want to do anything but go to London was inconceivable. She could feign an open mind but it was pure pretence.

'Finn thinks I should have it.'

Marianne had felt like shouting that Grace should *never*

have told Finn about the pregnancy. Both daughters had been indoctrinated, successfully she had thought until now: *Don't have sex until you're ready to bear the consequences of a pregnancy. But if you do get caught, don't tell the boy or your best friend. Tell nobody. Come home to me and we'll be on the first plane to London.*

This had been the mantra she had communicated. What did Finn know? she thought resentfully. How would he suffer?

'Do you still like Finn?' she'd asked.

'I don't want to have a baby.'

Able to breathe again, Marianne had said, 'Nobody will force you to have a baby, darling. It'll be like bringing on your period.'

'I always liked him more than he liked me,' Grace had said, and Marianne had had a sad image then of Grace trotting along beside him worshipfully.

'I didn't know you drank alcohol, Grace.'

'I don't.'

'Was that your first time?'

Grace had nodded.

So Finn had introduced her to drink as well as sex. Marianne tried to rid herself of the idea that her daughter had been casually seduced by a careless boy. 'Did you not think of birth control?'

Grace, crimson, had said, 'He told me that he was using a . . . condom.'

Finn had been waited on by an army of nannies, housekeepers and au pairs, who had entered and left the house as if by a revolving door. He was incapable even of bringing his plate from the table to the dishwasher. Clare complained that he never 'followed through'. He'd followed through this time, Marianne thought blackly.

'Marianne.'

'Clare.'

There was a small, unfamiliar pause.

'What are you having?' Clare asked.

Clare nursed her first drink as Marianne disposed of her second.

'I need to get hammered,' Marianne said. 'Same again?' she asked, heading back to the bar.

Clare shook her head. 'I can't stay late. Joe's at a function.'

'We have things to talk about. Surely Finn can hold the fort.' Marianne had every intention of being understanding with Finn. But she'd found it hard to say his name.

'I really can't be late.'

Marianne waved to Roddy, the owner, feeling uncertain. The moment Clare had arrived she'd felt an alien reserve spring up between them. Perhaps she'd imagined it.

'How are you keeping?' Roddy asked.

'I'm fine,' she lied.

'Vodka, soda, lime?' he asked, smiling. 'Loads of lime cordial?'

Ordinarily they would have engaged in a bit of banter about films or the state of the economy. Now she simply nodded, barely able to muster a smile.

Marianne couldn't read Clare's features, but tried to stay positive. She had already said to Clare that nobody should be told. 'Not even Pete or Joe,' she said, thinking, Especially not Joe. His strong anti-abortion line was well known. 'The more we can contain this better.'

'Agreed,' Clare said, and Marianne had felt relieved.

When Marianne had settled back on her seat – was it significant that they were sitting on either side of the table rather than side by side? – Clare said, 'I think two things. First, we leave it two days to meet with the kids so that things can calm down. We all need to get perspective on our feelings. It's natural we might feel a bit muddled after such a shock. Second, we meet in a neutral place so that everyone stays in control of themselves.'

'Okay,' Marianne said. 'Good idea.' She wondered what 'perspective on our feelings' implied. There was only one perspective surely. And what about 'muddled'? Against her nature she did not dive in and ask Clare what she had meant. At some basic level she felt it vital to maintain the equilibrium, the sense of them being at one, because a new wariness had crept in between her and Clare. It was almost as if they had both begun to stand behind their respective children. Where was the easy shorthand between them that allowed them to talk?

Clare had told her nothing of what Finn had said, and Marianne had not elaborated on her conversation with Grace, except to say that she was very upset. In fact, the appointment was already made for the termination, although Marianne would not divulge that until they all met.

'What happened with Finn when you spoke to him?' she said. 'You're not going, surely?' Clare was buttoning her cardigan.

'I'm really sorry,' Clare said. 'We can go through all this when we meet. I have to go.' Marianne felt a firm dry peck on her cheek. 'Don't worry, Marianne, we'll get through it.' And then she was gone.

13

When Clare had met Marianne in the pub she had still not succeeded in tracking down Finn. His phone was switched off and she had rung around his friends in vain. It was ten o'clock when she finally caught up with him.

Finn walked to the car.

'I was ringing you.'

'Sorry. I had the phone off.'

'I know.'

He was entirely still.

'Get in,' she said. She drove for a while, circling the neighbourhood, unseeing, hardly able to think straight.

'Stop sign, Mum,' Finn said, and she screeched to a halt.

For once she had his full attention. Usually she fought to be heard or had to ask him to remove his ear-buds. Under any other circumstances this would be gratifying.

'I'm sorry, Mum,' he said.

She stemmed the welter of apologies. 'It's too late to be sorry, Finn. How many times did you sleep with Grace?' she asked, although Marianne had said it was just once.

'Just the one time,' he said, not meeting her eye.

Once had been enough.

'I'm so sorry, Mum,' he said again, and she felt a hot lump in her throat. She could smell his fear, and saw him as a small boy, in his yellow fleece and yellow wellingtons, aged three. Yellow had been his favourite colour.

A thought lacerated her. Had she attended to the specifics of Finn's life, had she not handed over authority and responsibility to a line of au pairs, nannies and other minders, they might not be where they were.

She remembered the notes she had failed to find in his schoolbag of dress-up days and cake sales she had never contributed to, and the times she had asked other women to pick him up from swimming or other school events.

'Was it the night you and Grace went to the disco in West Cork?'

Finn nodded. Over and over again Clare had replayed the scene in her head, wishing she had been more insistent, that she had stood up to Marianne. She tried very hard not to blame Marianne. At the most basic level it wasn't fair, particularly when Clare had had doubts about the part she might have played in the drama: at the beginning of the summer she had found a condom in Finn's room. Now she could picture the small blue packet winking up at her, accusing her. At the time, she had contemplated mentioning it to Joe, but she hadn't wanted to start yet another fight between father and son. Instead she had told some parable to Finn, hoping it might penetrate the recesses of his teenage brain, talking generally about the merit of abstinence.

'Had you both drink taken?' she asked.

Finn nodded again.

'You were drunk?' she asked.

'Yeah.'

'Grace too?'

'Yes.'

'Did you feed her drink, Finn?'

'I couldn't stop her.'

'Is that the truth, Finn?' she said, suddenly harsh. 'Do *not* lie to me now.'

'I'm not, Mum,' he said, so she believed him. 'Grace isn't the angel you think she is.'

'Was that not her first time drinking?'

Finn shook his head.

Marianne was clearly out of touch. Clare wondered if Finn was the only person Grace had slept with. Like mother like daughter, she thought, and was ashamed of the cheap, ungenerous thought. She felt a spasm of guilty anguish then for Grace.

Joe had not come home from his function. For once she didn't really care: Finn occupied her. Finally Joe sent a text in the early morning: 'Made dogs of ourselves. Suffering now . . .' After the function – some legal bun fight – it hadn't been worth while 'making the trek' back from the north side. Philip had offered a bed. It was rare that he saw Philip: 'It was good to catch up.'

Clare told herself that the men had probably egged each other on. It was true that they didn't see each other very often. Clare missed Philip vaguely. He had a quiet intelligence she'd always admired. But Joe and he had seemed to drift apart.

'Why do we never see him?' Clare had asked once. 'We were friendly with him and not Louisa.'

Philip's ex had been a barrister too. She had not fancied life as an academic's wife. Married now to one of Joe's more successful colleagues, she stayed at home swaddled in cashmere, taking art-history courses. She also had an interest in interior design.

'Honestly, I think Philip's found it hard to deal with my success. You know what they say? Those who can't do, teach. Philip became an academic because he knew he couldn't cut it at the bar.'

She reread his message, her brain performing the necessary loops to find the rationale in what he was saying. The

Law Library was said to be a hotbed of sex. Bright young things arrived each year and dazzled. Those were the rumours if you cared to listen. Clare had heard wives say they were careful to check whom their husbands had taken on as devils each year.

She spoke to nobody about such things, not even Marianne. There ought to be certain constraints even between friends in discussing such private matters. She mistrusted the modern mania for disclosure. Some things were better kept private.

Her marriage functioned. Clare had always let Joe move away from her and drift back. Some men did not want to be completely domesticated. She was neither sanctimonious nor self-regarding enough to characterize herself as 'a good person'. Nor was she a martyr. But she was seduced by the idea of doing her duty. It had been the bedrock of her life since she was ten. As far as her family was concerned, she had made her choices a long time ago. She was a middle-aged woman.

No one had a God-given right to be happy. That was an American idea. It was out of step with real life. Romantic love, like happiness, was, to some extent, a myth. Yet she thought of Joe fiddling with his phone. Recently texts had been arriving at odd times. Phone conversations were truncated by her appearance. But then her defence mechanisms kicked in. Life was a series of checks and balances, she told herself. She had a good life and was grateful for it, as she should be.

Clare listened to the early-morning sounds of her children. It was past the time to get up. Finn was almost certainly comatose beneath the pictures of buxom temptresses tacked to his walls alongside anaemic males wielding guitars. She would have to wake him or he would be late. Clare didn't feel like seeing Finn. One part of her wanted to scream at him; the other wanted to hug him.

Clare found her dressing-gown. Cian was probably slumped in front of a glowing screen, his fingers flying across the keyboard, a half-eaten bowl of cereal positioned where it would be knocked over.

She moved to the door of her room and looked up the stairs. Cian's door was ajar. 'You up, Cian?' she called, with one foot on the step.

Silence.

'Cian?' she called.

He stuck his head out of the door. 'Yup,' he said, and disappeared.

'Good man,' she shouted.

She angled her head, tuning into the fracas that had burst into life upstairs. Footsteps pounded across the ceiling overhead. Jack and Hugh were most likely having a 'riot', as they called play-fights. Their bedroom would be strewn with clothes and wet towels.

Clare moved up the stairs, hearing a mixture of laughter and snuffling. The voices drifted down.

'Get off me.'

The sound of ringing slaps.

'Ow.'

'Fuck off, you bender.'

While racism was utterly taboo, casual homophobia remained an integral part of the average schoolboy's vocabulary.

Another thump.

Inevitably she would be called on to intervene when it went too far. Much of the time that was what parenthood amounted to, she thought, endless bargaining and intervention.

There were times when Clare guiltily thought that a life without children might not have been entirely unpalatable. She could have become a forensic scientist.

Sometimes she thought she'd had four children because she wanted to be the sort of woman who had four children. Also she considered the number four immutable. Four kids sent out the signal: *Strong marriage. Nothing to see here, folks.*

'Fuck off,' she heard.

'Boys, language!' she called.

There was the creak of floorboards. A door opened. It was Finn. Ordinarily he would have stumbled past in the direction of the loo, in his boxers, his eyes encrusted with sleep. Today he acknowledged her. 'Morning, Mum.'

He was fully dressed. He was waiting for her to say something. 'Morning, Finn,' she said. 'We need to shake a leg.'

'I'll put on the kettle,' he said.

14

Two days after the bombshell, Marianne and Clare met with their offspring.

'It's going to be fine,' Marianne told Grace, as they walked from the car. 'I'll deal with Finn.'

The maître d' hustled them to the back of the restaurant and Marianne immediately suspected his motives. Were they being kept out of sight? She and Pete had been asked recently to leave one neighbourhood place. Other diners had not been able to stomach their food at the sight of Pete.

'Do you have a table up front where it's brighter?' Marianne asked tersely.

'Your friend requested a booth at the back,' the waiter said.

Clare was signalling at them from the leatherette seats. Strangely, Marianne thought of West Cork. She saw a row of swimming togs and towels, imperfectly hung on the line, flapping in the wind. She was the organizer, really, the one who loaded all the gear into the car and decided what they would eat. Clare was surprisingly clueless when it came to logistics. She pictured the kids in the garden, shoving each other, yelping and playing.

All those years she and Clare had rubbed sun cream on small shoulder blades in anticipation of Irish sun that didn't really come, wiping each other's children's dirty faces, sometimes even their bottoms. She forgot about the wails at sand being kicked in someone's face. She forgot about the twins' endless fights, the petty squabbles between the adults (meaning between her and Joe), and thought only of the good times.

Finn and Grace had run into the sea with the smaller ones trailing after them, their teeth chattering with the Atlantic cold. The idea of desire between them was absurd. She wondered if they would have another holiday together. Ever the optimist, Marianne sensed that if they could keep the men out of it the situation could be retrieved. Women had co-operated through the ages to deal with the big events in life, births, deaths and unwanted births. If she and Clare could manage this together, then things could be salvaged, she thought, putting her arm around her daughter and guiding her to the table.

The remains of their meal lay in front of them. Although Finn had dug into his food with gusto, wolfing down most of his mother's chips as well, Grace had barely touched hers. The atmosphere was leaden, although Finn seemed relatively relaxed. Grace had sat down with obvious dread, staring at the table, but he chugged at his Coke looking faintly sheepish.

Marianne kicked off with an awkward little preamble about how both Clare and she would do everything in their power 'to remedy the situation'. She sounded too formal, as if she was addressing a seminar. 'There's no shame involved here,' she went on, 'and while we're upset, very upset,' she flung back her shoulders to rally herself, 'we're not angry. What's done is done, as they say.'

Finn traced patterns in some sugar he had tipped onto the table. Grace began to pick at her chipped nail varnish, her face small and strained. Not once did they look at each other. Love's young dream was over.

'We want to sort this out. If we all work together . . .' Marianne looked at Clare. 'Clare?' she said, willing her on.

Clare said: 'There's no use crying over spilt milk. This is a very costly lesson. But of course we'll support you both.'

'It's vital that we keep this among ourselves,' Marianne said. 'Attitudes to abortion in Ireland can be . . . complicated.'

Finn popped a sugary finger between his lips. 'My father is anti-abortion.'

Marianne was just processing this comment when she saw that an angry patch of red was spreading from Grace's neck to her face.

'Finn doesn't want me to have an abortion.' Her voice wobbled. 'He thinks it's murder.'

The word hung heavily in the air. Marianne was glad that the banquettes behind them were empty. 'Well, that's nonsense,' she said recovering herself. 'At this stage it's just a tiny ball of cells.' Why was Clare not jumping in to support her and cut short Finn's mawkish teenage sentimentality? Marianne felt a spike of anxiety. She had a feeling that somehow the compass needle had shifted.

'That's not true,' Finn said, in a faintly combative tone that was alien to Marianne and again echoed strangely of his father. A tone that smacked of entitlement, she thought, studying the finely moulded face, untouched by the adolescent acne that Grace had only recently beaten.

'I looked it up. The baby is about the size of a kidney bean at eight weeks but it has fingers and toes and a brain.'

Grace's face collapsed. Marianne frowned and stared meaningfully at Clare. Finn was turning into the enemy. The father was refracted through the son.

'It certainly does not have a brain at eight weeks,' Marianne protested. If you had used protection properly, she thought, looking at Finn, who was now pouting, there would be no 'kidney bean'. With his elaborately teased hair he resembled a sullen cockatoo.

'Actually, in his brain, nerve cells are starting to connect to form neural pathways,' Clare said, and Marianne felt acid in the pit of her stomach, 'primitive ones at this point. Teeth are forming under his gums and he's starting to move.'

He.

It was a second before Marianne trusted herself to speak. 'As I said, Finn, it's important we keep the fact of Grace's pregnancy to just us four,' she said, unable to meet Clare's eye, 'so that Grace can go to London for a termination and not be afraid that she will be judged.'

'Why is it only Grace who gets to decide?' Finn asked. He was now poised on the edge of his seat. Ordinarily he lolled.

Never once had Marianne ever imagined any roadblock to her plans. Inwardly she both chafed and quailed at what she saw as his presumption. She was in no mood to pander to this bolshie new version of her godson. She needed to pin Clare down. 'Because it's Grace whose life would be utterly ruined were she to do something as moronic as having a baby when she's still a child herself,' she said, the previously pleasant tone gone.

Finn shoved his hands into his pockets.

Clare opened her mouth to speak. At last, Marianne thought. She closed it again.

'Go on,' Marianne said. 'You were about to say?'

Clare said softly and hesitantly, 'Grace, I'm sorry to have to ask you this, and I hope you won't take it the wrong way, but is Finn the only person you have had sexual intercourse with?'

Grace, who had been gazing off to the side of the table, looked at her. Then she twisted in her seat and bumped against the table so that her drink spilled. She slid out of the booth and shuttled off.

Marianne gasped. 'God almighty, Clare,' she said. 'Why the hell did you say that? It was totally uncalled-for! Grace!' She stood up, feeling as if somebody had been sitting on her chest. 'What the hell? Seriously.'

Clare was clearly unhappy. 'I had to ask for Finn. I wouldn't be doing my job as a mother otherwise.'

15

An air of gloom hung over Stoneville. Marianne had finally rung. It was a long time since they had gone three days without speaking. The conversation had been short.

'Grace felt bad enough, let me tell you, Clare, without that gem you came out with. I hate this word but she basically feels you implied she's some sort of slut.'

'I'm sorry for upsetting her, Marianne. I understand why she's upset. But it's a question I felt I had to ask,' Clare had reiterated. She had felt vaguely penitent but firm too.

Marianne's tone, she thought, had been a little hectoring. 'I need to cool off and then I'll be in touch. We need to sort this out. And soon, obviously.'

Clare sat in her armchair brooding. Grace was her goddaughter. She remembered picking up her small soft body from her cot. As a little girl she had had a comically mannered way of speaking.

It was late. There was silence in the house. Clare had checked on Finn. He was lying on his bed, listening to his iPod.

'Mum, I think we should tell Dad,' he had said earlier, moodily slurping his pasta.

Under his white school shirt Clare saw the edge of a Cuban freedom-fighter's face. It was positioned, she knew, beneath the word 'revolution'. If ever there was a boy less likely to foment revolution it was Finn. He'd probably miss the start time or get the day wrong. The only truly energetic thing about him was the vigorous way he vacuumed food.

'Like, they can't be the only ones to decide about this. Do you not think, Mum?'

Clare had wondered about this. 'Finn, Marianne asked us not to tell anyone. If Grace decides to go to London –'

Finn had cut her off: 'She can't just decide to flush our baby away.'

Our baby.

'What do you want to do, Finn?' Clare had asked. 'How would you like this pregnancy to end?'

Finn had fallen silent. There was a dribble of sauce on his chin. 'I don't want it to be killed.'

She had persisted: 'Would you envisage the baby being adopted?'

He had looked flummoxed. She sympathized. Clare was confused too.

Then, more gently, she had probed, 'Do you see yourself and Grace keeping the baby?'

The discussion was surreal. In another way, it was probably the most real conversation mother and son had ever had. Clare had often fretted that Finn had never really been tethered to her. She had been slow to bond with him when he was born. His head had been conical from the suction so that he had looked like an alien. She had felt almost nothing when they plopped him on her stomach, although she had made the right noises. She had also lacked confidence that her proximity soothed him. The obstetrician had been kind. He had sat on her bed and talked to her, sensing, she realized now, her detachment. Was it because Joe hadn't made it for the birth?

At the time she had become aware of a young devil floating about in fishnet tights with sharp opinions and a body straight out of a Modigliani painting. Back then Clare had not yet become practised in the art of switching off and sitting it out as she would learn to do. She had found that she could outlast them all if she was stoic.

Clare had needed Joe with her to welcome their firstborn into the world, to make her feel that he wanted this too. She had sleepwalked through the first few weeks, barely managing to function. Love for her son had entered her heart incrementally. Finn had always seemed slightly apart from her: perhaps some early memory had caused him not to rely on her.

'Grace and I aren't, you know, meeting any more . . .'

Meeting. The most casual of connections where a girl or boy was not even accorded the status of girlfriend or boyfriend.

'I'd gathered that.' Yet he seemed to be proposing that they become co-parents.

'I want to tell Dad. That's what I want to do.'

Should Finn be deprived of the right to fatherly guidance, a reassuring hand on the shoulder? The television was turned low. Images flickered on the screen. Clare watched the man who played the latest James Bond emerge from the sea in eye-catching blue swimming trunks. Ordinarily she quite enjoyed Bond movies. Years ago Marianne had dragged her to art-house films, often with subtitles. Some had had improving themes or were shot beautifully – 'The light was so amazing.' People had sex that caused them great angst and little happiness. Invariably the films were slow-moving and sad so Clare had left the cinema feeling weighed down.

Life was challenging enough. As a doctor, Clare often felt she was more of an agony aunt, paid to listen, than a medic. After a long day of listening to other people's troubles her preference was for slapstick, big-budget action movies with defined heroes and villains, films with happy endings.

Clare was tired, yet she didn't feel remotely drowsy. A decision loomed. If she were to tell Joe, things would change.

Marianne would be furious. Marianne and Joe were the flip sides of a coin. Both would be certain they were right: neither allowed for shades of grey.

Clare checked the time again. Joe had not come back. Her insides somersaulted. It had been some time, but she could read the signs. They'd been here before. This time, though, something was different.

The first night Joe had ever approached her, Clare had looked behind her, unable to believe he might be seeking her out. The formerly fat girl who had never had a boyfriend would not have had the confidence to presume. He had asked if she wanted a drink. So when she thought about what had come later, when she doubted that he had chosen her, she told herself that he had pursued her. He had wanted Finn. He had wanted the four children and the stable home.

She couldn't explain what it had been like to be acknowledged. And not just by him romantically, but socially too. She had no longer been Marianne's large quiet friend. She was Clare, one half of 'Clare and Joe', an entity that demanded attention, thanks to Joe.

She had felt an immense relief after they had walked down the aisle together, job done. It was if she had passed a test she'd never thought she would. After the reception, Clare had shed her dress and spent the remainder of the night vomiting into the toilet, crippled with embarrassment at the noise that would be penetrating the thin walls of the hotel. As wedding nights went, it could not have been considered a success. The photos, which were slung in a box, seemed to confirm this impression, depicting two stiff matchstick people.

Marianne's wedding had been an occasion of plenty in a marquee on the family's sloping lawn. Their friends had floated around, giddily trying to approximate adult behaviour at one of the first weddings of their generation, until the champagne had become too much for them and they had cheered, hooted and raved through the early hours, like the college kids they were.

But Joe was hers. She had changed her name to Corcoran with pleasure, although Marianne had berated her for this when she came back from India. Clare had wondered if that was a back-door way to castigate her for the marriage.

Over the years she had turned her face away from certain possibilities, hopeful that he would boomerang back to her. Sometimes she asked herself how she could overlook the obvious. But it was more possible than people thought. At a young age Clare had thrown her emotional eggs into Joe's basket. She'd had Finn quickly, then the other boys in rapid succession. It was hard for her to conceive of a life without Joe. Parts of the marriage worked. And although in many ways she was somewhat retiring, she had always known and been proud that Joe was a significant sort of person, which had continued to be the case: his profile in important and influential circles had grown over the years, which lifted her from the humdrum. Now, thanks to some animal instinct or woman's intuition, she could feel him being pulled away from her by some superior female force.

She checked her phone again. Nothing from Joe.

It buzzed. Clare registered, with disappointment, that the text was from Ruth: 'I hope you are feeling better. R.'

To her credit, Ruth did not pry.

A key turned in the front-door lock. Clare heard the sound of soft footsteps approaching. 'You're up late,' Joe said, coming into the room.

'Yes,' she said, trying to read his face. He had the loose, blurry look that meant he had been drinking. She wanted to know and she did not want to know. She would do almost anything to keep him, she thought, shamed by the thought.

'Joe . . .' Her heart was skipping, dum-de-dum-de-dum. 'Good night?' She was buying time.

He didn't meet her eye, but his tone was cool and unflustered. 'Grand.'

He would never lie unless directly challenged. Then he would convince her that she was paranoid, imagining things.

Clare set the sort of feminine trap she despised.

A few months earlier Joe had looked up from a property supplement. 'We'd be crazy not to move in this economic climate. There's serious value to be had.' They had driven out to Dalkey where he had shown her an enormous house with its own tennis court and direct access to the sea. It was the sort of place a movie or rock star might live. She had resisted the idea for a number of reasons. The children would have to take the DART to school or move. She didn't want to migrate away from Marianne. They had moved five times in fifteen years, starting out with a dingy flat, leapfrogging to bigger and better homes. Sometimes she thought it odd that Joe could want more space when they had so much. Joe had pushed and she had resisted.

But it had not escaped her notice that recently such house talk had died away.

'I've been looking at some houses,' she said.

'Really?'

'You said there was so much value to be had.'

'Oh, I don't know,' Joe said, turning over a paperweight. 'Maybe now's not the time. This house is fine. I thought you were against moving anyway.'

'I've changed my mind.'

'We're fine here.' Then, 'I'm done in. I'm going to hit the hay.'

She was losing him. She couldn't lose him. There had been too much loss in her life and she couldn't bear more. She couldn't have a schism in her family life. She needed the certainty of being married, even if it was not always very certain.

Clare performed some mental gymnastics. Finn would tell Joe anyway. It wasn't right to keep something so fundamental from a husband, not about his child.

'Joe, I've something to tell you,' she said.

16

Emily persuaded Marianne to go to a charity lunch at the Irish Art Museum. 'Come on. I haven't seen you in ages. We need a catch-up, kiddo. Ticket's on me.'

'I don't know. I have a lot on at home.' That was an epic understatement.

'We never have fun any more. What's happened to us?' Emily said.

Marianne knew what she meant although she found it hard to imagine that Emily's life was dull. Marianne rarely dressed up and went into town as she had done in previous years. Such jaunts had tailed off even when their financial circumstances had been more secure. When she went for a drink with Clare or Pete, it was in the suburbs. Most of the time she preferred not to confront the fact that she was a middle-aged woman to whom nothing *risqué* might happen again. She liked to see herself as somebody who might wake up with a stamp on her hand. A person whose days of demonic drinking, walks of shame and breakfast in the afternoon were not over. In this she knew she was deluded. The timing now was seriously off for her to be reconnecting with her fun side.

But Marianne needed a break. The oxygen had been sucked from their house. Only Holly was still happy.

'I want to make my Confirmation,' she had said, as Marianne drove her to school.

Marianne considered how to answer. 'I don't think so,' she said.

'Why?' Holly asked.

In Marianne's head there was a tangle of reasons as to why this wouldn't be happening. While in general she liked to think she had no animosity towards the Church, seeing the attraction of the more vaudeville aspects of the Mass, with the singing and incense as she did, she also considered herself a rational being. There was a strong whiff of hocus-pocus about the institution's diktats. Was there not something hypocritical, too, of continuing to demand its intercession at critical junctures in one's life, if one didn't participate at other times?

'"I'd rather live my life as if there is a God and die to find out there isn't, than live my life as if there isn't and die to find out there is."'

'What?' Holly said.

'Albert Camus, a famous French philosopher. I don't agree with him as it happens.'

'Tell me why I can't. I want to.'

Marianne became uneasy because, in some way she didn't care to identify – it didn't reflect well on her – she thought Catholicism wasn't quite the thing. 'A lot of things have happened in the Church, scandals and such,' she said, grateful, as she often was, to the Church for supplying her with ammo to justify her misgivings about it, 'and I feel disillusioned. To be honest, I'm not sure I believe in God and Heaven and all that.'

Holly looked upset. 'That's awful, Mum.'

'Well, I don't know,' Marianne amended. 'I'm not sure.' She continued, 'One of the reasons we sent you to your school is that they respect all traditions in a nice, broad way, without picking one religion and saying it's the best.'

'Nessa goes to special classes outside school and Dad said I could.' Holly folded her arms across her chest.

'Jesus,' Marianne said.

'You shouldn't blaspheme, Mum,' Holly said piously.

Marianne sighed. 'True. Dad and I will have to talk about it.'

'Plugged-out Pete' was her new private nickname for him, and he was clearly not so plugged out that he couldn't make a unilateral parenting decision.

Holly began to reel off the names of children in her class who had made their Communion and who were now receiving instruction for their Confirmation outside school. She would switch tack as many times as she had to to get her way. Though good-humoured and generally placid, she could be dogged. In fact, she was a steamroller when she became fixated on something.

There was the also the fact, Marianne thought bitterly, that she and soon Grace would be excommunicated by the Church for having abortions. How easy it was for men, supposedly sexually chaste and without wombs, to judge and cast them out.

She would go to the lunch because she needed time out from contemplating the fact that her daughter was pregnant by her best friend's son. She didn't want to think about Pete either, who was lost in a miasma of martyrdom, unable to care about such earthly things as their finances or to notice that his daughter was the colour of chalk.

Getting ready that morning, she was mentally halfway down the road. In particular she felt a shamefully strong urge to escape Pete, which didn't make much sense as he had already gone to work. Her pressing need to make sure he was okay was at loggerheads with her desire to escape. She wanted to be with him at every waking moment but felt suffocated if she was. At breakfast today she had rejoiced, knowing that she would be leaving her house. The truth was that she had wanted to run down the road and be shot of him for a while.

She particularly wanted respite from the way he siphoned off her natural joy.

Now Marianne and Emily stumbled over the cobblestones in their heels.

'I remember being here at a party during the boom. Courtesy of the bank,' Marianne said.

'Different times,' Emily said, raising an eyebrow. 'Good times for me from a work perspective.' Emily was head of an art foundation, which was basically a collection of dealers. The name was supposed to give it more legitimacy. There were dubious aspects to the art business too, which Emily admitted when squiffy.

That party had been champagne-fuelled. The courtyard had been teeming with people. The bank had taken a table and the smell of money had been overpowering. Deep Pockets had held court all night, ordering bottle after bottle of champagne, a man for grandiose gestures. And in his clique they had laughed too readily at his jokes, transmitting to him, 'You're the man.' The arty crowd, too, had courted him, fawning over him and his 'wide open' cheque book. Their critical faculties had been dulled by the money and they had been high on hubris. Now it was a lost world.

'These cobblestones were not made for walking on,' Emily said, her hand flying to the hem of her dress, which billowed in the breeze. Her shoes were remarkable. Perhaps she had bought them in a fetish shop. These days, she dressed in *avant-garde* Japanese-designed outfits that made her look like a member of the *Starship Enterprise*. Her hair was sleek, her skin well tended, her body considerably less lumpy than it had once been. She had never married: 'When I think about the certainty of it, that for ever more one guy will climb into bed next to me, I feel like putting my head in gas oven.'

Emily preferred to have friends with benefits: 'We holiday

together, go for a meal or to the theatre, and get back to our respective homes without financial ties or obligations. It works for me.'

She had never wanted children. 'Just didn't feel it,' she said simply. 'I like my nieces and nephews, in most cases, but I've never felt overcome by the urge to reproduce.'

Marianne found it difficult to imagine the oceans of time you might have if you were not responsible for others. There was no denying Emily seemed very content.

'It's a beautiful building,' Marianne said, eyeing the stone edifice. 'I always think when I come here that I should bring the kids more often. I used to when they were small, to the drawing classes on a Sunday. I sort of forget about it.'

'I meant to tell you,' Emily said. 'I met Fusty the other day. Remember him?'

'Of course. God, there's a blast from the past. What's old Fusty up to?'

Emily made a face. 'Getting treatment. I met him at the centre.'

Emily was a director of a drugs-treatment clinic. The leftie do-gooder tendencies had been diluted, but not entirely abandoned.

'Oh.'

'He's not in good shape. I barely recognized him.' She bit her lip. 'He's lost a few fingers. His teeth are stained. The poor devil's a shadow, really.'

'Heroin?'

'Yeah. He turned out to be one of the casualties. He was inside for a while. We talked briefly. I gave him my number. I'd like to help him. It was awkward and really sad . . .'

'Very sad,' Marianne said.

'He was good-natured, just a bit mixed up.'

'I know.'

'Things happen in life sometimes, don't they?'

Marianne said nothing, not trusting herself to speak. She wished she was at home.

Emily sighed. 'Oh, God, here comes my sister-in-law. Look at that face. I reckon she's aiming for immortality she's had so much work done.'

'Ladies!'

'Susie,' Emily and Marianne chimed.

Susie was permanently 'on', at least in public. Aggressively thin, she was married to Emily's brother, a short, barrel-chested property developer with a turkey neck, who owed a billion plus to the state. She mouthed something at them and scuttled off.

'What's wrong with her?' Emily said.

There was a little flurry, and Marianne saw a constellation of women move off like a flock of starlings.

Both women watched Susie. Then Marianne saw a man with a camera bearing down on them. The women had fled at the prospect of the lens. She felt a current run through her. 'Can I take your picture, ladies?' he asked.

Marianne sidestepped him, averting her face.

'Yes,' said Emily, reaching for her lipstick. 'Work,' she said to Marianne, who had turned her back. 'Who's this for?' Emily asked.

'I'm freelance,' the photographer said. 'Would your friend like to join you?'

'No,' Marianne said.

She walked a distance away. A young woman held out a tray of glasses. Marianne accepted one. This was not an extravaganza. Life had to go on. The economy needed people to do things. But half the country had been wiped out and she was drinking champagne. It was business for Emily. But Marianne should not have come.

*

A self-conscious woman, with a red gash for a mouth, gave a speech. She spoke haltingly, as if that might imbue what she was saying with meaning. She talked of how the shrunken economy had seen horizons contract and how it was the role of the artist to broaden them again. Although normally this would resonate with Marianne – she was for the arts – today she struggled to follow the talk.

A video played in the background of a naked man rolling in flour. A narrator delivered a jargon-laden monologue that Marianne couldn't follow. Occasionally the artist gave a sort of ululating wail. Apart from that he was silent.

'This guy is the talk of New York,' Emily said, lowering her voice. 'He does a combination of multi-media art and installations. His father was a truck-driver, his mother a hooker. They lived in a dirt cabin in the Deep South. That makes him hot. Which means his "work" fetches huge prices.'

'If his father was employed in a building society and his mother was a teacher, would it have the same resonance?' Marianne murmured.

'Definitely not,' Emily said, with a droll expression.

Now Marianne wondered when she could escape without being rude.

When the 'piece' had come to an end, there was a thunderous round of applause. Susie stood up beating her small hands together. 'We need to support the arts,' she said. 'Without art we are barbarians.'

Emily whispered: 'Some of the art my brother and Susie have ended up with is barbaric.'

For Susie, art was a way to graft meaning to her life. Being 'interested in art' was a way to justify consumption, albeit consumption of a prestigious type. Or maybe Marianne was beginning to think in a rancid way.

'How's Pete?' Emily asked then, settling back in her seat.

'He's very religious.' She gulped some wine. How to explain the dense silences that set her on edge, followed by the occasional bursts of chatter? 'If I'm honest I'd almost prefer it if he hit the bottle. The religious thing is odd . . . I'd thought he and I would be bedding down now in our lives . . . not falling apart.'

Emily tsked. 'I'm so sorry, honey. I have to go and talk to this guy. Duty calls. Won't be long.'

Marianne ate the remains of Emily's dessert. It wasn't hard to rationalize her greed. She deserved some cake. Susie didn't eat cake. To Marianne, she looked ravenous in a literal and metaphorical sense.

The noise had risen in accordance with the amount of wine consumed. Little had been said about the distressed economy.

'Everybody's sick of gloom and doom,' Susie had said earlier. During the boom she had once confided in Marianne that she liked to 'rip out' her kitchen every year and start again. Even then, during those crazy days, that revelation had made Marianne feel queasy.

She realized that Susie was talking to her. 'I saw you fled from that photographer earlier,' she said. 'Me too. Glen would kill me if I got my picture taken at a lunch. It sends the wrong signal, doesn't it?'

Yes, optics were what mattered to Susie. Susie talked about the need to cut back. She chirped about her supposed economies. Thrift was trendy. But it was a smokescreen. In many cases, small fortunes had been hived off and salted away out of reach of the banks. Emily had said a well-known department store sent unmarked vans and personal shoppers to Susie's home and those of her cronies. Shopping had become an underground activity for the wives of the publicly indebted. Otherwise it was more or less business as usual.

Susie jawed on. Marianne wondered if she had had an abortion. Some women in the room certainly had. Marianne had heard politicians, mainly male, refer to 'an Irish solution to an Irish problem'. By this they meant forcing women to go elsewhere so that it remained true that there was no abortion in Ireland. Marianne thought of Grace and what lay ahead.

'Susie, you'll have to forgive me, but I need some air,' she said, standing up too quickly and jogging away from the table.

She made her way out of the room. A woman nodded to her. Earlier she had encountered women she knew but they had not lingered to chat.

Marianne had drunk one glass of champagne and two glasses of wine. That was not a lot for her but she ought not to get drunk. She would go home soon. She threw her head back, glad to feel the air on her face as she stepped into the courtyard.

A little later she found her way to the bathroom in the basement, passing Emily in conversation with an arty twig of a person in black with bleached hair.

Emily didn't see her.

She passed a well-known socialite. 'Hi,' she said, stupidly relieved when the woman greeted her.

Marianne regretted the desserts. Recently she had found herself taking comfort in food. The eating would have to stop. Her genes had 'form'. Slim enough in their youth, the women in her family often expanded after a certain age. She was on her way to being fat. She would be fat and disgraced. A winning combination. She decided against adjusting her makeup and entered a stall. She was just reaching for the flush when the heavy door to the Ladies opened.

'Did you see Pete Campbell's wife scoffing the desserts?'

Heat shot into Marianne's face.

'It can't be easy,' said another voice. 'Ed said her husband wouldn't make it down Grafton Street at the moment without being beaten up.'

'Serious?'

'None of that shower from the bank would. Is it any surprise? Jesus, would you look at my eyes?'

Marianne recognized neither voice.

'What's wrong with them?'

'What's right with them? I'm going to have them done. There's a guy in Paris who's supposed to be brilliant. Gillian told me about him.'

'What's his name?'

'Can't remember off the top of my head. Anyway, getting back to your woman's husband . . .'

'I didn't know he was that senior,' the first voice said.

'He was in all the photos. You just have to look at the papers.'

Marianne had almost stopped reading them. It was the only way she felt she could cope.

'He's been let go, you know.'

Her knees felt unsteady.

'Did they do that on the QT? You'd be surprised at the wife, out swanning around in the circumstances.'

'As far as I know, yes – well, they'd hardly want him still sticking around. Ed says he's found religion.'

'How convenient. I'm sorry, I don't buy it. What – a conversion on the road to Damascus? More like a rat deserting the sinking ship. Bastards the lot of them.'

'Ed says they should all be strung up.'

'And that Susie one. Did you see her at the top table? Christ knows how much her husband owes to NAMA. Wouldn't it make you sick? Neck for iron.' Marianne leaned her head against the side of the stall.

'Where will we go after this?'

'Well, now that my dear, darling husband has agreed to look after his own children – "babysitting", he calls it – I'm damned if I'm going home.'

'It's too early for Residence.'

'The Four Seasons?'

'Nah, the Shelbourne.'

'Residence afterwards.'

'It's a deal, babe.'

The door slammed and Marianne was alone.

17

The kitchen resembled an urban farmyard, with water, mud and sticks. The twins were making crannogs – ancient Irish dwellings built on water from wood. The sheer scale of their vision was quite majestic, if exhausting, Clare thought, cutting twigs to size. There was a breadth to their vision that she admired.

Sometimes she thought that the way boys were taught didn't necessarily play to their skills. It had been a feat for dynamos like the twins just to sit at a desk. She would not mar their enthusiasm by raising the issue of transporting such mammoth structures to school. It was nice that they weren't culling random facts from the Internet and throwing them on a page, complete with muddy-footprint or genitalia illustrations.

'We did this thing today in Religion,' Jack said, lifting his head. Of the two boys Jack was, on balance, grubbier, although it was hard to call. Clare had to beat them both into showers and peel from their bodies the acrylic sports gear they wore day and night.

'It was something about if a tree falls in a wood do you hear it?'

Hugh laughed loudly. 'If I fart and no one is there to smell it, does it make a smell?'

Jack crammed a biscuit into his mouth. He laughed and there was a mini explosion of crumbs.

Clare eyes were heavy. It was too late to be doing this project. She had been told about it at the last minute and enlisted as their assistant – they had been largely ignored recently. Upstairs Joe and Finn were talking. The distraction from what might be taking place was welcome.

As if by telepathy – surely she must know that a seminal conversation was taking place – Marianne called. Clare hesitated. Things had been off-key between them since the revelation of Grace's pregnancy. Obviously, now that she had told Joe there was every chance that things were set to veer even further off course.

'You got a minute?' Marianne said.

She was knocking the edges off her words, which told Clare she had been drinking.

'Sure,' Clare said. 'Back in a minute, boys.' She heard the clink of ice cubes.

'I had a terrible day.' Marianne pattered on about a lunch she had attended. Although not wanting to be judgemental, Clare thought it odd that Marianne would socialize at a time like this. She decided it was best to say as little as possible until Joe had finished talking to Finn.

Although Clare was jittery, she felt less besieged by doubt. Her once flimsy reasons for telling Joe had solidified to the point at which she felt entirely justified in what she had done. Telling Marianne was a different matter, though.

Suddenly Clare tuned in to what her friend was saying. Pete had not being going to work.

'Can you believe it? All that time he was going to the cinema or sitting in the park,' Marianne said. 'I feel so awful.'

'He obviously felt ashamed,' Clare said. 'Men can behave strangely when their livelihood is threatened. It's not just about income, it's about their status and self-worth too.'

Marianne heaved a sigh. 'It's like some sort of Orwellian nightmare. At least we have an appointment with the shrink tomorrow.'

Clare heard the splash of pouring. 'I'm very sorry, Marianne.'

'I know.'

There was a pause. Again Clare felt that the fluency of their conversation was gone.

'We need to sort this mess out, Clare.'

Clare frowned. It was the way Marianne had raised the topic. Was she being canvassed indirectly? Was Marianne trying to get her on-side by mining her sympathies?

'Yes,' Clare said. 'How's Grace?'

'Bearing up,' Marianne said. 'And Finn?'

'Okay, under the circumstances. The boys need me to help them with their homework.' That was true, she thought, adding it to her justifications for ending the conversation.

'Oh.' Marianne sounded dashed.

Clare felt mean but she quickly rallied. Joe was not the enemy and neither was Finn. She did not want them depicted as such. They were her husband and son. She was defending her family.

'We must talk,' Marianne said.

'Tomorrow,' Clare said.

18

The psychiatrist's office was stuffy. He had a straightforward way of speaking, particularly when Marianne thought of the baffling circularity of her conversations with Pete's lawyer.

She felt a little under the microscope. She could smell the alcohol exuding from her pores, and she hadn't washed her hair, pinning it back instead in an unflattering tangle. Also, she had consumed not one but two croissants for breakfast, the buttery flakes of which clung to the hem of her sweater, pointing up her lack of self-control. She imagined the psychiatrist's notes: 'Wife slovenly. Possible problem relationship with alcohol and food.'

After she had confronted Pete about the loss of his job, she had got drunk. He had been on the computer surfing through websites when she had burst through the door on jelly knees from the charity lunch.

'You came back because you knew I wouldn't be here,' she said.

'I thought I'd work from home.'

'Except you don't work. You've been fired. And you haven't told me, your wife,' she said, her diaphragm heaving.

'I haven't been let go,' Pete said. 'I've been put on medical leave. The bank suggested I take some time off.'

A dove fluttered its wings on the screen. Marianne read, 'The true testimony of one man finding God.'

'Where did you go every day?'

'Mostly into town.'

'In your suit.' She was winded by the image. 'Jesus Christ, why did you not tell me, Pete?'

'I couldn't,' he said. 'Marianne, I won't be employable any more. Not with the bank on my CV, the photos in the papers . . . My reputation is gone.'

'What did you do to deserve this treatment?' Marianne asked, wondering if there was some sort of delusional self-aggrandizement on his part or whether she was failing to grasp the situation.

'As I told you before, I could have blown a whistle if I'd really paid attention to what was going on.' He continued, 'I let everyone down.'

She looked at the defeated sag of his shoulders. Then, in a bullish voice that was meant to convince both of them, she said, 'We'll survive.'

To her horror he had begun to cry. Loud, racking sobs, like a seal barking – for one crazy moment she imagined him balancing a ball on his nose. They were in uncharted territory, she realized. Pete had never cried before. At Grace's birth he had stood stoically by the head of the bed, holding her hand, until just at the moment of birth a film of moisture had briefly covered his eyes.

But he was not a man to express his emotions. And certainly not like this. She approached him almost shyly, patting his shoulder, then trying to enfold him in her arms. It felt totally alien. Usually it was he who pulled her head onto his chest at moments of drama.

'We'll get through this,' she said, and insisted they should speak to his lawyer.

'Why?'

'It sounds to me that you've been as good as let go. They're clearly trying to get rid of you.'

They sat on the sofa with the mobile phone between them on speaker.

'It was suggested to Pete that he take some time out.'

'Yes,' said the man who had become an overpriced fixture in their lives.

'Can they do that?'

'Yes, if he's failing to execute his duties properly.'

'They just want him out of the way.'

'It's possible to infer that, certainly, but difficult to prove if Pete is not honouring the terms of his employment.'

'Meaning he was doing his John the Baptist routine at work . . .'

'I wouldn't have put it like that, but if he's been articulating views that are openly damaging to the bank's reputation . . .'

'What reputation?' Marianne said faintly.

'All is not lost,' the lawyer said. 'The bank needs to tread carefully where Pete is concerned. It may be that he's suffered work-related mental injury.'

'Meaning?'

'Meaning we may be able to claim that Pete became adversely stressed due to the pressure-cooker conditions he found himself working in, and that the bank as his employer has been negligent in failing to protect his mental well-being.'

'Does that not mean that we'd have to make out he was crazy?'

'Again, I wouldn't phrase it like that. But in order for Pete to recover compensation we'd have to prove stress-related mental injury.'

'Could we argue that his religiosity is a symptom of his stress?' Marianne ignored Pete, who was shaking his head.

'Yes. We could construct an argument around that.'

'Which would be a lie,' Pete protested, tapping Marianne

on the arm, 'and I have no intention of lying. There will be no such case. I'm past that sort of carry-on.'

'We could also maybe run an argument that Pete has been constructively dismissed and argue that the bank did not follow the precepts of natural justice in dismissing him.'

'No, no, no,' Pete said, and Marianne shushed him.

'But could Pete go back to work?'

'I don't want to go back there.'

'Technically Pete could go back to work if he was certified medically fit.'

After each exchange with the lawyer she had been no wiser about what might happen. She had pictured him, a rotund man with an unfortunate penchant for pink shirts, which matched his lobster-coloured face, writing down how long they had spent on the phone, and felt frustrated.

After Pete had gone to bed she stayed up until the sky got light, drinking, glugging it back. She had smoked too, going out to a garage and buying her first pack in eight years. She had thought of the women in the Ladies at the charity lunch, their disdain, then of Grace, what lay ahead, and drank even faster until eventually she had lurched to bed.

Now her head felt like a boiled egg. Pete had insisted that she sit in on the consultation. The psychiatrist spoke briskly.

'How have your energy levels been?'

'Fine,' Pete said.

'He was hyper before the Xanax,' Marianne said.

'How are you sleeping?'

'Not as much as I used to.'

'You're barely sleeping,' Marianne put in.

'I wouldn't say that,' Pete said, in a calm voice that made Marianne feel almost violent. 'I don't feel tired.'

'How would you describe your mood?'

'Good.'

'Do you feel guilt about what you perceive to be your role in the bank's difficulties?'

'I do.'

'He lied about being asked to take time out,' Marianne said.

'Yes,' the psychiatrist said, 'so you mentioned . . . Would you say you felt overwhelmed by your guilt, Peter?'

'Initially I was,' Pete said, 'but now not as much because I take comfort in my faith and in the idea of redemption.'

'His new faith,' Marianne interjected. 'Pete was never religious . . . Is his new-found love of God not a sign –' Marianne broke off.

'A sign of . . .' the psychiatrist prompted.

'Of mental problems,' Marianne said.

'Extreme religiosity is worrying if it doesn't ring true with a person's character.'

'Which I think is patently the case here.'

The headlamp beam of the psychiatrist was on her again.

Pete was shaking his head.

'Do you agree, Peter, with what Marianne has said?'

'No. I think a person can change,' Pete said.

Marianne's sympathy began to ebb away.

'In my profession there is an impetus in certain quarters to bring back the spiritual dimension in mental-health approaches, the perspective being that recovery from mental illness can be seen essentially as a recovery of spirit.'

Pete smiled. Marianne didn't.

'When we experience a trauma, the things we thought were safe become unsafe. We feel a need to create security. We may join a group so that we no longer feel alone or helpless.'

'Exactly,' said Pete, nodding.

'You're not alone, Pete,' Marianne said. 'You have me and the girls.'

'Because some of Peter's work and social ties or bonds have been cut he may feel the need to make new attachments,' the psychiatrist said.

Pete continued to nod.

'However, while it's not up to me to judge your relationship with God I think we need to monitor the situation to ensure that your reliance on religion is not abnormal in the context of what might be termed acute stress. While the practice of religion can be associated with better outcomes, it can also be harmful where negative beliefs are harboured.'

Marianne was careful to keep her face neutral. Inside she cheered.

The psychiatrist continued, 'I'm a little worried about your moods, Peter, the loss of your appetite and the relative falling off in your sex-life.'

Pete, who had always been enthusiastic in bed, had little interest now. And Marianne had not gone unscathed: Pete's religious zeal did not exactly inspire lust. Nobody wanted to get frisky with one of the twelve apostles.

Here Marianne thought of her conversation with Holly. There had been an unsavoury side to Marianne's objection to religion that she had skated over. She preferred not to dwell on it. Now, however, out of fear and frustration, she confronted it. There was something unsophisticated about Catholicism: it conjured up images of backward peasants, with miraculous medals, flat feet and bad clothes. Marianne would never have voiced it – she liked to spout about a new pluralistic and tolerant Ireland and could see the contradiction easily enough – but the truth was that, at some fundamental level, she was tolerant but not of Catholicism. If Pete needed religion, he should have gone for something more attractive, like Buddhism, which invoked images of monasteries set on picturesque mountains rather than the

Popemobile and garish rosettes pinned to children's suits. She knew she had to camouflage these feelings.

'I'm going to take you off the Xanax and put you on olanzapine, otherwise known as Zyprexa, which might slow you down a bit.'

Marianne, too, could have done with something to take the edge off.

'Marianne,' Pete said, touching her arm. He had stood up.

'I'd like to see you next week, Peter,' the psychiatrist said.

'Thank you, Doctor,' Marianne said, leading Pete out, as if he were a toddler.

Marianne listened to him rabbit on. This uncertain, credulous Pete was new to her. He was not as attractive. He had always loved her for her. After the children had been born and her body had expanded, with dimples and stretch marks, he hadn't cared. He didn't care all that much when she lost her temper and was unreasonable. He fought back but they worked it out. He loved her for being Marianne and she ought to do the same. She was a bad wife. She wasn't much of a mother either, she thought, remembering Grace.

19

While Marianne was perspiring in the psychiatrist's office, Clare sat in Wilde and Greene, a coffee shop near the surgery, waiting for Ruth. Her fridge was often full of food she bought here. Although it was a pricey way to shop for a family of six, she blocked out the cost. Marianne might make her own pesto, but to Clare, roasting pine nuts and chopping what sounded like a field of basil was a waste of time when there were jars of the finished product to be plucked from a shelf.

Clare failed to understand how people could go into raptures over a bottle of olive oil or a piece of cheese. Marianne was evangelical about food, spending hours rooting around small artisan markets. Clare often cited the perils of buying food from sources whose hygiene standards might be questionable. Marianne rubbished such concerns. Family meals were sacrosanct to her. Clare's family often ate their dinner from trays in front of the television. Sometimes they had takeaways. Once when Cian was still in nursery he had said loudly that the man in the van brought his dinner. Clare had been mortified.

Generally Clare dashed in and out, loading her car boot. She didn't linger. Today it was as if the place had been invaded by women. She had stood in the line to pay for her coffee, marvelling at the torrent of talk. Her previous certainty of having done the right thing had partly evaporated. The more resolute Joe was about what should happen, the less certain she became. Had she opened Pandora's Box? It was for this reason that she was taking the unprecedented step of confiding in Ruth.

Ruth waved from the doorway. Somebody gave a shriek of laughter. Clare felt marooned in a sea of cheer that seemed only to emphasize her gloom.

'Hi,' Clare said.

'Would you like something else?'

Clare shook her head. 'No, thanks.'

She waited for Ruth to come to the table. By nature and upbringing Clare was self-reliant. Now she craved reassurance. She watched Ruth negotiate the queue deftly.

A number of years previously Ruth had answered Clare's ad for a practice manager.

'I have a medical background,' she had said, 'but no references. I understand that this might be a problem.' She had been dressed in a subdued way and there was something in her demeanour that drove Clare to take the chance of employing her. She had been a GP too long not to sense a story, but her trust in Ruth was surprisingly instinctive and she had quickly come to value both her reserve and her advice.

It had been Ruth who had encouraged Clare to modernize. Now the surgery incorporated a holistic medical practitioner, although Clare had been sceptical.

'It will complement your practice, Clare,' Ruth had said, and she had been right.

'Do you not wonder about what Ruth did before?' Marianne had asked, on several occasions. 'What's with the secrecy?' She had accused Ruth of a lack of feeling. 'She's so cold. It's ironic that she's in the caring profession.'

Clare had never been to Ruth's home. Ruth had consented to come to Clare's once in a while although she had never stayed long. There was no question of reciprocal hospitality. Clare, who was schooled in the art of not asking questions, had no problem with this aspect of their relationship. Ruth had morphed from colleague to friend but there were lines they didn't cross. Now, she felt, Ruth was the only person she could turn to.

Clare began to talk and Ruth sat erect, listening intently. 'Oh dear,' she murmured.

When Clare had finished, Ruth was silent for a moment. Then she said, 'I don't think you had any choice but to tell Joe. You're anti-abortion, as I am, and you have to be true to your beliefs and values.'

Clare's face set in an expression of guilt. She liked to think she occupied the middle ground. But where was the middle ground when it came to abortion? Yes, it was heinous, but a voice she tried to quell told her that there might be times when it was the lesser of two evils.

'I think you have to explain to Marianne, in the least hurtful way possible, your qualms about Grace going to London.'

Clare nodded. Ruth didn't appear to notice any change in her expression, any signal of her doubts. She ascribed entirely pure motives to her, and Clare believed she didn't deserve such a favourable judgement. There were complex factors at play. Clare knew she was kicking against the way Marianne had tried to bulldoze her in the restaurant, just assuming that she would fall in with her plan.

'You're supporting your husband, too, and his beliefs. When you're married,' Ruth said, 'you have to support your partner, even though it can be difficult.'

There was a note in her tone that caused Clare for a moment to step outside herself and her concerns. Ruth came from a moneyed background. It was in the timbre of the voice. But her face spoke of hardship. Now her head pivoted away. 'There are things you do in a marriage if you want to keep it together.'

What did Ruth think of Joe? They were polite when they met. Clare had seen her listening to Joe tell an anecdote at the sixteenth birthday. It had gone on a little too long but had been greeted by applause and he had instantly embarked on another. Ruth, she recalled, had unobtrusively excused herself.

The coffee shop was quietening a little. 'I'd better get back,' Ruth said.

It had felt momentarily good to unburden herself, but Clare didn't feel any better. She had agreed to meet Joe at home. Then they would call around to Marianne and Pete's to thrash things out. Joe had a cause. He was energized by causes. There were times when Clare had wondered if they both searched for things to occupy them so that they looked anywhere but at themselves.

20

All four parents faced each other in Marianne and Pete's drawing room. The air crackled with tension. The conversation hadn't advanced. Predictably, Marianne and Joe had taken up their positions behind respective battlements.

Pete and Clare floundered in no man's land for the most part, looking from Joe to Marianne.

Clare was nervy, and with good reason, Marianne thought acidly. When she arrived she had planted a kiss on Marianne's cheek. Joe had shaken hands with Pete as if they were about to strike a deal. There had been something vaguely aggressive in his courtesy, she had thought.

When Clare had detonated her bomb, Marianne had been sitting at the kitchen table flanked by a bottle of wine and a packet of cigarettes, brooding over a blurred image of herself and a humdinger of a headline: 'Banker's Wife Enjoys Champers Lifestyle at Art Museum Beano'.

'It's very unfortunate,' her mother had called to say. 'You ought not to have gone to that, Marianne.'

'I know,' she had said. 'I'll be down to see you soon, Mum. I'm sorry I haven't been home. There's a lot going on at the moment.'

'We know that, Marianne. Of course we do.'

As soon as she'd hung up, Clare had rung.

'Don't you start about the bloody photo! I've just had my mother on the phone,' she said, wrapping one leg around the other.

'It's not about that.'

A silence.

'Marianne, Joe and I are coming over to talk.'

Marianne's head snapped up. 'About?' she said.

'I told Joe.'

'*What?*' she sputtered. 'You didn't! Clare, you *didn't*.' Something seemed to be jammed in her throat.

'He's my husband, Marianne.'

'Jesus. We agreed,' Marianne said.

'Finn wanted to tell him.'

There was a pounding in her ears. 'Finn is relishing the drama,' Marianne said, her voice rising. 'Finn has a lot less to lose than Grace.'

'You're not being fair to him.'

Marianne had started to think negatively about Finn. He was spoilt. All of Clare and Joe's children were overindulged. Joe's lavishing on them the latest electronic gadgets related to some fundamental sense of childhood privation, the filling of a hole. Finn's drive had been smothered by pampering and material goods. He had nothing to strive for when they lived in such luxury, where iPods, watches and items of clothing were replaced when lost or damaged. Like his brothers, he spent inordinate amounts of time permanently wired to the latest gizmo or plonked in front of a giant screen.

'Jesus, Clare, *I*'m not being fair?' Marianne flashed. 'You gave me your word.'

She had sent the girls to the cinema. Holly had been happy to go. 'Can we get popcorn and sweets?'

But Grace had protested. 'I don't want to go to the cinema.' She wanted to do nothing except stay cocooned in her room listening to her iPod. 'I just want all this to be over,' she had said.

In the end she had gone, insisting on going into town

rather than to the local cinema so that she was certain of avoiding friends. The idea of her discovering that Pete and Joe knew of her pregnancy – and the hysteria that was sure to follow – was awful, Marianne thought, looking out of the window.

The drawing room, she realized, was not very clean. It felt airless and a little grubby. The flotsam and jetsam of family life lay everywhere. There was a large cranberry-coloured mark on the couch, which she had thrown a cushion over. The paint on the dado rails was flaking. Neither she nor Pete looked fit to receive visitors either. In contrast, Joe was kitted out like some ad for a gentlemen's outfitters while Clare, as always, was simply and neatly dressed.

Marianne held a fortifying tankard of wine. Nobody else had joined her. Joe had worked his way into the centre of the floor, as if it were his house. Marianne had motioned for him to sit down but he had ignored her. Now he was talking at them.

Marianne had told Pete about their daughter's pregnancy just before Clare and Joe had arrived. He'd had difficulty in grasping what she was saying. 'Oh, Jesus,' he had said helplessly.

Not much Jesus can do for us in this situation, she had thought, steeling herself for Clare and Joe's arrival. She had worried that Pete might cry again. The shining 'giving it up for Jesus' expression he had worn recently, which she had found so provocative, was replaced now with a defeated look that unsettled her in a different way. He had the appearance of a man who had crawled from the wreckage of a high-speed car crash.

'Grace?' he had said. 'She's just a child, for God's sake.'

'She's sixteen,' Marianne said. 'Sixteen-year-olds can get pregnant.'

Now she said to Joe, 'Leaving aside that this is fundamentally Grace's choice, do you really think Finn is ready to be a father? Just the other day I heard him discussing the possibility of entering a banana-eating competition. His plan, I believe, is to beat the world record for peeling and eating as many as he can in a minute.'

'There's no need to be disparaging about Finn,' Joe said, his neck reddening.

'I don't mean to be. I'm trying to illustrate a point. That Finn is not ready to be a father,' Marianne said, topping up her wine. 'I guess what I'm saying is that we're not on board for bringing a child into this world, especially a child that is the result of a drunken one-night stand between two minors.'

'What do you think, Pete?' Joe said.

Marianne eyed Joe. There had been contempt in his tone. Not that Pete noticed, but Marianne did, and she cared on his behalf. Her husband, who no longer kept up with current affairs and ignored their finances but prayed by the bed.

Pete spoke in a way that suggested he was not fully present in the moment. 'I'm floored, Joe, to tell you truth. I'm lost for words.' He paused. 'I don't like the idea of abortion any more than the next . . .'

Man, Marianne thought, finishing his sentence.

'Obviously I hate the idea of my daughter being subjected to such an ordeal . . .'

Marianne fixed him with a look.

'. . . but Grace is a child herself. I'm not sure I can see an alternative.'

'And obviously we don't want our sixteen-year-old daughter's body to be used as a host for a baby nobody wants, most especially her,' Marianne said.

'I'm not sure it's entirely correct to say that nobody wants the baby,' Joe said, and Marianne gave him a hard look.

Joe, with his Victorian attitude to child-rearing, had moved into another room after his children were born, on the grounds that he needed his sleep. He believed in the concept of Family rather than *his* family, she thought. His arm was resting on the mantelpiece now in a proprietorial and presumptuous way. He spoke as if he were addressing an audience. Clare, his subaltern, was listening to him dutifully. He spoke about 'right and wrong'.

Marianne followed his argument with growing hostility. She imagined the satisfaction she might get from kicking him hard in the shins. But she reeled in her temper. Joe was a significant adversary. It was possible that he belonged to one of the secret societies that worked anonymously to preserve a Catholic Ireland. She remembered him saying, 'An open mind is a mark of foolishness, like an open mouth.'

But she wouldn't be cowed by him. So when she cut across him she was annoyed to hear a nervous edge in her voice. 'The appointment is made at a clinic in London for Tuesday week.'

Joe and she stared at each other. There was something strangely intimate about the look. As if they shared the knowledge that, for the first time in their chequered history, they were about to do open battle.

'I think we need to be reasonable about this,' Joe said, jangling his keys in his pocket.

He thought he could fix every situation to his liking. Marianne recalled when Finn and another boy had been caught dealing dope in school. Finn had not been expelled. Joe had brought his position and legal experience to bear on the school so that the other boy, from a much less vested family, was slung out instead.

'Where do you stand, Clare?' Marianne demanded.

'I'm not sure,' Clare said.

'You've got to be kidding me,' Marianne snapped. Pete tried to shush her. 'You're not seriously suggesting that Grace should continue with this pregnancy? . . . You're anti-abortion now, are you?'

Flustered, Clare said, 'I don't know, Marianne. Things aren't as black and white as you might want. I have to think about Finn's interests too.'

Marianne's stomach turned over. 'Clare, you're not seriously suggesting that they become parents? Would you like the happy couple to marry and set up home? In your basement or ours?'

'Melodrama isn't helping anyone,' Clare said quietly.

'Agreed,' Joe said, pacing a short distance away from the fireplace, then back to it.

Marianne ignored him. 'Quite apart from anything else, like the fact of her age or that she doesn't want a baby or that she and Finn are minors who do not love each other, Grace is destined for Oxbridge. Her teachers tell me that she may even win a scholarship. I don't want this awful thing to ruin her life.'

'And that gives her more rights than Finn because she's more academic? That gives her the right to destroy a baby?' Clare said.

'Jesus Christ, Clare, destroy a baby? She *is* a baby. Are you now following the dogma of the Holy Apostolic Church too?'

'There's no need to mock Clare's faith,' Joe said, inflating like a soufflé. 'It may be a joke to you . . .'

The tectonic plates beneath the discussion had begun to bash against each other and fissures were opening. All pretence of emotional detachment was gone. Marianne jabbed at the air. 'I'm an agnostic, Joe.'

Joe pressed his palms into his eye sockets as if severely

tested by her stupidity. 'Yes, of course you are. It's a hallmark of metropolitan sophistication to renounce the religious tradition you grew up in.'

Now there was a flash of the old Pete. 'Jesus Christ,' he said, 'listen to yourselves. This is not some rerun of a college debate from decades ago. This is our children we're talking about.'

'Agreed,' Clare said.

Marianne thought of the night Finn had been born. Clare had clutched her hand so hard that she'd thought the bones might shatter. Joe had waltzed into the room just after the baby had been placed in Clare's arms. Marianne didn't know now what Joe did or did not get up to outside the bounds of his marriage but she had her suspicions. 'Mr Business went to Mass every single Sunday. Mr Business went to hell for what he did every Monday.'

'What the hell is that supposed to mean?' Joe asked.

'How dare you?' Clare was incensed.

'Folks,' Pete said.

'I dare,' Marianne said, eyeballing Joe.

'I don't have to stand for this,' he barked.

'Always the hurler on the ditch, Clare,' she said, her body humming with anger. 'I went to London and you came with me.'

Clare's voice was suddenly cool: 'I came with you to support you as a friend but that doesn't mean I approved.'

An awful silence stretched before them.

'This conversation is over,' Marianne choked out.

21

Joe was calming down. He had stalked out of the drive.

'God bless,' Marianne had shouted after them.

It was what Joe usually said when he took leave of people.

'Bitch,' he grated.

Clare had been forced to trot to catch up with him. Ordinarily Joe's words were measured but he had thundered, 'She may disrespect her husband but she won't disrespect me, I tell you.'

Clare had hung back briefly to speak to Marianne. Although she was angry she had wanted to soften the blow of what she had said. 'I just want to clarify, Marianne, that I was happy to go with you but I wouldn't have an abortion myself.'

Marianne had not been placated. 'I don't care. You told Joe when you said you wouldn't. That has us where we are now.'

'Finn wanted to tell Joe. It's his right after all.'

'Just go, Clare.' Then she had called after her: 'Clare, just one thing.'

Clare stopped.

'Was that dinner really cancelled?'

'Marianne, I said to Joe –'

'Just answer yes or no.'

'No, but –'

'I thought so.' Marianne closed the door with such a bang that Clare felt the draught in her face.

Now she inched closer to her husband.

'Marianne is spoilt,' Joe said. 'Always was.'

Joe had always thought Marianne 'uppity'. There had been times when Clare had almost wondered if he hated her. She saw glimpses of something in his expression when he discussed her. 'She's coping with a lot at the moment. Pete isn't well. And there's the public aspect to things. And now this.' She'd felt compelled to say that in the interests of fairness.

She thought of the sneering tone that Marianne had taken with Joe – the childhood rhyme, what it implied. She felt angry with her. Then she seesawed the other way, thinking of the hurt on Marianne's face.

'You and I are lucky in that, values-wise, we've always been similar,' Joe said, and Clare felt a pulse of pleasure.

Already the dilemma was pulling them closer. During adversity some couples fell apart but others were drawn together.

That evening Joe had not gone out. He was at home with her. And his phone lay neglected on his bedside locker. Ordinarily she was asleep when he climbed in beside her. Tonight was different.

'I felt she was putting Finn down,' Joe added.

Clare did not point out that just the other day he had complained about Finn that 'the summit of his ambitions' was 'to get a tattoo'.

Now he said, 'Marianne ought not to think she can play God.' He pummelled a pillow and placed it against the headboard. 'I get the distinct feeling that Pete isn't as gung-ho as she is about a termination. In any case, the baby could be put up for adoption.'

Clare gave him a sidelong look. There had been a girl at school who had disappeared in the fifth year. She had been popular, with a mane of hair, good at games, quick to laugh. One morning she had not come to school. They had been given no explanation and had been shushed when they asked about her. Afterwards they had heard, through someone's older sister, that she had given birth in a mother-and-baby home. The baby had been put up for adoption.

Clare had wondered at the grandparents giving away their own flesh and blood. She had remembered the girl's parents attending the school concerts in the draughty hall. There had been nothing to mark them out as anything other than loving parents. It was not right to be judgemental about these things. In her practice, Clare had discovered that people had all sorts of complex reasons for making decisions that, on the surface, might seem inexplicable. But Clare had thought it cold. 'I couldn't put my own grandchild up for adoption, Joe.'

'I agree with you,' he said. 'We could keep the baby and raise it.'

Small kids bored her. She was better with older children. She loved her boys but she had found their babyhood taxing. She had not been sorry to pack away the baby paraphernalia. Often when one or another had been sleeping she had tiptoed past, not wanting to rouse them. Other mothers had spoken about wanting to wake them up.

She was not a natural at parenting. Scatty Marianne had somehow mustered the patience to devote herself to finger-painting and baking, even if she softened the edges with Chardonnay. She rubbed noses with the little treasure on her hip or kissed a tummy and made rude noises. When Marianne said that as a mother you got out what you put in, Clare found herself performing an audit that left her feeling miserable.

She mistrusted the idea that failings could be attributed to an 'unhappy childhood'. But it seemed obvious that the early loss of her mother had had an effect on her own mothering. She had enviously watched Gretta move in with Marianne after the birth of both girls. In a curious way Marianne had been Clare's mother figure, ready to dole out advice on colic or teething or answer her questions. It had been Marianne who had buttressed Clare's belief in herself as a parent. 'You're a great mother, Clare,' she had said, when Clare had doubted herself.

But Clare had sometimes questioned that Joe thought her a good mother. Joe said that mothers were among the most important people in society. He had tolerated her career, having made clear that he thought Clare's true place was at home. It was one of the few matters on which Clare had refused to let him sway her.

She did not think of herself as a feminist. She was not political and the battle of the sexes did not interest her in the way it did Marianne, who could talk at length on discrimination and oppression by the patriarchy. Clare had changed her name, her husband always drove the car when they were in it together, unless he was drunk, and before sat-navs she had handed him the road atlas whenever map-reading was called for. But in a non-confrontational way she had quietly fought for her independence.

Now Clare began to think wildly. Might a baby jump-start things between them again? Maybe this was an opportunity. Sometimes when she looked at her kids she saw them as guinea pigs she had practised on as she tried to become a parent. Perhaps now, having learned through her mistakes, she could have another shot.

Clare found herself persuaded by Joe. It was all very well to fudge the issue but certain realities could not be ignored. When you aborted a child you were snuffing out a life and playing God, as Joe said, no matter how you smoothed it over with rhetoric. That was the bald fact of what Marianne was proposing.

'We have the money,' Joe said, propping himself on his elbows. 'We can get help. This is a secure two-parent family.'

'It could be fraught with problems,' Clare said, wondering what role he imagined Grace would play in the baby's upbringing.

'There's a lot to be thought about,' Joe said.

As he talked through the possibilities, Clare found herself back at the airport all those years ago, waiting to break the news that she was carrying Finn. It had been a day she had tried to bury, with the words Joe had spoken. 'You wanted to abort Finn,' she said now.

'My God!' Joe shot up on his elbow. 'That's crazy talk. What in God's name are you on about?'

She still remembered how the scene had played out in the café.

'I stood by you. We've had four children, Clare.'

He touched the side of her face. 'C'mon,' he said.

She felt herself fold at this rare display of affection. It was pathetic that such a small gesture should mean so much. But it did.

'No more of that nonsense now,' he said, putting his arm around her. 'Clare.'

'Okay,' she said.

'Good.'

He changed tack. 'You never told me that Marianne had an abortion.'

'It was a long time ago.'

'I can't say I'm surprised.'

Clare said nothing.

'Who was the daddy?'

Clare shifted uncomfortably. 'I promised never to tell.'

22

As she banged about the house the next morning, Marianne ignored Clare's texts. It took quite some effort for her not to reply. In her head she composed a string of angry, stinging, self-righteous invectives. But she checked herself: her uncharacteristic withdrawal would punish Clare far more. *Judas*, she fulminated. Clare's attempts at explanation were pathetic. All these years she had sat in judgement on Marianne.

Marianne's anger with Clare was all that stood between her and immense hurt. She needed to stoke the fires of her fury or she might collapse. She busied herself by cataloguing the wrongs perpetrated against her and Grace. Clare had more or less called her daughter a slut. She had squealed to Joe, breaking her word. Not only had she sat in judgement on Marianne, but she had excluded Pete and Marianne from a stupid dinner.

Marianne's brain did a loop and she thought of a French film that had been shown when they were at college, a modern retelling of the Virgin Birth. Mary had been a basketball-playing schoolgirl. Joseph was at the same school. The clergy had denounced it as heretical. People had picketed the cinema. Marianne had found the whole thing hilarious. Clare had been pained. Now she decided that Clare was as religiously fixated as her husband, both of them foot-soldiers of the Vatican.

Marianne concealed the prohibited items she had just dropped into the green bin by covering them with newspapers. The bin for general refuse stank, overflowing, in the corner.

'We can't lift the bin, missus, if you haven't paid your charge. It's all in the system,' the bin men had said, when she'd pleaded with them.

Marianne eyed a crate of wine bottles that sat on the drive awaiting recycling, evidence for all the world to see of her growing consumption. A fox drifted across the garden wall, his long tail dragging behind. 'What are you looking at?' she asked.

She decided against distributing some of the rubbish in neighbours' bins that night, as she had done before. Damn Clare, she thought, as the fox jumped down in a leisurely way, and damn Joe. The previous night Joe had sent a text demanding they should meet up.

She would ignore him. She was equal to him. She slammed the lid onto the bin with more force than was necessary. He was an ideological thug.

She sensed the curtain of the house next door twitching. Pete was still being paid but the trip to London would cost money. She had hoped Clare would contribute.

Pete's lawyer had written that morning for an interim payment. Marianne slapped her way back into the house, pulling her dressing-gown around her as a draught whooshed up to chill her dimpled buttocks. Her ire gave way to depression.

Quite apart from the horror that lay ahead – she felt her nostrils stream – her mothering was in the dock. Marianne had never cared that she might be out of step with the *zeitgeist*. She had looked at the frazzled corporate lawyers, bankers and doctors and felt not one jot of envy. She did not judge working mothers but it annoyed her that stay-at-home mothers were portrayed as virtual malingerers.

She knew it was a heretical thought but secretly she had always felt there was something to be said for separate domains in marriage. She would never have admitted it. It was the sort of thing Joe trotted out when he extolled the virtues of having a family. But in fact it kind of worked that the man brought home the bacon at the end of the day when the wife had a meal on the table so that they could enjoy each other, rather than bickering about chores or seething with secret resentment.

Marianne had lived with the weight of her mother's disappointment for as long as she could remember. Gretta had always been an odd mixture of old-fashioned – 'I always had the dinner on the table for your father when he came in and a slick of lipstick on' – while harbouring a barely concealed disappointment that Marianne had not 'done something' with her degree. 'Why else did we educate you, if not to get out there and have a career? My generation did not have the option.'

Gretta had welcomed the birth of Grace with open arms, but she had said, 'You're in your intellectual prime. Now that you've had the baby you should be making plans to get back to work,' although 'getting back to work' was a euphemism as Marianne had never worked properly. But while Marianne had occasionally felt nettled at these hints of dissatisfaction, she had been broadly confident about her choices. She needed no further validation. She was a good mother and wife (particularly when she had a cleaner). Or she'd thought she was.

This was the foundation stone upon which she had based her identity. But what kind of mother ended up with a pregnant teenage daughter? A bad one. Her life's work was in question.

The slate-coloured sky hung low over her head. It was a cool, cheerless day, which was entirely appropriate. Having gone inside, Marianne plugged in a radio outside the bathroom door. Then she switched on the light. By now she was marinating in a stew of self-pity. The bath was grimy. Earlier she had found mould on the bread so she had given the girls money for lunch. The ironing had mounted up. Marianne didn't iron, really. There were worse things than wrinkled clothes.

She resisted the siren call of the biscuits that were downstairs in the cupboard. The other day she had ripped open a packet and scoffed half in one sitting. The stratagem of not having any in for easy consumption didn't work. It simply resulted in a late-night trek to the local garage. Trying to cut back on food meant that she thought about it incessantly.

Marianne wondered where Pete was. The night before, when they had worn themselves out discussing Grace and how they might best shield her from what lay ahead, they had shared a moment. It had felt like their old life. They had lain in bed and he had placed his hand on her thigh before pulling her to him. 'I love you, Marianne,' he had said.

'I love you too.' She had moved towards him, relieved that her response was not feigned. That she could get around the roadblock of his new-found faith was an achievement. Afterwards, during the post-coital chat, Pete had agreed to pretend that he was ignorant of Grace's pregnancy.

'I promised her I wouldn't tell you. The idea of you knowing fills her with horror,' Marianne had said.

She paused in her scrubbing. Wiping her forehead, she suddenly realized that the voice coming from the radio was Pete's.

'I was trained to carry out management systems like some sort of high-level automaton.'

She stared at the radio.

'I went to a private school, and right from then I ceased to think independently.'

The cloth fell from her hand.

'I feel that I was part of something wrong . . . I can't turn my back on that fact . . .'

Still Marianne didn't move.

'That was Peter Campbell, as part of a report on the banking crisis,' came a second male voice.

'Christ almighty,' Marianne said, as her phone began to vibrate.

23

While Marianne tackled her bath, Clare went for a walk with her husband. It had been Joe's suggestion. 'Let's clear our heads and strategize,' he said, holding out her coat.

They strolled beside the Grand Canal, Clare watching her husband's face like a hawk. She was struck by a rogue thought that threatened to spoil her pleasure. Why couldn't it always be like this? Why did it take such a drama for Joe to direct his energies towards his family, to take an interest in her?

'I love the canal,' Joe said, slowing his pace.

'Yes,' Clare said. In fact she had never given it much thought. Clare was not a visual person. When others marvelled at a view she tended to murmur agreement for politeness' sake. Joe would extol the virtues of their sea view in a hotel while she would be wondering how comfortable the beds were.

Now, though, she looked at the canal as he might. It was picturesque. The sun bounced off the red-brick buildings, lending the scene a rosy glow. Swans glided on the water, and there was no evidence of the urban debris that sometimes bobbed in it – shopping trolleys, boots, miscellaneous plastic and other ugly objects that tangled with the rushes: even Clare couldn't fail to notice that.

Joe stopped and began to quote poetry. When he reached a line about a couple kissing, Clare wondered if he might kiss her. When he didn't she asked, feeling a bit flat, 'Patrick Kavanagh?'

'Correct. Kavanagh saw the beauty in the everyday.'

Clare caught a glimpse of Joe as he had been at college. Certainly he had been focused and driven, but he had been intense and thoughtful too. There had been an expansiveness in his thinking that she had admired. He'd considered the bigger picture, not just his own patch. He'd had ideals. And although he had not been particularly privileged he had felt that he was as entitled as others to succeed. And because he had been like that, and because he had achieved so comprehensively, their children would never understand how their parents had had to scrabble.

Maybe, Clare thought, the awful thing that had happened to their son had caused them both to look up from their daily lives and consider who they were and what they had. Maybe this was some sort of turning-point.

'Kavanagh had a wonderful faith – Oh, there's James Wolfe.'

Clare saw a couple coming towards them. She recognized the name from the newspapers. Wolfe was a well-known financier.

They stopped to greet him and the woman Clare presumed was his wife. Introductions were made and the men talked briefly about business before they began to joke about golf.

The women exchanged conspiratorial glances, as if to say, 'Aren't they a gas?' Maybe it was because she felt more secure than normal that Clare felt she did a reasonable job at playing her part as Joe's wife. She uncrossed her arms and ventured another smile at the wife, who was hovering on shoes that were said to help you burn more calories.

Joe didn't like Wolfe, although from the bonhomie it wasn't obvious.

'Ah, go on out of that . . . this fella . . .' Joe said, patting him on the back.

Clare remembered an all-male party the man had held.

Joe had gone to the loo after the first course and phoned her to say that there were Russian hookers at the party, supplied by the host for his guests' pleasure. 'I feel compromised.' He had sounded angry. 'I can't leave but I will as soon as I can. I just wanted you to know.'

Clare had been grateful for the call.

The financier, Joe said, had a girl in every port. Maybe he compartmentalized his life, but so did she. Did his wife know about the roving eye and the hookers? Clare watched the woman lean in towards her husband.

'I saw you in the paper today,' the financier said.

'Yes,' Joe said, and gave a brief run-down on his no-to-same-sex-marriage campaign. 'All donations welcome,' he said, rounding off.

'I'll leave that kind of thing to you,' the man said, smiling in a way that prompted Clare to wonder what they thought of Joe. She was both proud and protective of him even though her own misgivings about the campaign had multiplied.

The man was small and had a simian look about him, like a toy monkey, she thought.

When they had moved on, Joe said, 'Slippery bollocks. He's like a barracuda.'

Clare saw with regret that his jovial mood was gone. He began to walk more quickly so that she almost had to run to keep up.

He heaved a deep sigh. 'Do you know, Clare, you'd get sick of people portraying you as some sort of right-wing loon. Ireland is overrun with secular fascists. They're anything but liberal. It's a question of anyone but Jesus. Mark my words, this country is at a crossroads. And if we continue to teach our kids that personal happiness is all that matters, as per the liberal agenda,' here he frowned deeply, as if personally carrying the weight of the country's licentiousness, 'then we're sunk.' Mainly Clare thought of life as peopled by those just trying to get by. 'It comes down to this: do we want our kids to live in a society with abortion on demand, readily available pornography and gay marriage?'

She must mention the campaign. She thought of her short-sighted melancholic son. She thought of him dying to have a nickname, wanting to belong. When she looked at Cian she visualized him behind a pane of glass, cut off, banging his fists, wanting to be heard. She thought of her brother closeted by his own family. Yet she allowed Joe to press forward, reluctant to say anything that might damage their new solidarity.

'We live in a country where they're thinking of banning prayers in the Dáil! I ask you! I can tell you something for nothing. I respect the rights of others to practise whatever faith they want, to have no faith, but I do not want our kids growing up in some sort of spiritual and moral vacuum where anything goes, and that's a fact.'

Joe moved from the general to the specific. 'This is a crossroads for Finn too. This is where we say to him as parents that, no matter how hard it might be, he picks up the tab for his actions and that we will help him to shoulder his burdens. I honestly believe, Clare, that we're fighting for our way of life.'

'But Finn is not some cause, Joe,' she heard herself say.

'I'm not saying he is,' Joe said, wagging a finger. 'I'm drawing an analogy. Of course Finn's welfare is paramount. I wouldn't say this to anyone else,' he went on, and Clare felt absurdly flattered, 'but sometimes when I look at Philip and Matt, both divorced, I feel depressed.'

Clare interpreted this to mean that Joe not only respected family values but he respected their family and, by extension, valued his life with her. She thought of Marianne's insulting rhyme and felt renewed anger. What right had anybody to judge another like that, to peer beyond the hall door and say that they knew their marriage?

Clare thought of Finn at home, cross-legged on the floor, eating pizza and watching *Simpsons* reruns, bereft in his own way.

'Grace has stopped answering my calls, Mum,' he had said.

At the most basic level this must have been anathema to Finn, having a girl ignore him. He had been cut out of the equation. No respect had been paid to him on any level. This was one of those pivotal moments, she thought. Family must come first. She must row in beside her husband.

'If it had been years ago, before the law was changed, we could have notified the guards,' Joe said. 'We've got to stop them, Clare.'

24

Family dinner was grim. Grace toyed with her food although Marianne had cooked her favourite. Whether this was from nausea or a pre-emptive strike against an expanding body, Marianne didn't know. Devoid of makeup, Grace's drawn face looked waxen. Earlier she had asked, 'Do you think I'm doing the right thing, Mum?'

'I do, darling, I really do,' Marianne had said, attempting to put an arm around her.

But Grace had twisted away, not allowing herself to be touched. Her body was toxic to her. 'I'm worried that afterwards I'll feel really guilty, like Finn says.'

Marianne fought back panic. 'Finn doesn't know what he's talking about.'

There were no anecdotes or exchanging of the day's news. Pete had lost his teasing tone with his girls. He and Marianne no longer had their 'back and forths' so the girls had no reason to unite in sisterly disgust at the parental flirtation.

Marianne was finding it hard to look at him. Pete's lawyer, who had heard the radio interview, had called to say that Pete ought to quit, saying he was sorry as it implied liability for wrongdoing. Pete had been unrepentant.

'But how is this going to affect your chances of going back to work?' she had asked, thinking of their overdraft.

The family sat in oppressive silence, save for Holly's chatter. Pete had made a small speech about some anti-capitalism protesters. 'I admire them,' he said. 'They're fighting for their principles. Not a lot can say that.'

Nobody seemed particularly interested.

Holly was wolfing down seconds, seemingly oblivious to the gloom.

'Slow down, Holly, you'll get indigestion,' Marianne said.

'I won't,' Holly said. 'I never do.' She was surveying Grace's food. 'You eating that?' She nudged her sister. The other day she had requested two lunches. 'I always eat my lunch on the way to school,' she had said. 'Then I've nothing for break.'

In her skinny jeans Holly's thighs looked like thick carrots. You could see the outline of two chubby knees fighting their way through the fabric. As strongly as Marianne felt that her daughters should not be defined by their size or have their self-image dented by weight talk, she might have to encourage Holly to eat less.

'Grace needs to eat her dinner,' Marianne said.

'Dad says that I can make my Confirmation,' Holly said.

Grace snorted.

'I don't have the energy for this right now,' Marianne said.

'You sound like a pig when you snort,' Holly said to her sister.

Grace ignored her.

Then Holly said, using her youngest-daughter cute voice, 'Dad said that it's my choice if I want to. Didn't you, Dad?'

Pete nodded.

'I live in an asylum,' Marianne said. 'Why don't we turn this place into a convent while we're at it? I could become a nun. Pete, you can go on the radio with your crazy talk –'

'What crazy talk?' Holly and Grace looked from one parent to the other.

'I can't stop you doing that but I'd prefer you not to try to imbue our daughter with magical thinking.'

'Religion is not the impediment to human development

that you think it is, Marianne,' Pete said. 'It's a way of looking at the non-rational forces in our lives, things like art and love. What's wrong with pursuing basic human goodness? Religion, if you think about it, is a call for altruism in society.'

'It's a fucking cop-out for losers who can't cope with the idea that they'll end up in the ground and be eaten by worms or reduced to ashes as their bodies are burned. End of,' Marianne said.

'That's not a very nice thing to say, Mum. And you shouldn't curse,' Holly said.

'No, I shouldn't,' Marianne said, grinding her teeth, 'but it's one of the few pleasures left to me.'

She was aware that they were all looking at her in disapproval.

'Why are you doing that with your teeth?' Holly asked. 'It makes you look kind of crazy, Mum.'

'I feel a bit crazy.'

'There's nothing wrong with wanting to explore the meaning of life,' Pete said, almost dreamily.

'"Everybody wants to save the earth but nobody wants to help Mom with the dishes,"' Marianne said. 'P. J. O'Rourke.'

'Who's he?' Holly asked.

'An American commentator,' Marianne said. 'Meanwhile, back on Planet Earth . . .' she continued, feeling a catch in her throat. She finished the sentence in her head: . . . I have to take our sixteen-year-old daughter to London for an abortion . . .

Somebody was knocking at the door.

'I'll get it,' Marianne said, sliding from her chair. She felt hollowed out.

She opened the door in time to see Finn bounding down the steps. 'Finn, wait! I'd like a word.'

Finn turned back and waved.

Marianne stooped to retrieve a brown parcel. It was addressed to Grace in a messy, almost illegible scrawl that sloped across the front. 'Finn,' she called again.

But he had begun to jog down the street. Marianne watched her godson disappear from view. Then she hesitated briefly before tearing it open.

25

The next day the sky was leaden. When Clare awoke she felt grey when she thought of the obstacles ahead. Marianne had not taken her calls. Her texts had gone unanswered. She would try to avoid them until she and Grace went to London.

'Well, obviously she's had the right to travel since 'ninety-two,' Joe said, 'so an injunction is out the question, more's the pity.'

Clare silently offered a prayer of gratitude that this was so.

'It seems to me that Grace is the weakest link, although obviously we need to tread carefully and take a softly-softly approach.'

'Joe,' Clare said, alarmed, 'remember how fragile Grace must be. We can't do anything to destabilize her. We wouldn't want anything on our conscience, God forbid.'

Joe said nothing.

'I'll talk to Marianne,' she offered.

In the surgery Clare scribbled on her pad. Work, which had always provided solace, no longer did. All she could think of was what she might say to Marianne. They had arranged to meet that night. A young mother sat in front of her, exhaustion etched on her face. A small girl squirmed by her side, tugging at her sleeve. 'I want to go, Mummy.' Then, 'What's that?' she asked, pointing at the stethoscope.

'It's for listening to your lungs and your heart.'

'What's that?' She pointed at the light.

'Sssh, Sorcha.'

The baby on the woman's lap gnawed at a rubber teething ring, one cheek aflame and covered with small raised bumps. 'He just cries and cries at the top of his lungs until I think I'm going round the bend.'

Young babies swallowed you whole. When Finn was an infant, Clare had thought she would die of tiredness. She had worked on a call roster, one night a week in Casualty on the respiratory team. Often she had been barely functioning. She remembered a night when she hadn't being able to quell Finn's crying. Strangely numb, in an almost disembodied state, she had rung Marianne. 'I think I'm going to shake him,' she had said dully. 'He won't stop crying.'

Marianne had appeared with tiny Grace in a sling and sent Clare to bed. When Clare had woken up, the flat was clean, the shopping done. Marianne had often stepped in when Clare's childcare arrangements proved inadequate.

Now Clare said, 'He's teething, obviously, but he has a middle-ear infection. The good news is that he's going to get better very quickly.' She handed over a prescription.

She couldn't picture either Grace or Finn with a child. The image was ludicrous, she thought, watching the mother pat her daughter's head.

'My mummy doesn't let me eat nuggets and chips but she lets me eat crisps.'

'Sorcha's only just getting over the sore throat,' the woman said.

The little girl resumed her questioning in the too-loud voice of a very young child, then said, 'Look, Mummy, look at the picture!'

'Sssh,' the mother said.

'She's grand, a brilliant big sister,' Clare said, in the falsely enthusiastic voice she used with very young children.

'I want to go, Mummy,' the little girl said.

'You need to take care of yourself,' Clare said to the mother. 'Is there anyone to help out for a couple of hours so that you can have a sleep?'

The woman shook her head. 'Wouldn't I love it.'

'It's important you don't get overtired,' Clare said, standing up behind her desk, thinking how useless platitudes were. 'Allow me.' She opened the door.

'Thanks, Doctor.'

'Mummy, I need to go pee-pee.'

'Hold it, pet, for two seconds. Can you do that?'

'Mummy . . .'

'Give that bruiser here to me,' Clare said. 'You take her.'

'Are you sure, Doctor?'

'Of course,' Clare said, holding out her arms. 'You're a big fella,' she said, putting the baby over her shoulder. She attempted to manoeuvre the cumbersome double buggy with one hand. 'These are awful things,' she said to the baby, who was dribbling on her neck. She went to her desk and reached for the phone. 'Ruth, could you come in for a sec, please?'

A moment later Ruth was there. 'Take this little fella here,' she said, offloading her cargo. 'Big fella I should say. He weighs a ton.' She fiddled with the iron bar on the back of the buggy. 'I used to hate these things.'

Silence.

Clare looked up. Ruth had gone pale. 'You okay?'

'Fine.'

'That was quick,' Clare said to the young mother, who was back.

'She didn't need to go.'

Ruth gave the mother her baby without a word. She was

not a chatty person but she was unfailingly professional. Now her manner seemed almost rude. 'I'll be outside if you need me,' she said, and Clare wondered what had triggered her discomfort.

Later Ruth came in and placed a cup of coffee on Clare's desk.

Clare wondered if she was trying to make amends for the strange lapse in courtesy.

'Need anything else?'

'No, thanks . . . Ruth, is everything okay? You seemed a bit . . . strained earlier,' she said.

'I'm fine,' she said curtly.

The door shut behind her. Clare sipped her coffee. Ruth had almost bristled at the question. And Clare had confided something of monumental significance to her.

Her mind flicked to Finn. He hadn't wanted to go to school that morning.

'I have respect for you, son, in standing up for your principles,' she had heard Joe say to him. He had not been egging Finn on exactly, but Clare had felt uneasy.

Now she could hear raised voices. Over the years there had been incidents with methadone patients desperate for a fix.

The door burst open.

'I told Marianne she could see you at the end of surgery,' Ruth said. She seemed flustered. 'I explained,' she said, turning to Marianne, 'that you have a packed surgery.'

'And I explained that it won't keep,' Marianne said rudely.

'That's fine, thanks, Ruth,' Clare said, and Ruth closed the door behind her.

Marianne's face was puffy. There were small purple pillows under her eyes. Sitting down, Clare began to rehearse what she might say. 'Take a seat,' she said, indicating a chair.

'No, thanks. I'm not staying. I'll get straight to the point. Finn dropped over a DVD to Grace, which, thankfully, I intercepted.' She added, '*Juno*.'

'I haven't seen it.'

'Well, I'll enlighten you, shall I? It's a romantic comedy in which the teenage girl puts her baby up for adoption and is seen to be really pleased with her decision afterwards. Neither she nor her cute boyfriend seem to suffer any grief after they give their baby away. They just move on with their lives. Like that,' Marianne said, snapping her fingers.

'He's sixteen, Marianne.'

'It's indulgent and sentimental,' Marianne continued, 'and extremely unhelpful. I was going to raise this tonight. However, about an hour ago he directed Grace to a website about girls who kept their babies and were relieved afterwards. There were also testimonies from girls who deeply regretted having abortions and are scarred to this day. You can imagine what that did to Grace. Tell Finn to back off, Clare.'

'Marianne, can I ask you something? Do you not worry that Grace will be damaged by having an abortion?'

'I worry that Finn's behaviour will damage my daughter.'

'Do you not remember how upset you were after you came back from London?'

'I was more upset by the way that bastard treated me,' Marianne said.

'I don't believe it was just that. It had a fairly major impact on you, as far as I can remember.'

'Believe what you want.' Then Marianne changed the subject. 'So you judged me for having an abortion?'

'I never judged you. But, as I've said before, I would never have one myself.'

'Great,' Marianne said sarcastically.

'What if Grace regrets it?'

'She'll regret it more if she has an unwanted baby at sixteen.'

'We'll take the baby,' Clare said.

Marianne laughed, her mouth twisting. 'I've heard it all now. Let me get this straight: you're proposing to raise what would be my grandchild down the road from our house? Oh, yeah, that would really work. And you want Grace to have this baby for you as some sort of junior surrogate, then hand it over?' Marianne shook her head. 'And who would look after the baby? Would you hire a nanny to raise it?'

'What's that supposed to mean?'

'Well, you're not going to be at home supervising the homework and making the dinner, are you?'

'I cannot believe you said that.'

'I'm not saying you're a bad mother.'

'That's exactly what you're saying. I have a career, Marianne. I run a busy medical practice so, yeah, I probably take short-cuts at home. And I need help to run my life.'

'And I don't have a career?' Marianne shot back. 'Working in the home doesn't count? Is this what you've always thought behind the "I respect your choice" shtick?'

There was no blueprint for this. They had debated these questions before, of course, but not in this ugly, no-holds-barred personal way. Now it was as if some awful boil had been lanced.

'Well?' Marianne demanded.

When Clare didn't answer Marianne changed direction. 'Joe is leading you along by the nose. As a result, our kids are going to suffer.'

'That's my husband, Finn's father, you're talking about. Joe also wants the best for his child.'

'You always choose to see what you want to see,' Marianne

said scornfully. 'You were ever thus. You did the same when Donal died.'

Clare sprang out of her chair as if she had been electrocuted. 'Don't you dare drag Donal into this!'

But Marianne would not be silenced. 'You told your children that he died in a farm accident. And although you know he was gay you deny it. You barely mention him. You've always been in total denial about how his death affected you!'

Clare picked up a pen and threw it at her. 'How dare you!'

Marianne started. 'I dare because –'

'Shut up,' Clare said, trembling. 'You burst in here, you insult my husband, you insult me and you insult the memory of my brother.'

'That's the point. I'm not insulting you or him. So what if Donal loved men?'

'*Just shut up, Marianne! Stop talking about him right now!*' she shouted.

'Fine.'

With great effort, Clare modulated her voice. 'That's you all over. You make assumptions. You wade in. You assume I was upset that Donal was gay. You never stop to think that it might be –' Clare stopped.

Marianne moved towards her, perhaps to try to comfort her.

'Don't touch me,' Clare said. 'You have no idea about me or why I might have been upset. And it's none of your damn business. Let's stick to the subject. Not once have you stopped to consider Finn's wishes or attempted to understand what he might be feeling.'

'Finn, who introduced my daughter to alcohol and –'

Clare cut across her: 'Get real. Grace was drinking before Finn and she ever did anything.'

'That's not what Grace said.'

'Well, maybe, Marianne, not everything Grace says is the unvarnished truth. Like teenagers the world over. You need to wake up or you're in danger of becoming one of those ridiculous mothers who blames everyone else's child except their own.'

Marianne's face grew pink. 'Grace was not quite sixteen when Finn and she slept together.'

It was a moment before Clare spoke again. 'You're joking.'

'I'm a mother who must protect her daughter, no matter what.'

'Nobody threatens my family,' Clare said. 'Get out.'

Marianne reached for the doorknob. There was a tremor in her voice as she said, 'Keep your son away from my daughter.'

26

Marianne's pulse was galloping, like a runaway horse. She was being lashed by rain, which slanted down, stinging her face. She had thought the drama quotient couldn't rise but she had been wrong. Finn stood in front of the car, blocking their passage. He had been stationed there, drenched, when they came out.

'Finn, please move. You'll catch your death. Look at you, you're soaked,' Marianne said, half out of the car with one foot on the ground.

'You don't care about me.'

That was not the case. Marianne had watched the vacuous but pleasant boy come into the world. She had changed his nappy. She had stretched him out over her knees and burped him. Clare was not a baker, so for years Marianne had made his birthday cake, a dinosaur one year, a superhero another and finally a football stadium, which had been the most elaborate project. She had kissed better the cuts on his knees. She had nursed him through mumps when Clare had to work. He had been sick on her after he had eaten her homemade chocolate ice cream. But her need to protect her daughter outran her sympathy for him.

'That's not true, Finn. I do care. I care a lot. I know you're upset but this isn't helping anyone.'

Now he looked young and vulnerable. He was not his father. He was a confused child. And she had done him an injustice. She had discounted him.

Grace simply looked beaten. She tried to hide it but her chest was visibly bigger. Her skin had broken out from stress or hormones. The pimples pushed buttons that went deep. For years Marianne had tried to convince a wet-eyed Grace that her acne would go, that she was beautiful, but none of her attempts to shore up her confidence had worked. Grace's acne had blighted her life until the most draconian potion had worked.

The rain continued to barrel down.

'Grace, we can be together if you don't go to London,' Finn said, planting his hands on the car bonnet.

Grace shrank in her seat, her cheeks wet as he pleaded with her.

'Finn,' Marianne said, 'this is just making it harder.' She left the car and inched towards him. She looked around hopelessly for assistance. Pete was lurking at the back of the house.

'Don't get up,' she had said the night before. 'If Grace sees you mooning about looking hangdog she'll cop on that you know.'

Now Marianne looked at neighbouring windows. She was terrified that Finn might use the A-word and they'd attract an audience.

'Finn, I know how upset you are,' she said, wondering how to shush him. 'I'm so sorry. But there is no other way. In time you'll see that. I know it doesn't seem like it now but you'll both get over this.'

Finn continued to stand in the middle of the drive. His face upset her deeply. She wondered if she ought to move forwards to embrace him.

Romeo and Juliet! This, she wanted to say, was why teenagers ought not to have sex because they were unable to face the consequences of getting pregnant.

'Mum,' Finn said, and Marianne turned.

'Clare.'

Clare ran to the front of the car, crunching over the gravel. She was in her running gear. Her vest was transparent with wet. Marianne could feel water trickling into her own shoes.

'Clare, I'm sorry but if we don't go we'll miss our flight,' Marianne said.

Finn's head was bowed.

He had begun to sob noiselessly. Clare pulled him to her. 'Finn,' she said, attempting to put her arm around her son's shoulders. She was forced to stand on tiptoe. 'Come away, Finn,' she said.

'Clare, I really appreciate –'

Clare cut her off: 'Marianne, if you go to London, if you go ahead with this, I do not want you to contact me when you come back.'

The words were like a slap in Marianne's face.

Grace was now convulsed with sobs.

'Clare, for God's sake, please – listen to yourself.'

'I don't ever want to hear from you again.'

'You don't mean that.'

'I do,' Clare said, jaw clenched.

'Clare . . .'

But mother and son disappeared down the wet street. Marianne could barely see them through the water on the windscreen. But she could see enough driving past them to realize that only Finn's head turned.

In the Ladies at the airport Marianne was drying her hair under a hand-drier. She was in shock.

'Marianne, how are you? Off anywhere nice?' asked a woman she knew from the gym.

After what felt like an unnaturally long pause, Marianne

began to detail their fictitious plans. 'We're going to London to see a play on the Leaving Certificate course.'

'That's sounds lovely,' the woman said, smiling at Grace, who had emerged from a stall.

When she had gone, Grace said wryly, 'There was a bit of a pregnant pause, Mum, while you were coming up with that bullshit.'

Marianne wanted to cry then for her witty, brave daughter. Instead they sidled off to the departure gates, Marianne hoping fervently that they wouldn't meet anyone else she knew. Waiting to board and watching Grace sip from a bottle of water, she felt rage. They were skulking off to England in a way that could only increase the stigma.

During the flight, Marianne shovelled pretzels into her mouth, plunging her hand almost feverishly into the bag. Then she savaged some nuts. As the trolley rattled up the aisle she worried about who might be on the plane.

Grace had lapsed into silence, wanting only to read her magazine. Marianne thought of what lay ahead in London. She had been older than Grace when she had gone. After that day in Bewley's she had only seen him once or twice in the distance. Her letters to him had remained unanswered.

Then, years later, she had spotted him in the National Concert Hall. He had been so close she could have reached out and touched him. He was with his wife. He looked quite similar, older and faded. He was reedier than she had rembered. He had turned and she was sure he had seen her before he stepped away to lead his wife downstairs, then outside, amid the stream of music lovers, onto Earlsfort Terrace. She had followed them to the door, hanging back a little, calculating the age that their child would have been.

Of course, later she had felt regret for her selfish disregard of his wife. But she had been twenty-one. He had been older and had wooed her with Thackeray and Eliot. He had charmed her and called her 'fey'. She had been a silly young girl infatuated with an older man. Much later she heard that he had run off with a student with whom he had had a child. She wasn't surprised. But she had felt nothing.

Now Marianne and Grace were in a taxi on their way to Brixton, with London looming on either side of them. Marianne had briefly considered taking the tube and saving on the fare, but the thought of being shunted down walkways and up escalators, the concentration it would require to navigate their way through the fetid air, had seemed overwhelming.

Marianne thought of Clare. She had been about to draw her to one side to apologize. There were things she needed to say. She regretted mentioning Donal. She had done it because she had been hurt at the idea that Clare judged her or, worse, Grace.

She wanted to say that she thought Clare was a good mother. Who was she to cast judgement? Marianne no longer felt secure about her own mothering. Her image of her daughter as a teetotal bookish prig had been shattered.

'Why didn't you tell me that you drank?' she had asked Grace.

Silence.

'Why did you try to blame Finn? Why didn't you tell the truth?'

Grace hadn't given a satisfactory explanation. Marianne had thought Grace incapable of calculation. Now she remembered Grace's brown legs encased in the briefest of shorts in West Cork. She remembered the hours Grace had spent titivating herself. She had entirely missed the teenage longing in her daughter.

Marianne wanted to tell Clare that she should never have

made the threat about statutory rape. It was a disgusting thing to do, born out of fear and a primitive need to protect her child. Something atavistic had happened. She and Clare had lined up behind their children like cavewomen. They must not let this destroy a lifetime's friendship. Marianne loved Clare.

She turned to Grace. Grace was not a good traveller. Now she looked frog green. 'I need to get out,' she said. 'Stop.'

Marianne leaned forward and spoke to the driver through the partition. 'Please stop. My daughter needs some air.'

Marianne and Grace got out. Marianne watched as she doubled over and threw up the meagre contents of her stomach. 'You're all right, darling,' she said, holding back the heartbreakingly childish plait.

27

Clare and Finn sat in the darkness of the cinema. She had given them both the day off.

'I'll reschedule things,' Ruth had said, without asking any questions. 'Consider it done.' Whatever had troubled Ruth seemed to have passed.

Mother and son sat with a giant tub of popcorn and two fizzy drinks between them. Clare had not been to the cinema with Finn for years. In fact, they hadn't been alone together for a long time. She found herself unsure in his company.

'Some day you'll meet somebody and marry and have a family,' she had said to him.

Finn hadn't replied so she had felt self-conscious.

Her thoughts looped back to Marianne, as they had when she'd parked her juggernaut of a jeep. Marianne considered Clare's car a vehicular anachronism: 'Four-by-fours are so environmentally unfriendly, Clare. And the person in the other car doesn't stand a chance. Only Irish people and redneck Americans drive them.' But Clare knew that for Marianne her real crime was being behind the times. Marianne saw herself as principled. With a rush of bitterness, Clare decided that much of her posturing was about the desire to be in vogue.

Marianne displayed a copy of Warhol's *Chairman Mao* in her sitting room. Clare found it strange that such a ruthless dictator should adorn a wall. Could you refer ironically to Maoist witch-hunts? Was it possible to be witty about a nightmare like the Cultural Revolution?

'Post-modern irony, Clare,' Marianne would have said, then gone on to speak of 'Warholian genius'.

Marianne had made insinuations about Clare's mothering and had threatened Finn with a rape allegation. Clare hadn't mentioned this to Joe for fear of what it might provoke. It had been up to her to defend their son.

A tsunami of protectiveness swept through her as she glanced at her firstborn silhouetted beside her. I love you, she thought, as Finn reached for the popcorn. She never told any of her children that she loved them. The words formed but she couldn't articulate them.

Marianne, Clare thought, had crossed the Rubicon. She had said the unsayable. In the past they had always flattened out their differences successfully. Or maybe she had always backed down. This time Marianne had gone too far.

Joe was right: Marianne professed to be a liberal but she was narrow and judgemental. As Clare sat marshalling arguments against her friend, certain memories barged to the front of her mind. Old grievances grafted themselves to her pain. The airy casual letters about lazy days spent globetrotting. In Marianne's Jane Austen phase they had begun, 'My dearest Clare'.

She visualized Marianne lifting her luggage from the carousel in Baggage Reclaim after yet another idle summer, sending home to the Bank of Mum for cash infusions. Marianne didn't understand why Clare couldn't come out and party with her, that she had to conserve her limited funds for the college year. She had scorned Clare's job in a fast-food outlet, mocking the hairnet she had been required to wear.

An accumulation of slights and wrongs from the past clustered together so that the friend she loved morphed into a selfish stranger who had little consideration for Clare, her marriage or indeed her family. And now she was facilitating the abortion of Clare's grandchild.

Worst of all, she thought, was the way in which Marianne had felt entitled to speak about Donal when he was not here. She could hear the coffin creaking as it was lowered jerkily into the waiting pit. The wind was rustling the tall trees that lined the graveyard.

Clare's shoulders were heaving.

'Mum,' Finn said, 'you're crying.'

28

The strange thing about the clinic was that it looked so ordinary. There was nothing to suggest from its façade what went on inside. There were no shouting campaigners positioned outside as there might have been in the US.

Throughout the lead-up to this event Marianne had avoided feeling that there was anything momentous about what Grace was going through. In order to convince Grace that the procedure would not be traumatic, she had to keep telling herself the same thing. She had simply blanked out her feelings. And when she had felt herself flagging she had reminded herself of Joe's attempt to coerce her child. That had spurred her on.

Marianne had stayed calm during their first visit to the clinic when she had given a false British address and changed their surname. She had debated this. Should she preserve Grace's anonymity, thereby highlighting even further for her daughter the furtive and therefore shameful nature of what they were doing? In the end she had thought it better to be cautious.

The pregnancy had been verified by ultrasound. Marianne had watched the cold gel being smeared on her teenage daughter's belly and forced herself to prattle on as if this was routine. A time had been set for the next day's termination.

The clinic had recommended a nearby B&B. Alexandra had wanted them to stay with her but Marianne had said no. 'If Grace thought I'd told anyone . . . It's better this way.'

There would be no condemnation from Alexandra. Marianne had not told her who had made Grace pregnant: to do so would have been a betrayal and replicate what Clare had done to her.

Now, on the second day of the ordeal, they presented themselves at the clinic clutching Grace's small bag. Marianne would go to a nearby café where she would meet Alexandra, although Grace didn't know that.

Grace had opted to have a general anaesthetic. A London Irish nurse –'Me mother was from Tullamore, Dad from Listowel' – had talked to them in the small room as they waited for Grace to be taken down to theatre. Marianne was grateful for her upbeat manner as earlier another nurse had been brusque.

In the waiting room the day before, Marianne had wondered if they were being judged for Grace's youth. She had dressed with more care than usual to appear 'respectable', which was pathetic.

When it was time, Grace was wheeled along a corridor with Marianne accompanying her. Somewhere in the nurses' station a radio played a jaunty song about teenage love – she wanted to ask them to turn it off. There was a queue. Two women lay on trolleys ahead of Grace. Marianne ricocheted between the past and the present. The years seemed to fall away and Marianne became her daughter on that trolley. She stood in that London corridor and she could smell the fear and shame.

'Don't be scared,' Marianne said. 'It won't hurt, it'll be over in a jiffy and then things will go back to normal.' She continued to babble. It was only in movies that people said anything wise or inspiring at such a seminal moment.

As she spoke she thought of Grace shinning up the bars and out of her cot when she was small. Marianne would wake to see a small figure in a sleepsuit defiantly pushing open the door of their bedroom, a bottle in her hand. The warm body then climbed up and lay between her and Pete. She could hear Grace reading aloud, in the determined voice of a five-year-old, with no heed to punctuation so that one sentence ran into another. In all the years of raising Grace, she had never bargained that they would end up here.

Then it was Grace's turn. Marianne's smile was carved into her face as if it had been chiselled there by a sculptor. In an awful inversion of a game they had played when Grace was a baby on Marianne's hip, she leaned over the bed so that they almost touched noses.

'I love you, Grace. I'll be here when you get back.'

She watched as Grace was wheeled down the corridor. When the blonde head disappeared through the double doors, Marianne sagged against the wall. Nothing could have prepared her for this. When Grace or Holly had a cold she had almost felt it by proxy. This was like being skinned alive. At first Marianne cried soundlessly, a hand clapped over her mouth to smother a noise that didn't come but was reverberating deep inside her.

Marianne had thought she might never have a baby. She had not gone for a check-up after she'd come back from London. She had just pretended that the whole thing had never happened. And she had had endometriosis.

The day she realized she was pregnant with Grace, it had been raining. Pete had waited for her in his banger with the hole in the floor. They had parked the car on a hill so that it would start again. Gripping the pregnancy testing kit, they had made for the nearest pub. Marianne had peed on the stick as Pete waited outside, talking to her through the door. He knew about the abortion. He had never judged her. He had only wanted to hurt the professor.

Marianne had opened the door to tell him she was pregnant. They had barely known each other.

'I love you,' he had said.

Eventually the London Irish nurse reappeared.

'It's okay, Mum,' she said.

Marianne followed her outside to the chilly drab street. The nurse smoked and talked. She was kind in a garrulous way.

Marianne realized that she had begun to bawl because passers-by were eyeing her. It was a primitive sound. Muscles quivered in her legs. Mucus ran from her nose. The nurse produced a tissue and then another.

Marianne sat in the café across the road from the clinic. Faces swam in and out of view. Teacups clattered. The coffee machine emitted its steam rattle. Alexandra was talking. Marianne was doing her best to follow what she was saying.

'You look great,' she'd said to Alexandra, when she arrived.

'Liar,' Alexandra shot back.

It was one of those false things you blurted when you got a shock. Facially, Alexandra had changed almost beyond recognition. It wasn't so much that her features had coarsened, more that they had vanished. She was blade-thin in the way that suggested illness, either mental or physical. The lovely hair was still blonde and thick, but now it was cut short. The clothes were simple but stylish, a man's shirt over trousers with a bangle on her arm. And she held herself in that graceful way still.

'It's been ten years,' Alexandra said.

'That long?'

When she sat down, she said, 'This is very hard for you . . . your daughter.'

Immediately Marianne's vision blurred.

'You don't have to talk about it.' Alexandra began to speak

about other things, of past difficulties. Her life now was lived inside the lines. 'It has to be,' she said, 'so that I stay sober.'

'So Foucault's gone?' Marianne said.

Alexandra smiled. 'He died of Aids from indulging in sadomasochism in bath-houses.' She exuded sadness. 'I've become a yoga bore,' she said. 'I've replaced booze with it, thereby swapping one addiction for another.' She worked in a health-food shop. 'They're where the unhealthiest, most neurotic people in the world hang out,' she said.

'You were always brilliant at poking out new places,' Marianne said, remembering the young Alexandra.

Alexandra smiled her gap-toothed smile. 'I met a woman from my boarding-school the other day,' she said. 'It turned out that she lives around the corner from me. She said she'd expected to hear my name some day and that at school she'd assumed I'd be famous and end up being Somebody. She seemed terribly disappointed on my behalf. Do you feel you realized your potential?'

Marianne shrugged. 'Today I don't know what I think about anything. Are you in a relationship?'

'No. Post-rehab, Blaise and I split up, as you know. It was inevitable. He carried on drinking.' She paused. 'I can barely manage me. Is Clare still with Joe?'

'Yes.'

'I'm surprised, but she was always rigidly conventional.' She smiled. 'I remember you two having a big fight about not drinking on Good Friday. She was pathologically strait-laced.'

The mention of Clare's name was painful. Marianne shook her head. 'I was furious at the time, but I have a different perspective now. I mean, I don't get the religion thing but I look back and think she showed strength of character in standing up for her principles.'

'He made a pass at me, you know.'

'Joe?'

'Yes,' Alexandra said, her hair falling over one eye. 'The strange thing was, he wanted me but he hated me too. Lust mixed with contempt. Strange guy. He was so cocksure but patently insecure.' Marianne was surprised. She had always thought of Joe's confidence as impregnable.

'God, look at the time,' Alexandra exclaimed. 'I have to go.'

'Come to Ireland,' Marianne said, and hugged her.

'I will,' she said, but they both knew she wouldn't. 'Please let me pay,' she said.

'I wouldn't dream of it.'

'I hope your daughter . . .'

'Yes,' Marianne said. 'It was lovely to see you.'

'And you,' Alexandra said, blowing her a last kiss from the door.

Marianne stood at the counter. Alexandra was still funny and candid. But it had been depressing, too, and Marianne was glad she and Grace hadn't stayed with her.

There was a tattered paper on the counter. Marianne read about a woman who had been wrongly convicted of smothering her baby son; she had taken her life. The expert pathologist who had given evidence for the prosecution had been struck off. Marianne regarded the image of the slim blonde woman who was now dead. The shot of the pathologist showed an older man in a pinstripe suit being driven away in a Jaguar.

She looked at the line of photos of women in similar cases who had been convicted on the basis of the same man's evidence. The ring from a coffee cup meant that one or two of the images were partly obscured. Then Marianne stared. The hair was different. And she looked considerably more robust. But it was her.

PART THREE
November – December 2011

'And say my glory was I had such friends.'

W. B. Yeats

29

Clare shrank from the window. Marianne rang the bell again.

'Clare, please.'

She came most days. Ruth had been instructed to turn her away at the surgery.

'Are you sure?' Ruth had asked.

'I'm sure,' Clare had said, in a way that invited no further discussion.

On one occasion Marianne had tracked her up the drive. Clare had slammed the door of her jeep shut with her shoulder and walked into the house, ignoring her. Sometimes she brought news calculated to break Clare's resolve – about Pete, or how she was worried that Gretta was hiding something.

There was violence in ignoring somebody, denying their existence. It was cowardly, and yet Clare, besieged by contradictory feelings, could not yield. She had been in denial for so long about Joe, Donal, her father, that she didn't know how to move forward. She was stuck.

'Friends drift away,' Joe had said to her. 'Whether you ever had anything fundamental in common is a moot point. In any case, people change.'

Marianne's absence had left a gap in Clare's life. And the truth about her motives in supporting Joe, combined with the knowledge that the alternative to the abortion might have been worse, was weighing heavily on her.

She had convinced herself that she had wanted the baby, but now she could admit that she had been motivated by a compulsion to thwart Marianne. Even more, she had wanted to keep Joe happy. She often adopted an attitude that suited her need for stability and solidity in her life. She was a duck gliding along – the good wife, the devoted mother, putting her family first – while its feet paddled furiously beneath the surface of the water. She was beginning to see that she had worked overtime to avoid the terrible unsettling feelings that she could barely identify. This crisis had thrown her into turmoil – dark thoughts were bubbling up in her mind, like weeds pushing through gravel, threatening to overwhelm her. Clare watched Marianne pick her way carefully down the icy drive. She paused and looked back at the house. When she had gone, Clare rested her forehead against the pane.

'You okay, son?' Joe had asked Finn, the night before.

The truth was that Finn had slipped back into a version of his normal life. 'The baby' had been an abstraction whose hold on him had waned quickly. Occasionally there were bursts of anger against Grace, which Clare cut short. When Finn spoke of what had happened he seemed to view it through a lens of what had been done to him, so she tried to make him see that it had been the consequence of Grace and himself having made poor decisions.

She wondered if his upset stemmed more from a bruised male ego at not having prevailed rather than any sorrow about the ending of the pregnancy. But now that she had accepted the truth of her own mixed motives, she could hardly condemn Finn for hypocrisy.

Clare had been partly correct in her calculation that recent events would bring father and son together. That aspect of the gamble had paid off. Joe had stopped extolling the manifold achievements of his colleagues' kids.

He got the points for Med.
He's on the Senior Cup Team.
He's hoping to do an MBA.

But she had been naïve to imagine she might be the third corner on this triangle: now that the crisis had passed, Joe had moved away from her again.

He had come home to pick up some papers. 'I'm off,' he shouted.

'Wait, Joe,' she called. 'Joe.'

Quick footsteps down the stairs. He stopped on the second-last step. 'Hi,' he said, pulling his phone out of his pocket.

'Would you like to have lunch?' Clare asked, tilting her face up to him. Her usual lunch was a hasty sandwich eaten at her desk or perched in Ruth's small office.

'What?'

'Lunch. Would you like some?'

'I thought you were going to the dentist.'

'I've been. Check-up. And it's Wednesday, my half-day. Normally I take the twins swimming but they've gone to a party.'

'I need more notice than that,' he said.

'Okay. I'll catch up with stuff at the surgery. Ruth has been after me to spring-clean my office.'

'Great,' he said. He was jabbing at his phone again.

She bypassed her disappointment. 'Joe, we need to talk about the campaign,' she said.

His head snapped up. 'What about it?'

'I have concerns that it's homophobic.'

'Well, it's not,' he said, frowning. 'It's about protecting the sanctity of marriage.'

'Even so,' she said, 'I'd like to discuss it.'

'Fine. But not now. I have to go.' He moved towards her

and pecked her on the cheek. 'Don't forget Philip's book launch tonight.'

'Bye,' she said. Her words seemed to echo after him.

Through the window Clare watched him click his keys so that the door to his car zapped open. It had been an arid kiss, she thought, watching him motor through the gates.

Clare went into town. She wasn't good at using leisure time and wandered around aimlessly, surprised to find she was enjoying the experience. She was so programmed that she had forgotten how to relax.

On Coppinger Row, at the open-air food market, she purchased some olives and a piece of cheese (of a type Marianne would approve – but Marianne was immediately banished from her mind). Under her arm she also had some lavender soap that made her think of the lawn at home in West Cork.

Now she turned onto Castle Market Street. There was something distinctly continental about the scene, she thought, seeing smart people sitting outside bars, smoking and chatting, despite the freezing weather. She paused at a restaurant, attracted by the outside area, which was roofed with an attractive beige wood. La Maison, she read, slowing down to look inside.

'*Fondant au chocolat*,' she heard a waiter say.

A man was ploughing through what looked like a fish stew.

The room was very Parisian, she thought, noticing the wooden floor and bentwood chairs. Not that she was an authority . . . Ruth seemed to know Paris well. 'I like the Latin Quarter best, the fifth and sixth *arrondissements*,' she had said once, confiding something as she only rarely did, 'over by the Sorbonne and the Panthéon. Near the Jardin du Luxembourg.'

At a table in the corner, set against the backdrop of a beige wall, Dervla Feeney looked startling in a violently raspberry suit. Clare couldn't imagine wearing such a colour. What did that say about her? she wondered. She had never got the hang of clothes. In her earlier years she'd had neither time nor money to devote to how she looked. Now she dressed in a bland, formulaic way.

Clare waited until Dervla looked up, then smiled.

'Clare!' Dervla said. 'It's been a long time.'

'Yes! I was just in town . . .' Clare trailed off.

'How are things?'

'Fine,' Clare said.

'Good, good, good.'

She was more skittish than Clare remembered. 'It must be odd being back in Dublin,' Clare said, without mentioning the failed marriage.

'I like it, actually. I hadn't realized how much I'd missed it.'

'That's good.'

'You're working on a campaign with Joe?'

'Yes. It's very interesting.'

The waiter descended on them. 'Are you joining the lady?' he asked Clare.

There was a split second when Clare thought she might. Then old unresolved doubts returned. Long-forgotten hierarchies re-established themselves. She was transported back to a world of cliques and whispers behind half-raised hands. She was once again the overweight girl at college, shovelling damp carbohydrates inside her at lunchtime, lumbering across campus pretending to search out non-existent friends.

'I just popped in to say hi, and now I'd better push on,' she said.

'See you soon,' Dervla said.

Clare had the dispiriting thought that she seemed more cordial now that the threat of Clare's company had lifted.

*

In the Royal Irish Academy on Dawson Street, a judge of the High Court had given a witty speech incorporating legal in-jokes that had gone over Clare's head. She took a swig of her wine. This was the sort of night where Joe thrived and furthered his career. He was interested in people and they were interested in him.

She watched her husband of so many years, the father of her children, throw his head back and laugh at something the judge had said. It was a loud, confident laugh. He was so expressive with people in the outside world. She had assumed when they'd met that he would be like that with her. But at home he seemed to shut down some part of himself. She often found herself mining conversations for traces of affection. They had soldiered on for years, telling themselves that they were no happier or unhappier than anyone else. Was that true?

Clare recognized some faces. Colleagues of Joe, people they had broken bread with, some who had been at Finn and Grace's sixteenth birthday party. She had said one or two hellos, but she wasn't inclined to make conversation. They were technically friends of hers too, she supposed. She had once assumed that Joe's self-assurance, his social skills, would rub off on her. Now she wondered if they had compounded her nervousness.

Here Clare felt herself attacked again by that ruthless avenger, guilt. Before Joe, Marianne had been her main conduit to social interaction. Had she not hidden behind her friend, then blamed her for leading the way? She recalled how Dervla had brushed her off.

'Born insiders, most of them,' the man on her right was saying. He was large and meaty-looking. Earlier he had asked her where the loos were. 'The *crème de la crème* of the Irish judicial scene,' he went on, jerking his head at a passing man.

'There goes reputedly the next president of the High Court, one of the leading lights of the tribunal. They're all bright boys and girls,' he said. 'But, to be honest, all that verbal jousting gives me a royal pain in the arse. Cleaning up down in the Four Goldmines. It pays to be in the advice business, doesn't it?'

Clare murmured in an ambivalent way.

'"All professions are conspiracies against the laity,"' he said. 'Shaw,' he added, as if she had sought the source of the quotation.

She was framing a response when he spoke again. 'Criminology and criminal justice . . . As areas of law go, pretty interesting, I'd say. Not saying much, though. The book looks like a bit of a tome. Don't see myself tucked up at night with it,' he said, 'but an interesting fella, Philip.'

'Yes,' she said.

'Grounded.'

'Yes.'

'Nothing grandiose about Philip,' he said, and she followed his gaze to where Philip was nodding at something a little old lady, in a coat that seemed too big for her, was saying. A proud aunt, maybe. Philip looked well. Was it that he had changed his glasses? He was less stringy, having filled out in a way that suited him. He was one of those people who had improved with age, she thought, as he was accosted by an attractive woman in a wrap dress.

'Does Philip have a partner?' Clare asked.

'Not that I know of,' the man said, 'although I couldn't be sure.'

'How do you know him?'

The man's shirt was missing a button and he had a faint stain on his right lapel. 'We go for pints together from time to time,' he said. 'I'm a journalist.'

'Oh.' Clare wondered what she felt about journalists. She didn't really know any. Marianne wasn't keen. Once again she stopped herself referring to the compendium of Marianne-isms. Joe had been savagely angry over an item that had labelled him a fat cat who had earned millions from a tribunal. The implication had been that he had been feathering his own nest rather than helping rout out the corruption in Irish life, as those tribunals were supposed to do.

'I don't really read the papers,' Clare said.

'Heresy,' he said, tutting. 'You're probably right. They're mainly filled with depressing old shite. What do you do yourself?'

'Doctor,' she said, draining her glass. (Her third or fourth?)

'You're too good-looking to be a doctor,' he said.

Clare went crimson. She didn't attract compliments. He was mocking her. 'Are you making fun of me?' she asked, startled at her boldness and deciding that she was definitely pissed.

He looked genuinely taken aback. 'Jesus, no. What gave you that idea?'

Silence.

He was flirting with her. Clare's ears roasted. She was not somebody men flirted with.

'I'm Tony,' he said, offering his hand.

Tony. It was not a name she liked.

'Clare Corcoran.'

'Dr Clare Corcoran,' he said, and more colour flooded her face. He reached out to a passing tray and grabbed two glasses of wine.

'I shouldn't,' she said.

'Oh, go on. The only way to get through these things is warm plonk,' he said, pressing it on her.

She accepted the glass.

'The weird thing about all this politicking and beavering and trying to get on in life is that it won't really matter. We're all on a collision course with death.'

One of his front teeth was discoloured. 'That's quite fatalistic,' she said, deciding he was a drinker.

'I watched this great film the other day, *Life During Wartime*. Have you seen it by any chance?'

'No.'

He was a man with a need for conversation. 'I'd highly recommend it. One character is married to a paedophile, a psychiatrist who sodomizes boys and goes to prison . . .'

'Doesn't sound like my sort of thing,' Clare said, with a wintry laugh.

'I can see how it might sound off-putting. It's blackly funny. In a way, I found it uplifting. It's about forgiveness, really, and what it takes to lead a new life. Forgiveness is an interesting subject, particularly in the current climate. Can we forgive people?'

Clare said nothing.

'There's a quote – I think it might be the last one,' he said, and gulped some wine, '"Forgive and forget is like freedom and democracy. But in the end China will take over and none of this will matter any more." I think,' he said, smiling, 'that without the ability to forgive we're nothing.'

She thought of the footsteps receding down the drive. He was looking at her.

'I'm sorry,' he said, 'I'm talking too much. I always do when I'm arseholes.'

30

In the Village Café in Rathmines, Marianne waited for Joe. She did not want to be ambushed. It had been her choice of venue. She wanted to meet on territory that was familiar to her. She was known there. It was not his kind of place. Joe liked restaurants with carpets that deadened sound, heavy cutlery and linen tablecloths, places where he could be reminded of how successful he was.

Good jazz played, as was often the case. Through the glass doors Marianne watched papers whirl down the street. People set their faces into the bluster. It was one of those bright, windy days that ordinarily would have energized her. She had the beginnings of a headache. As she'd been walking out of the house, Holly had come running to waylay her. 'I've picked a name. Thérèse,' she'd said, glowing. 'After Saint Thérèse of Lisieux. The Little Flower. I'll be called Holly Elizabeth Thérèse.'

'Fine,' Marianne had said, putting up her hands as if she were being taken hostage. 'I give in. I surrender.'

Now she considered going outside to join the smokers puffing at the front of the café. She decided against it, not wanting Joe to have the satisfaction.

'Just an Americano, please, Aodan,' she said to the owner.

A group of older women in tennis gear were chattering at the next table.

'My budget for a coat would be around three hundred and fifty euro. To get a decent one. I mean, a yard of wool costs fifty.'

'Mary's daughter got married last week.'

'Ah, Mary, you scrub up well,' said a woman, eyeing photos.

'Once you're wearing black or beige there's no trouble,' said a silver-haired woman.

'The groom is lovely.'

'I bought the hat in Pamela Scott's.'

All the tables were full. The place hummed. A mountainous man ordered apple pie with extra cream. Two women sat at the table next to hers, their heads bent close to each other. Marianne saw that one woman's face was damp. She heard the words 'speed dating'. A little later the other dropped her Rice Krispie cake on the floor and they both laughed.

The idea that Clare would never forgive her was devastating. Clare had come with her to London even though she didn't approve of abortion. That was the sort of friend she was. The end of their friendship was like a death.

Joe was coming down the steps and through the door in his heavy winter coat, a scarf wound around his neck. She watched him eye one of the more eccentrically dressed customers, a woman in a ragged fur coat with wellington boots and what looked like a ski band around her head. She was smoking a long, thin cigar with panache. But Joe would not see it like that.

'Hi,' he said, sitting down.

'Hi.'

'How are you?'

'Fine,' she said warily. 'And you?'

'Also fine,' he said. He pointed at a speaker. 'Good music,' he said.

'Yes,' she agreed.

'Coffee?'

'A quick one,' he said. 'Black, no sugar. How's Pete getting on down at the Central Bank?'

Marianne decided to ignore the question. There was no satisfactory answer. And he was possibly being snide.

'I asked to meet you, Joe,' she said, 'because of Finn's Facebook posting. Clare won't take my calls or see me.'

He nodded.

'Clare reacted with great speed last night to my text and Finn's post came down straight away. But I need your assurance that this will never happen again.' She was speaking too quickly. 'You can imagine the effect it had on Grace.'

Marianne had woken in the middle of the night to see an anguished face at her bedside.

'Mum,' Grace had whispered, tugging at the bedclothes. 'Mum, I need you.'

In the bathroom, Grace had bawled, 'He wrote "Baby-killer" on my Facebook wall.'

'Oh, Grace, honey . . .' Marianne had wanted to disembowel Finn.

'How is she?' Joe asked.

Marianne considered the question. Grace had been managing to slouch into school and do her work until the latest débâcle. She had been back in contact with her small but tight posse of pals. She had been 'okay' until this. She had gradually been coming round. Now she lay in her room like a corpse.

'She was fine,' she said. 'This was a big setback.'

She hadn't been able to persuade Grace to go into school that morning. Curled up in the foetal position on her bed, she had cried, 'I can't, Mum. I can't.'

'Nobody saw it, darling. It was in the middle of the night. Clare made Finn take it down straight away.'

Marianne looked at Joe. 'Grace's biggest concern is that her peers will find out that she had a termination. We told people she was out of school with a virus.'

'Finn's very sorry for what he did. It was a rash act. You have our word it will never happen again.'

'Good,' Marianne said. 'How is he?' She felt compelled to ask.

'He's unhappy,' Joe said.

'Yes,' Marianne said, in a noncommittal way, trying hard to summon some compassion.

Joe tipped his head to the side as if considering something. 'Can you be so sure, Marianne, that guilt does not play a part in Grace's upset?'

'I can,' she said, her face hardening.

They were teetering on the edge of an age-old fight.

'Stop,' she said. 'It's pointless.'

He went to speak again.

'Enough . . . You won in the end,' she said, her voice scratchy.

'This is mine,' he said, meaning the bill.

She didn't thank him. 'Clare and I have fallen out. You got your way.'

'That's a fatuous thing to say,' he said coolly.

'I love her more than you ever have,' Marianne said.

'You've always been a self-dramatist.' All *faux*-amiability had left his voice. The force of his dislike was laid bare.

They were two animals, she thought, got up in human clothes, twitching with dislike as they sized up the enemy. The veneer of civilization had been entirely scratched away.

Marianne reached for her buttons. 'Please keep Finn in check.'

When she left the café it was only after a minute or so that she realized she was walking in the wrong direction.

31

While Joe and Marianne were fronting up to one another, Clare was taking Cian out of school. She drove along the Dublin–Cork motorway at what was for her a high speed.

'Just you and me hitting the road, like in a movie,' she had said to Cian. 'Think of us as going on a road trip.'

'That's mad, Mum,' he had said, looking up from the floor.

Now he seemed perplexed but pleased. Gradually he had become more responsive so Clare felt heartened. His iPod played in the car.

'I love Snow Patrol,' he confided. 'Lots of people don't like them because they're so commercially successful. They think that's a bad thing. But I don't.'

Clare felt giddy. This was possibly the most impulsive thing she had ever done in her life.

'You did what?' Joe expostulated, when she rang him from the McDonald's at Cashel.

'We've gone away for the night to West Cork,' Clare said. 'Cian had a bruise on his arm today.'

'The rough and tumble of a schoolboy's life, Clare, and what on earth has that to do with you going to West Cork, for God's sake?'

Clare could picture Joe's face, tight and disapproving. 'Our son is being bullied because he's gay, Joe.'

There was a stunned silence. Then Joe said testily, 'Don't be ridiculous, Clare. How can you possibly know Cian's sexuality at this stage?'

'He's gay, Joe. I've always known it, really.' And you have too, she thought. Joe was selectively blind. He hadn't liked it when Cian hadn't wanted to play football as the other boys had done. Cian had wanted to stay with Clare.

'Don't be silly now,' Joe would say. 'Come and play with your brothers.' *Stop being a cissy.* In the end Joe had stopped asking. She remembered a day when Cian was a small child. Joe had come home from work to find him wearing Clare's pearls and lipstick in their bedroom. He had been very angry. 'Take that muck off your face,' he had roared. Cian had quailed. And Clare had done nothing except hug Cian afterwards.

'The school doesn't seem willing or able to deal with it. At the very least Cian has been subjected to name-calling.'

'Boys bandy that word "gay" around all the time. It doesn't mean anything. Like I said before, Cian needs to develop a thicker skin.'

Clare had been on the Internet. What she had read had terrified her. Gay kids were up to three times more likely to commit suicide and they were far more likely to get depressed or take drugs. 'He's in the wrong environment for him, Joe. He needs to change school.'

'You sound like Marianne.'

'Leave Marianne out of this.'

There was a short, tense silence.

'Donal was gay. Look what happened to him,' Clare said.

'I'd say there was a history of depression in your family, Clare.'

Joe had adopted what she thought of as his cross-examining tone. No doubt he had an arsenal of arguments at his disposal. Clare looked through the window of the petrol station. For once she didn't care about marital harmony. Cian was in the car, munching a burger. He seemed less pale now.

He had once been a happy, if quiet, little boy. Now he was disappearing down some hole.

Clare went outside where she could see her breath against the cold.

'It's starting to snow,' Joe said. His voice told her once more that he thought she was being contrary.

'I'm not making the same mistake twice,' she said. 'We'll be back tomorrow. We can talk about things then.'

Majella and Clare sat at the kitchen table. Majella had opened the bottle of wine Clare had brought. They would go on to drink another. The kitchen, though familiar, seemed claustrophobically small. It needed to be painted. The settee in the corner was threadbare. But Majella had the gift of hospitality and Clare felt welcome.

Sophie, Clare's niece with the sunflower-coloured hair, had shepherded Cian in to watch television. She was a good student and her parents were very proud of her.

Through the door Clare heard her ask Cian about school.

'It's okay.'

'Do you not like your lessons?'

'I don't like rugby and stuff,' he said, after a pause.

Then they had chatted about other things.

Clare heard Cian laugh. It was a sound too seldom heard. She had said they'd come because Cian was having a hard time at school, and because she wanted to talk to their father.

Earlier PJ had offered to take Cian out. 'Time you were driving, young fella.'

'But I'm only fourteen,' Cian had remonstrated.

PJ shook his head. 'Go on out of that. I was driving a tractor at your age.'

'But it's dark,' Cian had said, pop-eyed.

'You're a bit of a devil for the rules, Cian, are you?' PJ asked, and Cian had nodded in his literal way.

Cian had driven past his mother, beeping and flashing his headlights. A wide grin stretched across his face.

PJ had gone to bed after a glass of wine.

'There's a bit of an improvement, no question,' Majella said, lowering her voice. 'He's out walking every morning now at least. And he's stopped combing the paper for news on the bank and the shares, and how the big guns seem to be getting away with things. It was eating him up. And it wasn't doing us any good. I said to him that he took a risk buying the shares and it went bad . . .'

The question of who was to blame for the losses was a vexed one. PJ had taken the plunge without any real understanding of what he was doing. It had been his decision: nobody had forced him to sell the land and plough the proceeds into shares. In another way, though, he and others like him were collateral damage: little people caught up in a maelstrom of avarice and dreams gone wrong.

'No sign of the estate being finished off?'

The village they lived in was bordered by a half-built housing estate.

'It went up for tax breaks. Nobody even comes to the completed homes. I suppose they can't rent them out when the others aren't done. It's an eyesore, but what can you do?' Majella said, shrugging.

'Does Sophie still want to do medicine?'

Majella nodded. 'The teachers say she'll get the points.'

'She can live with us in Dublin,' Clare said, studying her engagement ring. It was large and ostentatious and had been a replacement for the original. In fact she had preferred the first. This one jarred in Majella's company.

'Do you mean that?'

'Of course. Why wouldn't I? You and PJ were always so good to me.'

'We'll drink to that,' Majella said.

And Clare would find some way to pay the fees without insulting them, she thought, as her sister-in-law poured them another glass of wine.

When Clare woke in the morning the room was cold and she was hung-over. Her son was curled up beside her like a koala bear.

'Would you like to change school?' she had asked him, when she had fallen into bed drunk. 'Go somewhere that might do more of the stuff you like?'

'I would, Mum.'

Through the crack in the curtains she could see that the tops of the trees were snow-capped. Clare thought of her father up in the farmhouse. She had tried to make him move but he wouldn't hear of it.

The day before, she had driven down the tree-lined boreen wondering how she might introduce certain subjects.

'We're going for tea in West Cork, Daddy,' she had said.

When they were installed in the hotel Clare had said, unable to think of a more nuanced way to ask the question, 'Daddy, I was wondering recently if there was a history of depression in the family.'

She waited for him to speak, and when he didn't, she added, 'I seem to remember that Mammy went to bed sometimes.'

The pause seemed to stretch on for ever.

'She had good and bad days,' he had said then.

A little later she had piloted the conversation in the direction she really wanted to go. 'I'm thinking of moving Cian from his current school.'

'Oh,' he said.

'The others get on grand there but it doesn't suit him,' she said. 'He's been bullied, Daddy. That's why we came down. To give him a bit of a treat.'

Her father buttered his bread.

'He's been bullied like Donal was.'

The comment hung between them. Two generations of one family sitting together, she thought, still struggling to name things.

Then the white head lifted slowly. 'He wanted to be a gardener, you know,' her father said. 'One of those fancy ones.'

'Yes.'

'I think now,' he said, looking beyond her, 'that people should be let alone to do what they want.'

32

A makeshift collection of tents was pitched on the plaza outside the edifice that was the Central Bank of Ireland. They were blanketed with snow. The protest, when compared to others in neighbouring countries, seemed small. A woman with a loudhailer to her mouth cried, 'Why should the survival of bad banks be more important than the welfare of Irish citizens?'

Marianne sought out Pete among the protesters. This was not her first time here. As ever, she felt conspicuous. She found him next to a girl in her late teens with a mane of matted hair. He was holding a cardboard sign that read 'Real Democracy Now'.

'Hi there.'

'Hi, Marianne,' Pete said, smiling broadly, his too thin hands poking out of his coat. 'This is my wife, Marianne,' he said to the girl. 'This is Joy from County Laois.'

'Hi, Joy,' Marianne said.

'Hey.' Joy held out a grubby hand.

Marianne felt her gaze voyage up and down Joy's person. Inside her belted camel coat she felt matronly and stolid. Joy was young enough to be her and Pete's daughter. But then, compared to the majority of the protesters, Pete was Jurassic.

'I really respect Pete's struggle against his paymasters,' Joy said.

Marianne gave him a parcel. 'Sandwiches. And flapjacks. Homemade. Plenty for Joy too. An army needs to march on a full stomach,' she added lightly.

'We'll be going on our march later,' Joy said, accepting a sandwich from Pete. She looked at Marianne. 'Cheers ... Later, dude,' she added.

Pete seemed pleased to be fist-bumped. Marianne saw Joy migrate towards a wooden structure where coffee appeared to be served.

Pete ate his sandwich. His hair almost tipped his shoulder blades. He tugged his woolly hat down on his head. He looked the part. 'Really good,' he said. 'My favourite.'

'How's the rage against the machine going?' she asked.

'I know that you're doubtful about what I'm doing, but for the first time in ages I feel alive. Why should the citizens of this country shoulder a debt that was not of their making? Why should the survival of bad banks, like the one I worked for, be more important than the welfare of ordinary people?'

To stem the delivery of the political lecture, to which she had already been subjected many times, she said, 'The girls miss you.'

This wasn't strictly true. They had only expressed a fleeting concern about what Pete might be doing. Like most teenagers they were entirely egotistical and their lives were what mattered. That Grace was preoccupied was hardly surprising.

The inevitable media coverage that had followed Pete's involvement with the group meant that people frequently approached Marianne.

Holly had come home from school to tell her, 'Amy said Dad was on the news and he's gone mental.'

'Dad was on the news but he hasn't gone "mental",' Marianne replied. In fact, to her, he seemed to be unravelling.

'Dad's turned into an Emo,' Grace had said. 'He'll be drinking cider and smoking weed soon.'

'Grace!'

'Will he, Mum?' Holly asked.

'No,' Marianne had said, thinking that anything now seemed possible. 'Girls,' she said, in the schoolmarm tone they hated, 'Dad is part of a peaceful protest. He is standing up for what he believes in. It's vital that in a democracy people have the right to express themselves. We should be proud of him. Tell anyone who says anything rude about him what I just said, and if that doesn't work, tell them to piss off.'

The girls had liked that.

Now Pete swallowed his mouthful. 'How's Grace?' he asked.

'On the mend,' she said, hoping it was true.

He fell silent. Then he said, 'I still can't believe what happened.'

'No . . . Are you coming home tonight?'

'Hard to say.' He made a face. 'I might be needed here for security. It can get messy in the middle of the night.'

You're needed at home, she thought.

'And with the march later . . .'

Gardaí milled about in yellow vests and peaked caps.

'You won't get arrested, will you?' she asked, not for the first time. 'The girls and that . . .' She trailed off. 'We've had enough drama recently. Don't want to have to bail you out.'

'No,' Pete said, shaking his head. 'The gardaí have been brilliant, very supportive, actually.' There had been no clashes with the police.

Joy, who was now wearing a khaki army surplus jacket, was chanting, 'End capitalist corruption.'

'I want to show our girls,' Pete said, 'that you can see the world in a different way.'

Marianne cared in theory about a better world too, particularly when she had some good wine inside her. Then she worried about American foreign policy (boo), Aids in Africa (boo) and the plight of women in the developing world, to name just a few issues. She had a fridge magnet with the face of a Republican president declaring that a village in Texas had lost its idiot. The morning after a good rant, when she surfaced with the alcohol gone from her system, she inevitably felt a little less committed. Sometimes when she considered her politics, she wasn't entirely sure if she said such things because she wanted to think of herself as someone who wanted to change the world, whether she wanted others to peg her like that or if she genuinely thought she might help it along by adding to the debate.

Her mother had been staunchly admiring of Pete. 'The French take to the streets and strike, the Greeks riot, the Irish do nothing except drink and talk about what they should do. I admire Pete. And what does he have to lose? "Th' whole worl's in a terrible state o' chassis,"' she said, quoting from O'Casey's *Juno and the Paycock*.

Her mother was staunchly disillusioned with what had happened in the world and had become belatedly belligerent, like many of her peers. There had been a warm text from Coleman, too, which had been touching. It seemed that the financial meltdown had dampened their faith in the establishment and the world they had grown up in.

Pete's mother, though, was unhappy at the new protesting Pete. But, then, she thought mainly of the golf club and her small circle of suburban cronies. The limits of her world seemed to extend not much further than the area she lived in. 'Will the bank fire him?'

A good question. It was rare that she and Pete's mother agreed.

'So far, not a word from them,' Marianne had said.

Marianne had been moved when her neighbour angled her head over the railings between their houses to say that she thought Pete was 'very brave'.

Although she wouldn't badger him, Marianne wondered if Pete planned to work again.

'I need time out,' he had said making a T sign with his fingers. 'I was like a hamster on a wheel.'

Now he kissed her. 'Give my love to the girls.'

'Come home soon,' she said, as he was absorbed into the crowd that was gathering for the march.

Maybe they all would have to shift tracks now. People built new lives all the time, moving country in search of work, leaving their culture and language behind. Sometimes people were forced to build a whole new life. She thought of Ruth and what she had found out. A young man with what looked like a multicoloured sock on his head offered her a leaflet. 'I already have one, but thanks,' she said, making a decision.

The taxi dropped Marianne at the block of apartments. They had been built in the mid-seventies and had a dated, vaguely run-down look about them.

She knocked on the door. There was silence for a few moments. Then she heard sharp, staccato footsteps. She felt a thrumming in her chest.

'Marianne!'

'Ruth.'

'Come in,' Ruth said. She was wearing a sleeveless jacket that made her seem even smaller than she was.

Marianne glanced around the sparsely furnished living room. It was like a monastic cell. There were no photos or personal mementoes.

'Sit down,' Ruth said, indicating the one soft chair. 'Tea or coffee?'

'Tea would be nice.'

From her vantage-point she could see a galley kitchen

where Ruth was flicking on a kettle. This life, Marianne thought, was not about renunciation. It was more like mortification.

On the table lay a pair of knitting needles. 'You knit,' she said.

'When I can't sleep at night,' Ruth said, returning with cups. 'I think I know why you're here,' she went on, when she had sat down.

'Oh,' Marianne said, wrong-footed.

'You should make it up. You're such good friends. Clare is miserable.'

'She won't make it up,' Marianne replied sadly. 'But that's not why I'm here,' she added.

Ruth was scrutinizing her.

'I've debated for weeks,' she said, 'whether I should say anything. My instinct tells me that I should.'

Ruth wasn't going to help her.

'I'd like to say that I haven't always been very welcoming to you and that I regret it. That's the first thing.'

Ruth looked understandably cagey at this announcement.

'I know what happened in England,' Marianne said. 'With your son.'

Complete silence.

'I saw an article in a paper, by chance. I'm sorry . . . It must be . . . indescribable.'

Nothing.

Marianne felt panicky. 'You were a doctor,' she continued.

'Yes.'

'I read that medical evidence was kept secret that might have cleared you. The pathologist was struck off.'

'Yes. I have another son,' Ruth said. 'He's fourteen now. I've seen him from a distance, at school through the railings. His father and the psychiatrist have turned him against me.'

'But you were the victim.'

'My baby died of cot death. But I was drunk that night putting him down,' she said, flatly. 'I was insensate. I could never have registered or dealt with any problem that arose.'

She was not angry or philosophical, Marianne thought afterwards, but damned.

'I drank. My husband never forgave me.' Her face was devoid of expression. 'There is prison with bars. And then there is prison of another kind . . . I would talk to Clare. Life is short.'

33

Clare took a call about a leak in a rental property they owned. They were between management companies and Joe's phone was off. Reluctantly she got into her car, feeling obliged to investigate. Good tenants were hard to get. It had been Joe's idea to a buy a number of flats in the development. She had little interest in owning property. She had her practice and that was enough. Clare was just glad he hadn't been involved in a consortium like Pete.

On her way to Mount Merrion, she wondered if Joe was avoiding her calls. They'd exchanged words about the campaign, about Cian.

'I know you mean well, Joe, but I've given this a lot of thought and I think there is a homophobic element to the campaign. It sends a wrong message to young gay people. I think,' she searched for the words, 'that it's discriminatory, and I don't care what Irish law says.'

Joe, she could see, had been surprised that she hadn't backed off. Joe loved his children, not in a get-down-on-the-floor-and-play-with-them kind of way, but he loved them. Why could he not see that Cian was in trouble?

Clare wondered about the school's attitude. Generally they seemed sympathetic to the children. And they were not unkind to Cian. But she felt that while they dealt with the bullying it was in a literal way that did not admit to the homophobic element, either because they failed to understand the fact or didn't want to acknowledge it.

Clare drove past Donnybrook Stadium to Wesley disco,

where her sons learned to dance and kiss and do God knew what else. Going to 'Wes' was a rite of passage for most kids in south Dublin. But while her other sons sprayed themselves in clouds of cheap deodorant and aftershave, and fussed with their hair, getting ready as much a part of the courtship ritual as anything that went on at the disco, Cian kept himself apart. And thus he was locked out of yet another area of growing up.

Her standing up to Joe was new. Ordinarily she appeased him. They were both in uncharted territory. She worried that if she did not keep patting things down and instead shone a light on her marriage the entire edifice might crash. Yet she knew she was not for turning.

There was the Marianne question too. She couldn't stop thinking about it. She could no longer tell herself that it had been about Marianne's high-handed ways. Marianne seemed totemic of all that was wrong in her life.

The answer to the riddle had come to her when she recalled an image from the previous winter. She had been driving past Marianne and Pete's house when she had seen Pete chasing Marianne and snowballing her, Marianne shrieking and laughing. Clare had not beeped, reluctant to puncture the intimacy of the scene. Pete had kept pelting her. By the end of the road he caught up with Marianne, clutching her so that she had flung her head back, laughing in an unbridled joyful way. *Marianne had always had love.* That was it. And in some way Clare, feeling a flush of shame, had resented her for it.

Had she put Marianne on a pedestal? What had Marianne really done other than point out unpalatable truths? At last Clare saw that she had damped down all the awful feelings that had formed her life – feelings about her mother's death, her father's attitude to her dead brother, Donal's suicide, Joe's lack of loyalty. When the crisis over Grace's pregnancy had arisen, she had lashed out at Marianne because Marianne had always been loved and had glided through life, when Clare had had to struggle and settle for scraps. It was as simple and as complicated as that.

Still turning this over in her mind, she let herself into the vacant first-floor flat. The tenants downstairs had said water was coming through their bathroom ceiling. Stupid not to have arranged to meet a plumber – what was she going to do about it on her own? She looked past the scantily furnished living area. It wasn't a bad flat. There was plenty of light from the floor-to-ceiling windows. She and Joe would have loved to live somewhere like this when they were starting out. Their first flat had been ratty.

Clare stopped. Clothes were strewn on the floor as if someone couldn't wait to shift their activities to the bedroom. She stopped, staring at a shoe turned on its side. It was the sort of impractical article that she would never have worn. She moved forward uncertainly.

When Clare pushed open the door to the main bedroom, she was splayed beneath him, his bottom rising and falling, like an apple bobbing in a basin of water. It was a moment before they realized she was there.

'Jesus Christ,' Dervla said.

Joe's head snapped round. 'Clare.'

He leaped from the bed, covering his genitals with a pillow as if he had to keep them private from her.

Clare's every sense was heightened.

'Clare.'

She was breathing hard through her nose. She shook Joe off. 'Fuck off.'

The words were crude and unsatisfying.

She ran down the stairs. She saw Joe's new gleaming car, a feat of German engineering. Clare got into hers and gunned the engine. Years of suppression, of patting things down, had resulted in an explosion. Clare's anger burst up out of her depths, like a geyser. She drove her car repeatedly into the back of Joe's until the number plate hung down and flakes of paint littered the ground.

Whether or not she was observed, she neither knew nor cared. She drove home, the wheels spinning as if she was not in charge of the car. Her phone thrummed relentlessly.

She sent a text before shutting it down: 'Do not come to the house or I will tell the children.'

In the kitchen she found a pair of scissors. Behind her locked bedroom door she began to cut up his clothes, suit after suit falling to the floor, like clippings in a film editor's suite. She filled the bath with hot water and bleach, then tossed in Joe's expensive leather shoes. She flung his cuff links down the loo, although they lodged at the bottom of the bowl. She left the wedding photograph till last. Turning on the taps to muffle the sound she smashed it against the wall over the bath so that the shards fell into the water. Afterwards there was complete silence, save for her harsh breathing. Then her anger began to subside and her strength deserted her. She got into bed with her clothes on, removing her shoes as an afterthought. She lay there rigid in the dark, the shutters closed tightly.

How long had it been going on? She was condemned to replay in her head the image of Joe pounding away at Dervla. And she was forced to confront a reel of pictures that she had shelved. The painted talons of a young barrister proprietorily resting on Joe's arm at a legal function. Joe missing on the night Finn was born. The anonymous calls to the house before mobile phones had become an adulterer's dream. A letter she had received, which Joe had convinced her contained the ravings of an unstable fantasist. Had her myopia spanned the entire marriage?

Morning finally came. When the time arrived to slide out of bed, she didn't, like her mother before her.

34

Marianne sat opposite Matt in the Central Hotel, regretting that she had agreed to come. They had met on the street. He had proposed an early Christmas drink. It had started off quite well. Matt had taken charge, his hand on the small of her back, steering her along the slippery streets and into the hotel in a way she found male and reassuring.

'The snow makes you feel childish,' he had said, and she had warmed to him.

Women deposited shopping gratefully, having braved the Christmas bustle. The customers were a mixed bag. A man slapped another on the back. There was the usual mix of Christmas licentiousness and booze in the air. Marianne had felt vaguely infected by the communal exuberance.

At first the conversation grooved along pretty well. Matt seemed less bombastic than usual, and she began to remember his good points, the qualities that had originally attracted her to him. She even began to revise his performance in bed, in the spirit of Christmas goodwill. For a brief time they were their young selves, just with extra poundage. Marianne raised her gin and tonic, and for a moment she was the flirty, fun previous incarnation. Matt became the earlier replica of the man, the fundamentally sound Tayto-sandwich eater trapped inside a sleek senior counsel's body.

He had made a cursory enquiry about Pete but hadn't pursued it. For this she awarded him marks. She was enjoying time out. Pete had given up his protest outside the bank. Some of his fellows had not liked his introduction of Jesus into the political fray. She suspected he had worn them down with recitations of scripture. Plus he had gone in wearing a peaked cap that said on its brim 'God loves you but I'm his favourite'.

'It makes him look like a psycho,' Grace had said.

He was talking about going away on a religious retreat. He ate very little and had no interest in sex or his family. But he was canny enough to put on a good show for his psychiatrist. He could be in his room, or out praying and bowing in church, and then, Lazarus-like, up he trooped off to his appointment and seemed 'normal'. Conclusions were not easy to come by in psychiatry, it turned out, and the psychiatrist could only assess the data available to him. Marianne didn't blame him. Now Pete was mainly at home. There was a marked irony in that, she thought. For years she had carped that he was not there enough. Now he was around her too much.

Matt and she spoke about Deep Pockets: he had been killed in Argentina. 'His car smashed into an oncoming lorry,' Marianne told him.

'Do you reckon it was suicide?'

'He didn't seem the type,' she said, thinking of the boom days when Deep Pockets had sat behind a forest of microphones boasting about his bank's performance and delivering bullish pronouncements on the economy.

'There was drink involved.'

'He'd received death threats, I heard. His family too. Cosmic justice?'

'Too good a death for him,' she had heard one woman say on the radio.

Even with her intense dislike of Deep Pockets, Marianne couldn't summon up such downright hatred.

There had been a shift in Marianne. She could allow that

Pete had had input with what had happened with the bank. But she objected to him being singled out. Many others had played a part in the ship going down.

Then she and Matt had talked about Joe and Clare.

'Finally caught with his trousers down,' she said, her voice harsh. 'And with Dervla.'

'You never liked Joe,' Matt said.

'True,' Marianne said. 'Or Dervla. How long had it been going on?'

'Not for me to say.'

'The boys stick together. *Plus ça change.*'

He made a face. 'Don't shoot the messenger, but I never thought he and Clare worked. I think they got locked into something by that early pregnancy. I always thought he and Dervla should have married.'

Marianne felt a rush of sadness for Clare. She had been astonished to come home from India and find out that Clare had married Joe Corcoran and was carrying his child. At college she had read about Eros and Thanatos, the link between death and sex. Had Clare reached for Joe because of her brother's shocking death? Or was it more pedestrian than that? Had Clare just liked the wrong guy?

Marianne considered their circle of friends. They had been a golden generation, or so they had thought, with lives far easier than their parents', certainly than their grandparents'. And they had spent their capital, their youth, and ended up here. She had taken a lot in her own life for granted. She had been privileged and spoilt, bankrolled by others.

She listened to Matt's relentless parade of jokes and anecdotes. Mild pleasure swiftly turned to purgatory. She was reminded of a dancing bear with a dickey bow entertaining her as he unleashed his conversational pyrotechnics. He was clever and too conscious of it.

When there was a gap she said, 'I must go soon.'

Did Pete know that Deep Pockets had died? She had heard it in the taxi on the way into town.

'I made a mistake in leaving Anne-Marie,' he said.

He was further down the road to being drunk than she had realized.

'I married a girl for her face and her easy-going personality. That's about the sum of it,' he said, 'and it wasn't fair to her. She has many fine qualities. She deserves better.'

Marianne searched for something to say. She thought of his young wife with her slow-motion smiles and flickering eyelids. Her conversation had seemed to meander nowhere. She had only become animated when Marianne, trawling for conversation, had admired her dress.

Clare had said that there had been something sad about the wedding in Venice. It had rained, and while it had been held in a beautiful *palazzo* on the water near the Peggy Guggenheim Collection, there had been two sets of guests from different generations who hadn't mixed. Matt and Anne-Marie's kids had lurked in the background, there but certainly not by choice. The new wife had looked for benediction from Matt's friends that almost certainly wouldn't come.

'She was so lovely and she was mad about me. I lost my head, I guess. Anne-Marie and I had allowed things to run down. Now she wants to have a baby. The idea of facing into all that again . . .' he said. 'There's no fool like an old fool,' he added, and Marianne felt a little sympathetic.

'My daughter hates her,' he continued.

Marianne thought of the girl nuzzling her father's neck, craving his attention, and, for a brief moment, remembered how awful she'd been to Coleman. It was so long ago now and she found it hard to pinpoint why she had hated him so much.

'Do you ever feel like you've made a bags of things?' he asked.

'My life could hardly be considered a roaring success.' She noticed his chair had migrated closer to hers.

'Do you regret not becoming a writer like you planned?'

'You asked me something similar at Joe and Clare's. You made me wonder, actually.' She tilted her head. 'Am I supposed to feel like that woman in the song realizing that she'll never get to drive through Paris . . .?'

'You were talented.'

'That's debatable . . . I don't regret it,' she said. 'I think.'

Matt sat forward in his seat, and Marianne edged a little further back in hers.

'I probably shouldn't say this,' he said, smiling, 'but I always hoped that you and I might get back together.'

She didn't know what to say.

'We were good together,' he said, aiming for roguish but missing the mark.

Could he be that lonely? Did he really think they could change tracks this late in the game?

He leaned forward and placed his hand on hers. He was arrogant. She had given him no sign, sent no signal.

She withdrew her hand. 'I'm sorry, Matt.'

When she got home the kitchen drawers were upended, the contents strewn on the floor as if there had been a burglary. Small pools of water collected from melting chips of snow. Marianne deposited the groceries on the counter. Then she followed the Hansel and Gretel trail to where Pete was seated at a table in front of his laptop. The table was covered with newspapers. From where she stood she could see images of Deep Pockets.

'What the hell happened here, Pete?' she said.

She missed him singing in the shower, although she knew that if he did it nowadays, he'd probably warble 'Ave Maria'. It was like dealing with a different person. Her pity and love for him mingled with resentment. She was angry with him, too, because he could block out her and the kids. Whether he was a member of the establishment out working for a bank, part of a protest group or devoted to spirituality, it seemed to unfold in the same way. He was not there to help with the more mundane things in life, like cleaning the toilet or going to the supermarket.

Pete looked at her as if he was seeing her for the first time. Then he launched into a garbled narrative about Deep Pockets. 'He was very good to me,' he said, fidgeting. 'I know he did wrong. But I can't forget that when I was starting out he took me under his wing.'

'I know,' Marianne said.

The tempo of the conversation was wrong. The words tumbled out of him. 'I just made a donation to a charity associated with the Church. It's a good cause,' he said, 'a good cause.'

Marianne moved towards him. 'Jesus!' She was staring at the glowing screen. 'We can't afford that.'

'It's a good cause,' he said, standing up suddenly, his shoulder almost hitting her jaw. 'In a way I did it for him. To try and absolve him.'

She swerved. 'Pete.'

His eyelids fluttered. 'Get him through the gates, as it were,' he said quickly. 'He sinned. I hope he repented before he died.' He minimized one screen in favour of another, then read aloud, 'Matthew eighteen, verses twenty-one to twenty-two. "Then Peter came to Jesus and asked, 'Lord, how many times shall I forgive my brother when he sins against me? Up to seven times?' Jesus answered, 'I tell you, not seven times, but seventy-seven'" – God told me to.'

'I don't know what you're talking about.'

He looked past her. 'I wonder if the bank knows about this donation.'

'What do you mean?'

'They may be watching us. I don't trust them. It's possible. They might have had him killed. The car crash.'

'Pete, that sounds crazy. What are you saying?' Marianne felt a giant fist clench in her chest.

He began to jabber again.

'We'd better ring your psychiatrist.'

35

Clare inched her way across the icy car park through the thick silence. Her cheeks were cold. Snow covered the roof of the rectangular building. The scene looked Alpine – it might have been printed on an old-fashioned chocolate box.

Earlier Ruth had sat on the edge of Clare's bed as she had done each day for a week. It was odd to have her in such a personal sphere. She had moved in to look after the boys, arriving early in the morning and leaving late at night. Clare, who had not left her room, had the sense that the house was running more smoothly than it did when she was around.

Today Ruth had said, 'I thought you should know that Pete has been admitted to a psychiatric ward.'

An image of Pete with a cranky baby – one of the twins, maybe – slung over his shoulder while he cooked a meal came to Clare. He had been like a baby-whisperer. Squalling infants were calmed by the rhythm of his heart, it seemed. Pete had been endlessly kind to her in those early years when she had rung Marianne at all hours for help or advice.

After Ruth had gone, she lay on her back as pictures ratcheted through her head. She saw Marianne at the altar at Donal's funeral. Marianne had been so controlled, when she intoned: 'Do not stand at my grave and weep . . . I am not there: I do not sleep.'

A sort of Marianne show had played in her head, an inversion of what she had thought in the cinema that day with Finn. Marianne's kindnesses over the span of their long friendship now beset her. Marianne, who had helped her with the children. Marianne, who had held Clare's hand during Finn's birth, heavily pregnant herself and probably frightened at the preview of what lay in store for her. Marianne, who had lived with her in a grotty flat because she knew it was all that Clare could afford and had always shared everything she had. For a second the professor and his green Saab flitted through Clare's mind. It must have been hard for Marianne to go back to London . . .

Clare had sat up. She'd got out of bed, showered, dressed and found that, although she had been pulverized, the world had kept on turning.

Under the darkening sky she made her way to the hospital in the caravan of cars that crawled along as more snow fell. 'Essential journeys only', the radio man had said. She thought of her friends, Pete and Marianne. There was Pete, an outdoorsy, broad-shouldered man, who had made mistakes but was her friend.

Clare saw Marianne's face through the glass doors. It was scoured of all colour. She was wearing an incongruously cheerful red skirt. Clare went in. Marianne turned. 'You came.' She ran into Clare's arms.

'I'm so sorry,' Clare said.

Marianne buried her face in Clare's dark coat. 'I'm sorry too.'

'How's Pete?'

The only sound was snuffling.

When she had calmed a little Marianne said, 'The doctor used words like "manic" and "psychosis".'

'It will be all right,' Clare said.

The women sat side by the side in the café.

'They said there's a television room, a smoking area and a section for families where we can visit him. In a couple of days Pete will be able to come down to the restaurant. For now, he has a room next to the nurses' station.' Marianne was talking quickly as if to reassure herself. 'Nobody wears starched white coats. I couldn't tell who was a patient and who was a doctor. There doesn't seem to be anybody shuffling around sedated.'

'Things have really moved on,' Clare said. 'There are no locked doors or anything like that. The Nurse Ratchet idea is outdated.'

'It's still an institution.' Marianne sagged. 'It's still a lunatic asylum, just by another name.'

'Don't think like that.'

'I feel . . .' Marianne trawled for the words ' . . . so sad.'

Clare reached across the table. 'Pete's in the right place.'

'To think that he'd end up here.'

While Marianne was camped in the hospital Clare visited her every day. With the snow, they couldn't go for proper walks so they spent a lot of time in the cafeteria. Sometimes they stood outside while Marianne smoked. They had both said sorry.

Yet the notion of complete forgiveness was naïve, Clare thought. Their relationship would always be shaped by what had happened. And there were limits to honesty: Clare could not tell Marianne that she had envied Pete's love for her. She couldn't lay herself entirely bare.

One morning when they had ventured outside and Marianne was puffing a fag, Clare said, 'A baby would have been a terrible idea.'

That was her peace-offering. The subject of their children was tacitly dropped. It was still too raw, the wound still open. They instinctively knew it was a landmine.

But Clare had spoken of Donal: 'I couldn't bear you mentioning him, not because he was gay but because I let him down. I never acknowledged who he was, and that's always in the background. I think, What if? It's hard to accept that if I'd acted differently, things might have gone in another direction. My father couldn't accept that Donal was gay. I look at Joe, who's much younger and sees himself as cosmopolitan. He denies he's anti-gay but, like a lot of straight men, he's steeped in homophobia. I see it with the boys and the culture in their school. It's one of the last remaining taboos. Cian's gay' – Marianne had nodded, clearly unsurprised – 'and if I make it all right for him, I don't know . . . I can't go back but it would be something.'

Another day Marianne said, 'I'm sorry for being a smug, complacent cow. I'm sorry for making assumptions. I've never had to earn my living and that I could criticize somebody else's mothering is laughable. I was so out of touch myself when it came to Grace.'

One night they had gone back to Marianne's house and got very drunk. Clare talked about Joe.

'It's been on and off between them since college apparently. Joe said that he tried to end it numerous times. That hurt most, really,' Clare said, 'the idea that it was hard for him to end it because he loved her.'

Marianne lay on the floor in front of the fire. Clare spoke almost as if she was talking to herself.

'You say to yourself that everyone has to compromise. You tell yourself that romantic gestures are empty, that they count for nothing. It's not what you dreamed of when you were young, but that's life. It's not perfect. The moments of despair pass. But you're fooling yourself.'

There had been an essential contradiction at the core of their marriage: they had been together but mainly alone. At low points Clare had told herself that people decided their corresponding needs interlocked and they fancied themselves in love. You met a boy at roughly the right time – okay, she'd been ahead of schedule there – and things fell into place. There was no such thing as love *per se*.

Maybe Clare had reached out for something she'd thought would be stable. But her marriage had not been the safe haven she'd imagined. As the years had passed, she and Joe had been clamped together by convention. She couldn't explain any better why she had wanted Joe. She couldn't rationalize to herself why she had stayed so long. Was it because she had never had a model of marriage to follow? Certainly she had a dread of upheaval that stemmed from childhood. But maybe she was simply gutless, unable to do anything but turn a blind eye to deceit and accept endless lies. Maybe she had stayed with him out of cowardice and taken on the mantle of a victim.

'Would you have him back?' Marianne asked.

'No,' Clare said. 'I don't think he'd want to come anyway. He loves her. Our marriage has always been a sham.'

'You have four lovely boys and that's no illusion, four living, breathing emblems of your relationship.'

'They're certainly real,' Clare said, and they both laughed.

There were other light moments too. She enjoyed seeing Marianne goggle-eyed. For once it was nice to be the dramatic one in their friendship and she recounted every outrage she had committed against Joe in detail, ramming his car, cutting up his suits and bleaching his shoes. Marianne gave a shout of laughter. 'Clare!'

'It felt kind of good,' she admitted, 'briefly. And I smashed our wedding photo.'

Her laughter stopped then. That picture had foretold the entire story of her marriage – the pervasive anxiety, her desperate attempts to play the part of the happy bride and Joe's to look like he wanted to be there.

In smashing the picture, she had finally accepted the truth about herself and Joe. She felt bereft, but at times she felt lighter too. And now Clare believed, for the first time since her mother had died, that she might be able to live without fear.

Epilogue

Christmas aromas wafted through the house. The table was already set for the next day. Earlier Gretta and Coleman had been unloaded from their taxi. The whole process had taken time. Marianne had watched her stepfather walk slowly into the house. His neck looked spindly, protruding from the collar of his checked shirt.

'It's prostate cancer,' Gretta had said on the phone. 'It's inoperable.'

Marianne had listened, motionless, and when she spoke her voice was hoarse. 'Oh, Mum, I'm so sorry. I knew something was wrong.'

'This will be Coleman's last Christmas.'

Marianne had lowered herself into a chair.

'He didn't want to tell you. You have enough on your plate. And he wants to do it his way.'

Coleman's movements were slow; pain was etched on his face. He had been an industrious, independent person. Now he had been put to bed like a baby. When she was younger she had fought with Coleman, ignoring him and being rude to him, which had hurt her mother. Her feelings had been so intense. It had seemed so important that she set herself in opposition to him. She thought of the battles she had waged, the wrangling and misspent fury. It all seemed so petty and pointless now.

'I love him in a way,' she said.

They were in the kitchen, Gretta uncorking a bottle of wine.

Marianne shook her head. 'Not like Dad, but I love him.'

'I know,' Gretta said, her voice quavering. 'He knows. But we must make this a special Christmas.'

Insulating the girls from what had happened to Pete had been Marianne's chief concern for weeks. Now there was another secret to keep. She and Gretta told them that Coleman was sick; they were vague about the prospect of recovery. Holly had to be restrained from lolling on the edge of his bed for too long and interlocking her podgy fingers with his. She wanted to regale him with her new-found interest in Catholicism, particularly the saints.

Since he'd been in hospital, Grace had been pushing for details about Pete. It seemed so hard that she should have to register another shock but Marianne felt the natural self-absorption of adolescence would see her through. Holly had totally accepted her explanation that Pete needed a rest. All she cared about was that he would be there for her Confirmation. Marianne had accepted that Holly was going to get her way. It was ironic, given what she had thought of her for so long, that Ruth was going to be Holly's sponsor. It had been Clare's idea. Ruth was an Anglo-Catholic and took her religion seriously, in a way that Irish people generally didn't. Holly had taken to calling around to Ruth's flat to pepper her with theological questions.

'Is she badgering you, Ruth?' Marianne had asked.

'We're becoming friends,' Ruth had replied.

Marianne thought she could hear a smile in her voice. Ruth had said that some time she might tell Clare her story.

Earlier, her arms full of clothes from the tumble-drier, Marianne had come across Holly and her friend plonked in front of the television with bowls of cereal. They were playing Marianne and Pete's wedding video. The quality was mediocre, with lots of shaky images. Marianne looked considerably thinner with dated hair as Grace toddled up the aisle beside her in her little smocked dress. Pete looked so young and confident. Most strikingly he had looked sane. In one sequence, they sat on two chairs, Marianne nestling her head on his shoulder.

Marianne had crept from the room. Halfway up the stairs she sank onto a step and cried quietly. She cried for those two young people. She cried for Coleman too.

Gretta fussed over her granddaughters, as she had done with Marianne. With a combination of grimaces and eye-rolling, Grace let her mother know that she was beyond this. But still she trailed her grandmother to the kitchen for the special hot chocolate Gretta made, topped with marshmallows, straining to conceal her pleasure.

Grace looked less gaunt. She had begun to care about her appearance again. The sack-like clothes hung untouched in her wardrobe. Marianne had suggested that she 'talk to someone' but this had been resisted. *Wuthering Heights* had been replaced on its shelf. She had stopped wafting around the house, lying in her bedroom among her Austen, Eliot and Wharton books like some nineteenth-century heroine. She no longer squirmed when you tried to hug her. The crying jags had tailed off, too. She was definitely more communicative. Spiky teenage Grace had reappeared. The routine teenage *Sturm und Drang* were back. Marianne felt that perhaps the trauma was receding.

Finn had sent Grace a brief message that he was sorry about his Facebook comment.

'It's good, Mum,' Grace had confided, 'but I don't really like him much any more. I used to laugh at his jokes but he's not that funny.'

'Maybe in time you can be friends,' Marianne said, doubting it.

Earlier Clare had called around. She had said that, in his father's absence, Finn was trying to be the man of the house. He had cleared their path of snow, and those of the neighbours, fetching groceries for an old man who lived down the road. Joe was coming for Christmas dinner.

'I got a call from Philip,' she had said, as she was leaving. 'He wanted to wish me and the children a happy Christmas. And to say he was sorry he hadn't seen more of me over the years but Joe and he had fallen out because he thought Joe didn't deserve me.'

'Well, fair play,' Marianne said, smirking. 'He's a fast mover.'

Clare had gone a dark shade of red.

Stranger things had happened.

Grace was now discussing *The Great Gatsby* with her grandmother. 'I like F. Scott Fitzgerald,' she said, 'but he's not my favourite writer.'

'Those last lines of Gatsby are wonderful,' Gretta said, and intoned, in her vaguely dramatic way, '"So we beat on, boats against the current, borne back ceaselessly into the past."' Gretta paused.

Holly, who was sprawled on a chair next to Gretta, eating a mince pie, asked, 'Granny, are you sad?'

'No,' Gretta said.

'Is it because of Coleman?' Holly asked, unconvinced.

'Or Dad?' Grace said, her face darkening.

'I'm the opposite of sad,' Gretta said. 'I'm happy because we're here together. And because I think we're so lucky to have each other. It's the Christmas of women.' She began to wax lyrical about Robert Redford, who had starred in the seventies film version of *The Great Gatsby*. She clutched the stem of her wine glass with a theatrically lascivious look on her face. It was a pose designed to entertain her granddaughters. It worked. The girls exchanged horrified glances.

After Grace and Holly had gone upstairs, Marianne and Gretta fell silent. There was the occasional thud of feet from above. The muffled sound of chat, echoes of laughter. Coleman was about to leave them. Pete hovered on the edge of insanity. But these were signs that life would go on, as it always did.

During the day, there had been the usual dance between mother and daughter, as each stepped around the other in the way of mothers and daughters everywhere. Gretta had taken a roll of Marianne's middle between thumb and finger, and said, 'You'll have to watch yourself.' Marianne had bristled.

Then she had chided her for smoking. 'I can smell them on you. What sort of an example is that?' Marianne had pulled a face while the girls giggled.

'You're so childish, Mum,' Grace had said. Grace was right: Marianne always found that in the company of her mother she regressed. It was soothing and jarring in roughly equal measure.

Gretta sat down on the ottoman at the piano. Throughout Marianne's life her mother had entertained and calmed her at the piano. After her father died Marianne remembered waking in the small hours to hear rousing strains of Wagner or Beethoven wafting through the house. Sitting beside her mother at the piano was like coming home to a place where, other than during her wilderness years when she had kicked against it, she was soothed.

Gretta moved her foot up and down on the pedal. 'You okay?' she asked.

'Fine.'

Pete had been riding the crest of a wave of mania. Giving things away, apparently, had been a major sign. On the advice of the shrink, she had coaxed him into the car and spoken soothingly to the wild-eyed stranger until she'd got him to the hospital. She had driven all the way, hoping he couldn't smell the fear exuding from her pores. When they'd got there, she'd switched off the ignition and reached for his hand, as Clare would reach for hers later in the café.

His thin, pale face was illuminated by the car-park lights, which gave it a sickly hue. No marriage was ever perfect. Some people were just better at hiding deficiencies than others. Pete and she had fought often. In the early years the fights were conducted on an almost operatic scale, with Marianne throwing things. They had crept into bed in the grey light shivering, with nothing resolved, eventually falling into each other's arms.

They had fallen in and out of love, moving away from each other, as long-married couples did, then migrating back. She had almost hated him at times when they were still in the foothills of having small children. He had gone golfing once for an entire week when Grace was tiny and had never rung. She had threatened not to be there when he came back. She had felt utterly abandoned by him. But on the way to the hospital, she had looked at him, the father of her children, a crazy religious nut spouting cant, and had thought of how she loved him. Now he was doing occupational therapy, which was not far off the basket-making that had featured heavily in schoolyard jokes about crazy people.

She missed Pete's body next to her in bed. She missed him coming home from town on Christmas Eve with an unwrapped present slung in a bag for her. She had long ago given up hoping for nicely written cards or wrapping paper.

She remembered how she had felt instantly connected to him when they'd first met. How she'd thought about him all the way to India and how everything she'd seen when she got there had been filtered through the prism of 'I wonder what Pete would think?' She went through chunks of their life together scene by scene. He had always said he was delighted with his girls, that he didn't particularly want sons. She didn't entirely believe that. She thought of him jogging Grace, then Holly, up and down on his knee when they were little, singing to them in his off-key voice.

She found she had to stave off tears. Her mother, still playing the piano, was watching her.

'The line between sanity and insanity is narrower than we think,' Gretta said, turning her head, her fingers still running up and down the keys. 'There aren't just two categories of people. These things are on a continuum. Pete will get better.'

Marianne felt infused with the confidence her mother always instilled in her.

'I'm going to travel . . .' Gretta said, ' . . . afterwards. I'd like to go to India, I think, as you did.'

In the soft light she had the bearing of a younger woman. She said, 'This can't be the end.' She lifted her hands from the keys and swivelled to face Marianne. 'At my age, you realize we don't have all the time in the world.'

'How can you bear it, Mum?' Marianne said.

'I'm lucky to have been loved by your father and by Coleman. To love and to be loved . . . that's a lot.'

Marianne bowed her head.

'You're very strong. I'm proud of you, Marianne.'

'Thank you,' Marianne said, blinking.

'We are the sum total of our experiences, both good and bad. The question is how we deal with those experiences.'

She stood up and went over to the window. 'It's snowing again,' she said, looking up at the sky.

Marianne followed her. The street was deserted, save for two young revellers wending their way up the road bellowing, 'Fairytale of New York'. Their footprints were the only marks in the pristine snow.

Acknowledgements

Many thanks to Patricia Deevy for her invaluable help with this book. Thanks to Michael McLoughlin and Cliona Lewis at Penguin Ireland for their guidance. Thanks once again to Hazel Orme for her excellent editing skills. Thanks to my agent Sheila Crowley at Curtis Brown, London, for her calm and good humour. I'd like to thank Alison Walsh for her help with earlier versions of this book. Many thanks to Colin Hopps for his valued input. Thanks to Stephanie Bourke, for her help with the medical aspect of the book. Thanks to Margaret Gallery and Louise English for supplying two of the excellent quotations. Thanks to Aodan, Martha, Matt, Ivona, Gianni and all at the Village Café for the good food and humour. Thanks to Eamon and Eileen of Puca Technologies for affording me a desk and a place to make tea, and to Elliot Tucker of the same company for answering my dumbass technological questions. Big thanks to Jay Bourke for keeping a roof over my head and making it possible for me to write, and thanks to Conn Harte-Bourke for his wit and permanent good cheer. Thanks to Niall and Kay Harte, the world's most supportive parents. Thanks to my aunt Aine O'Brien for her encouragement. And, of course, thanks to Paula O'Brien for her immense support in countless ways.